Mitakuye oyasin
(We all are related)

Wicahpi Win
(Star Woman)

Bonnie J Hunt
Lawrence J Hunt

DEATH ON THE UMATILLA

WHITMAN MISSION MURDERERS ARE AT LARGE; A VOLUNTEER ARMY ATTEMPTS TO BRING THEM TO JUSTICE

by

Bonnie Jo Hunt

and

Lawrence J. Hunt

"If I give up my men that killed the settlers, to let them be tried by your law, will you give up your men that killed our women to let them be tried by our law?"
Captain Jack, Modoc

A Lone Wolf Clan Book, Vol. VI

DEATH ON THE UMATILLA

First Printing, 2001

Library of Congress Catalog Number: 00-092021
International Standard Book Number: 1-928800-05-X (Vol. VI)

Front cover adapted from J. M. Stanley sketch of old Fort Walla Walla and painted by artist Betty Hunt.

Cover designed by Jon P. Duda, Art Director
First Impression, Inc., Albuquerque, NM

Published by:

Mad Bear Press
6636 Mossman Place, NE
Albuquerque, New Mexico

Words of Appreciation

The Lone Wolf Clan series is the work of many people. We are fortunate to have the help and loyal support of a team of talented editorial advisors without whose assistance we would be lost. We owe a special "thank you" to Barbara Lee Hunt, Juyn Krumm and Susan Shampine whose comments, suggestions and corrections always are on the mark.

We also owe a special thank you to artists Betty Hunt, Kay Smith and designer Jon Duda whose artistic talents produced the attractive cover art work on <u>Land Without a Country</u> and its sequel, <u>Death on the Umatilla</u>. Reader comments are as laudatory of these book covers as they are of the printed word between them.

To Lawrence "Larry" Dodd, Archivist of the Northwest and Whitman College archives, we are indebted for his valuable help in identifying and providing a copy of the correct sketch of old Fort Walla Walla.

Three different buildings were erected on this site. The first one was built in 1818 as a link in Hudson's Bay's fur trading empire and named Fort Nez Perce. Because of its location near the mouth of the Walla Walla River, it gradually became known as Fort Walla Walla.

During the Cayuse War of 1855, the last "old" Fort Walla Walla was abandoned and the name transferred to a US military post about six miles east of Waiilatpu. Today this site is a pleasant suburban area of Walla Walla, Washington.

The location where all three "old" Fort Walla Wallas stood is presently covered by the backwaters of McNary Dam that block the Columbia River near the mouth of the Umatilla. The fortification portrayed on the cover is the Hudson's Bay trading post in existence during Colonel Cornelius Gilliam's 1848 campaign to apprehend those guilty of committing the Whitman Mission massacre atrocities.

An engraving published in Marcus Whitman and Early Days of Oregon by William Mowery - Copyright, 1901 by Silver, Burdette and Company.

FOREWORD

Death on the Umatilla is based on events that occurred following the 1847 Whitman Mission massacre in Oregon Territory. Soon after the tragedy Territorial Governor George Abernathy issued a proclamation to raise troops to apprehend those involved in the terrible tragedy. Unfortunately, the body of men who volunteered were largely an undisciplined lot who caused more problems than they solved.

Colonel Cornelius Gilliam, a veteran Indian fighter who had earned his reputation in the bloody Black Hawk and merciless Seminole campaigns, was chosen to lead the motley group. Like so many of his enlisted men, Gilliam was of debatable worth. The volunteer army scarcely was formed when he threatened to pull Fort Vancouver down because Hudson's Bay directors refused him powder, shot and sundry supplies.

To complicate the supply problem further, an advance party of volunteers sent up the Columbia River to secure the village of The Dalles was raided. Indian horsemen galloped in and drove away three hundred horses and cattle. The dearth of food turned the undisciplined army into a mob. The volunteers swept down on emigrant families, pilfering their wagons and driving away their livestock. When the volunteer army's own supplies from down river arrived the plunderers descended on these wagons, ransacking them in the same ruthless manner.

Perhaps the campaign to apprehend the Whitman Mission killers would have bogged down in The Dalles if it had not been for a body of French Canadians who joined Gilliam's forces at the last minute. This disciplined group, well supplied and well armed possessing a nine pound cannon, was led by Captain Tom McKay, stepson of Doctor McLoughlin who had ruled Hudson's Bay's Northwest empire for twenty-five years.

Although Gilliam welcomed the French Canadians, he disliked everything Tom McKay represented. McKay was Catholic, a half-blood and connected with Hudson's Bay. In Gilliam's opinion Hudson's Bay and the Catholic Church had plotted and encouraged the Whitman Mission massacre.

Throughout the Cayuse tribal lands, where the massacre perpetrators were in hiding, troubles of a different kind beleaguered the citizenry. In 1846-1847, the Cayuse people suffered through a terrible winter that had devastated their herds. The weather had been so bitter wild game dropped dead; their carcasses froze so hard scavenger wolves broke teeth trying to satisfy their hunger. Before the natives could recover, another ravaging tragedy struck -- a deadly measles epidemic. Almost every Cayuse family lost at least one member to the white man's deadly disease. Doctor Marcus Whitman was begged for medicines. He willingly gave them, but deaths continued unabated.

"Poison! Missionary doctor gives poison . . . . Medicine Man Whitman kills . . . wants everything . . . herds, land, everything you have . . . ," outside agitators proclaimed. As a result of this agitation the grief-stricken, desperate natives fell back on tradition; medicine men who allowed their patients to die had to pay with their own lives. Thus, the attack on the mission took place; the first person killed was Doctor Marcus Whitman.

Now, in the winter of 1848, the Cayuse face a third tragedy. An army of Blue Coats is marching up river to wreak vengeance for the massacre. Lodges, herds, villages -- everything -- including their very lives is at stake. Into this atmosphere and mood gripping the uplands march Colonel Cornelius Gilliam and his undisciplined gang of volunteers.

This is the sixth book in the Lone Wolf Clan series, a series that emphasizes the role of Indian people in Northwest history. Michael Two Feathers, Stickus and Joe Jennings, with whom readers of this series are familiar, continue to encounter unbelievable challenges. Blue Lizard, Gray Eagle, Pelican Neck Jasson, Yellow Beard Adams and others emerge in roles ranging from the tragic to the bizarre. But the backdrop of the period when eastern culture and native culture violently clash, takes the spotlight in Death on the Umatilla.

DEATH ON THE UMATILLA

I

. . . Then the Creator gave us Indians game and fish. We knew they were for us . . . .

Meninick, Yakama

The hunters were in a good mood. They joked and chattered about the game they would down -- the feasting and dancing that would follow upon their return to the village. At the rear of the column a solemn-faced youth of no more than sixteen years rode along, not taking part in the merriment. He modestly remained silent in keeping with tradition. When among his elders he did not speak unless spoken to.

Besides, it was his first hunt. He looked forward to making a kill. On his upper right arm he wore a rawhide band decorated with a blue beaded lizard. He wore it with pride. It was a gift from his mother, a woman who came from beyond the shiny mountains. The beaded amulet brought good fortune, long life and gave the youth his name, Blue Lizard.

Blue Lizard lived on the south bank of the Columbia River. Harvesting salmon and netting sturgeon were trades his people knew best. On this day the men were intent on bringing in deer or elk. During the cold winter months the coveted game descended from the heights to graze on willow bark and grasses that abounded in meadows along the river banks.

The hunters were excited. Who among them would make the first kill? Who would have the honor of taking antlers home to display to family and friends? But uppermost in their minds was the hope of returning to the village with a goodly supply of fresh meat. After existing on fish week after week a change of diet would be a treat.

As the hunters neared the game trails that led into the bottom lands, the merry chatter ceased. For a while they rode in silence. The leader held up a hand to signal caution. The column came to a stop. Except for a scolding blue jay, twitting small birds and a rabbit that darted from the bushes to scamper away, there was stillness. Then the horses pricked up their ears. Faint sounds of shod hooves striking rock, the squeak and creak of leather, rattle of metal and thump of bouncing packs and saddlebags struck the hunters' sensitive ears.

"Blue Coats!" the leader of the hunters uttered. He reined his mount off the trail and into a thicket of trees. So quickly did he act, his companions were caught off guard.

Blue Lizard, at the tail end of the column, had been riding along lost in a bubble of happiness. Never before had he felt so alive -- so in tune with Mother Earth. He tingled all over. The thrill of being included in this, his first big hunt, was like a dream come true. He hardly heard the leader's words or saw his signal of warning. Before he was aware of danger, it seemed the Blue Coats were upon him.

Frantically, Blue Lizard jerked at the halter rope, startling his shaggy pony. The animal reared. Riding bareback, Blue Lizard slid off the horse's slick hide into the trail side brush. He dodged into a thicket, dropped onto the ground and lay among the carpet of brown leaves as still as a newborn fawn. Two bearded, cursing Blue Coats stomped back and forth.

"Thet blasted redskin's here," one growled to the other. Suddenly, a muddy boot crashed down on Blue Lizard's back. "Aha! Here's the critter, hidin' in the leaves like a chameleon."

Before Blue Lizard could scramble away a loop of rope encircled his neck. He was lassoed and dragged into captivity like a wild mustang. The beaded lizard amulet was stripped from his arm. Desperately, he fought for it. His white-faced, black-bearded captor plucked it away and shoved it in his pocket.

"Spoils of war," the bearded man gloated, throwing another loop around him, shackling Blue Lizard's arms.

The Indian youth glared defiantly at his captor but inside he was filled with despair. His sacred talisman was gone. He felt naked, inept and defenseless without it on his arm. The rapid approach of another Blue Coat brandishing a saber, struck terror in his heart. His first hunt had turned from a thrilling adventure into a tragic nightmare.

Colonel Gilliam, commander of the Blue Coat column, rode up at a gallop. "All right, so you have a prisoner," he shouted. "That's not enough. We want to teach all of these bloody brothers a lesson. Quit lollygagging and get after the rest of them." He wheeled his horse about and jabbed his saber toward the forest, motioning for his men to follow him into the trees.

All week long Gilliam had been in high dudgeon. The campaign had gotten off to a bad start. One delay after another held the troops up. The Whitman Mission massacre had occurred in November. Here it was the first of February and not a single soldier had set foot in the land of the murdering Cayuse.

The military operation had been slapped together; every harum-scarum idiot in the Willamette Valley had put in his two cents worth. They demanded action yet did nothing but add to the confusion. Petitions were circulated. The Legislature met and harangued. Under Major Henry A. G. Lee a token force, too weak and ill-prepared to fight off anything but a small band of warriors, was dispatched to The Dalles. A delegation was sent to California seeking help. Any numskull should have known it couldn't get through. In winter months snow blocked passages through the Siskiyous.

Cornelius Gilliam eyed his troop with disapproval. He had been a fool to accept the command. These people didn't need a leader, they needed a herder. They had as much discipline and sense of soldiering as a flock of sheep. He had done his best to whip them into shape, but his efforts had done little good. Look at them, he sourly thought as the men fumbled with their rifles. The first encounter with Indians had them gawking like school children. "Don't stand there. Get after them!" the colonel shouted again.

Corralling the Wascopum hunters was like chasing mirages in the desert. The hunters had dismounted, unbridled their horses and slapped them on the rumps. The flight of their mounts led the Blue Coats dashing blindly after them. Finally, discovering the ruse, Gilliam's troops angrily returned to search the forest where the Indian column first had been sighted. Instead of fleeing, the hunters waited in the shadows, smothering giggles as the Blue Coats helplessly floundered back and forth. Then, as if to taunt their pursuers, the hunters began to flit from tree to tree. As soon as troopers caught sight of one, he vanished. The soldiers became confused, then furious.

"No! Not there. Over here. Dammit! It's like trackin' bees in a blizzard." The soldiers charged one way, then another. They fired at shadows, sunlit branches, scurrying squirrels and flitting blue jays. They would have shot each other, but Gilliam's screaming voice stopped the chaos. "Cease firing, you silly clods. You couldn't hit the broadside of a barn from the inside with the doors closed and locked."

The colonel galloped back and forth rousting his men from the woods. "All you've done is waste lead and powder," he thundered. "I never've seen such a disgusting display of marksmanship. Blind pigs shoot better. I don't know how anyone expects me to fight the Cayuse with beetleheaded cretins like you."

Adams, a man with a long white beard stained yellow by tobacco juice, took a chew and spit. "Cretins, are we? I guess the colonel should know. Takes a cretin to know a cretin."

The middle-aged leader of the hunters, listening in the forest shadows, chuckled. He didn't understand the words but no one needed to interpret what was taking place. The Blue Coats clucked and gobbled like a flock of disturbed turkeys. If he wished, his men could pick off a dozen. The chief with a face and neck as red as a strutting gobbler, made an especially inviting target. Later the Wascopum leader wished he had killed the lot of them . . . . It could not have made matters worse.

The leader of the hunters gave a birdcall whistle. His men came to surround him. Should they rescue their brother? The leader shook his head. "It is best not to make haste," he said. "Let us wait. Red-Neck is the chief. He talks much but no one listens. Our brother is safe."

Back on the trail Gilliam continued to harangue his men. "Give me your attention!" he said in a voice that carried across the Columbia River. "When you fight Indians you shoot to kill. You may not get a second chance. I'll say it again. It's the one who gets in the first lick that keeps his hair. Don't be fooled by their peaceful demeanor. They're as deceiving as a basketful of snakes. Take your eye off them for a moment, and they'll steal the laces out of your boots.

"A harmless Indian is as rare as an odorless skunk. There ain't any. Last week these so-called peaceful Wascopums raided The Dalles. Three hundred horses and cattle were stolen from under the fort commander's nose. I'll wager this bunch were among the thieves. That's why this prisoner is important. Before we finish with him he's going to lead us to the stolen herd."

"Bull manure! He's more apt to lead us on a wild goose chase." The sarcastic words were spoken by a redheaded Irish giant named Walsh. The swaybacked mare he rode looked squashed beneath his bulk.

Gilliam twisted in the saddle. "Who said that?" His steely gaze scanned the group of men. Failing to identify the culprit, he spurred ahead to take his place at the front of the column.

"Yuh redheaded cretin! Yuh near put yer foot in it," scolded Yellow Beard Adams. "Yer not supposed to think. An' never should yuh talk back. It makes officers irritated."

"Why don't thet guy talk American? What's a kre-tin, anyhow? Maybeso, somethin' outta the Scriptures? Yuh know, besides an all-fired Injun fighter, Gilliam prides hisself on preachin' the gospel. I don't know how he converts nobody. He swears like the trooper he is, an' ain't spoke a kind word so far on this trip, 'less it's been to hisself."

"Cretins, yuh dummy, are creatures like yerself, nuthin' but solid bone 'tween the ears."

"Silence in the ranks!" a sergeant's rough voice rasped. "What yuh think this is, a Sunday school outing?"

"Who the heck was thet?" queried Walsh, the red head.

"Second class cretin, I think," Adams said, hawking and spitting in the sergeant's direction.

Hidden by the dark forest that cloaked the hillside, the band of Wascopum hunters continued to watch and listen. They fidgeted with their weapons as two troopers threw the captured youth over a saddle like a sack of baggage. The boy's father still was not perturbed. His son was acting as he should. He was defying his captors. They would admire the young man's courage. Suddenly he gasped in dismay. The blue lizard amulet was gone. His son was unprotected. How could he leave him in these cruel hands? How could he face the youth's mother, who loved First Son above her own life? He hurried to the leader.

The leader frowned. He knew the power of talismans. Perhaps they should rescue the youth. He counted twenty Blue Coats. If they surprised them . . . ! Before he could think of a plan ribald sounds of shouts and curses came from the river.

The Wascopum leader groaned. More Blue Coats! A makeshift ferry loaded with men had landed on the south bank of the Columbia. In a flurry of noisy activity the soldiers waded ashore. Another ferry followed loaded with horses and wagons.

The Wascopum leader turned to his men. "We must hurry to the village and hide children, horses and women. The Blue Coat army that our scouts told us was coming, is here. Look at their numbers, as countless as fleas on a long-haired dog."

DEATH ON THE UMATILLA

II

*Did you know that trees talk? Well, they do. They talk
to each other, and they'll talk to you if you listen . . . .*

Walking Buffalo, Canadian Stoney

The forward detachment of Gilliam's volunteers pushed
onward. Breezes off the cold, rushing waters of the river chilled
them to the bone and slapped their faces with dampness. There
was the smell of snow. Tall firs alongside the trail moaned as
they swayed and twisted in the whistling wind. A deer bounded
out of the brush and darted up a forested slope. The sharp crack
of a rifle echoed back from the escarpments. The deer, unharmed,
disappeared into the shadows.

"Damn fool!" someone muttered. "Yuh gotta aim."

Gilliam rode back along the line. His red-rimmed, angry
eyes fastened on two youths. Although they had nothing to do
with the shooting, Gilliam pounced on them. "Who fired that
shot?" he demanded.

The nearest youth shrugged; the other made no response.

"Hey! You! When I ask a question I expect an answer."

It was obvious the unresponsive youth had Indian blood.
He returned the angry glare with an absent glance as if the colonel wasn't there.

Gilliam wheeled his mount around. Snapping his quirt
against the horse's flank, he galloped to the head of the column.
Just as he thought, these people were about as soldier-like as a
bunch of purple-bottomed apes.

"What's the matter with yuh, anyway?" asked Yellow
Beard Adams, who rode in front of the youths on a stolid white
mount that was better suited to pulling drayage wagons or hooked
to a plow. "When yuh go sojerin' yuh say, 'yes sir' an' 'no sir'.
Otherwise officers git upset. Look at him. Jest 'cause yuh didn't
speak, he's whalin' the bejesus outta thet poor horse."

"Why, yuh ol' coot, lay off these boys. Save yer wind fer somethin' serious. One don't hev to talk to officers 'less they hev to," Redhead Walsh scolded. "Why're yuh gittin' inta sech a lather anyhow? We ain't got started yet. This little fracas ain't nuthin' to what we kin expect. An ol' white bearded geezer like yerself shouldn't be here anyways. Beats me how yuh got outta yer rockin' chair. Yer only goin' to git in the way of us fightin' men."

"Ah, shet up. I'm jest tryin' to give these young fellers a bit of advice. Yer not so brimmin' over with smarts yerself," Adams retorted. "If yuh was goin' to take to soldierin' like yuh should, yuh'd trade off thet ol' swayback. Look at the poor critter. It's got curvature of the spine. First thing yuh know, thet backbone'll collapse. Yuh'll be fightin' those Cayuses afoot."

"Silence in the ranks. Eyes to the front." The sergeant was getting upset. These people had no respect for any rank.

"Yep, war's hell," the redhead muttered. "We should jolly well be serious 'bout it."

"Silence, I said," the sergeant glared, catching sight of Walsh's moving lips.

"Yeah! Yeah!" Walsh was known back home as never allowing anyone but himself to have the last word.

For a while the sergeant rode alongside the two talkative men. He had to admit the redheaded volunteer was right. Marching on the Cayuse was no place for an old white beard like Adams. Indian fighting was a young man's game. The need was for soldiers like the two youths marching beside the talkative geezers. But the dark one . . . . The two feathers he wore marked him as Indian. What was he doing here anyway? Rumor had it he had been a member of the murdered mission family, yet had emerged from the bloody business unscathed. Had he taken part in the killing of his own people? Was he a turncoat who joined the volunteers to spy on them?

Ah! If he caught this fellow out, every soldier in the troop, including Colonel Gilliam would have to take notice. With a commendation on his record . . . . The sergeant smacked his lips with satisfaction. He might reenlist and make a career of soldiering.

The dark faced youth knew he was under surveillance. Still he rode along as unaffected as though alone, taking pleasure in his surroundings. Here the troop passed through the Columbia River Gorge, one of Mother Earth's most colorful creations, yet hardly a single volunteer paid any attention to the scenery or vibrant sounds that came from every side.

Mother Earth spoke in many ways: through the whisper of the trees; the roar of the great waterfalls that seemed to drop out of the clouds; the babble of brooks gurgling their way to the Great River; the call of a loon, squawk of gulls, rustle of tiny winter birds . . . . There were the clean, fragrant, perfume of evergreens, the damp smell of moss and decaying vegetation, and sharp odors emanating from the rushing stream. To the native they all sent messages listened to and understood.

When he was attuned to the sights and sounds of Mother Earth, the dark faced youth felt at peace with himself. Why was it these men with white skin who believed themselves superior and more learned than native people, ignored these wondrous gifts of Mother Earth? Did the eastern civilization they came from make them deaf and blind to all these wonderful creations surrounding them?

Of course when it came to sizing up the natives who made their homes here, they were as avid as a flock of hungry buzzards. They wanted to know everything about the Indian, their questions often demanding and insensitive. Why should he tell about the feathers in his hair, the buckskin porcupine needle decorated wristlet he wore? If he told of the feathers' origin listeners would think him stranger than they already did. Besides, the feathers came to him in a very sacred way. It was not right to speak of the occasion to these insensitive people who used blasphemy as often as they did the King's English.

Yes, if he told of how, as a boy of ten, he had gone into

the mountains on a vision quest, they would look at him scorn-
fully. But that journey into the mountains had changed his life
forever. He had fallen under a spell that no one who had not had
the same experience would understand. Unlike most dreams,
when he awakened he was able to relive it -- to again enjoy the
ecstasy that gripped him while he was asleep.

Briefly, for a few moments memory of the event brought
him comfort. The morning air had been unusually crisp, clear
and pungent with evergreen fragrance. Overhead Father Sky appeared filled with fleecy white clouds. Out of the clouds two
specks emerged. Slowly, they made their way toward Mother
Earth. When they came near he could see they were feathers, not
ordinary feathers but ones that were alive. He knew they were
alive because they were violently quarreling, shouting at each
other words he could not understand.

The two feathers drifted eerily down to land alongside
his sleeping robe where they had lain quietly and motionless.
Yet, when he picked them up they seemed to quiver in his hand
and gave off a luminous glow that brightened the surrounding
forest. He was dumfounded. Here he was, a youth of ten, wit-
nessing a miracle.

The dream told him these feathers came from Father Sky,
beyond the clouds, where spirit people lived. That alone made
them sacred; and they had been sent especially to him! He was
filled with such wonder at first he thought he was still dreaming,
but no dream could fill one with such tremendous exhilaration.
He was not dreaming. His vision quest had been fulfilled. *Wyakin*,
the spirit that would guide him through the rest of his life, had
come to him. *Wyakin* left the feathers as a token the dream was
real -- the feathers were his special gift. In honor of the wondrous event, he took the name Two Feathers, although his mountain man father insisted he still be called Michael.

Tobacco stained yellow beard Adams, now made another
attempt to draw the brothers out, with no result. "Teach me to
mind my own business," he grumbled. "Those two are as talk-

ative as thieves in a hen coop."

The older brother grinned at Adams' discomfort. A man with open face, fair hair and the vigor and stature of one in his mid-twenties, was clearly no greenhorn. The careless way he straddled his horse, the weathered buckskins he wore, the sharp, direct gaze, the myriad of squint lines at the corners of his eyes and the determined set of his shoulders, said "here was one who already had experienced the ups and downs of life." Above his left eye was a purplish, distinctive scar shaped in the form of a crescent moon. If it didn't look so raw it could be mistaken for a birthmark.

The only similarity between the two brothers was their eyes. They were blue, the color of a clear summer sky. In the older youth's light face, beneath a shock of brown hair, they looked natural. Against the dusky skin and long black hair of the youth with Indian blood they appeared out of place. What made the latter's eyes even stranger was that at a moment's notice they could change. The tranquil shade of blue turned violet, like a threatening sky that preceded lightening and thunder. When that happened the dark-faced youth's behavior became unpredictable. Anything could happen.

The fact he couldn't cajole a response out of the young men rankled Yellow Beard. "Dammit all, we're goin' to sojer together, might as well be friends." The brothers continued to pay him no attention. Frustrated, Adams kicked his pale-eyed plow horse in the ribs. "Might as well give up," he decided. But it still didn't keep him from fuming.

The boys came by their quiet nature naturally. Their origins made them reluctant to talk about themselves or make close acquaintances. They didn't even know each other very well. Their father had been a mountain man, a silent fur trapper who never spoke of himself or his origins. Like so many adventurers who came west to seek their fortunes, Nathanial Jennings fell in love with the rugged land and its people. He took an Indian wife and adopted her way of life. Although Jennings continued to support his eastern family, neither family knew of the other's existence. Perhaps the brothers never would have met if eastern son, Joe, had not gone in search of their father. Even then it was only after the death of the big silent man, who fellow trappers called Little Ned, that the brothers did meet.

Joe, the youth with fair skin and hair, remembered that first encounter well. He glanced at his brother who now rode silently by his side. Why did the memory of that first meeting come to mind? Perhaps it was the captured Wascopum. Michael and the youthful prisoner were about the same age and had similar features. If Gilliam's volunteers had happened upon Michael he would have received the same callous treatment. In Gilliam's eyes, and in the eyes of many of his command, every Indian was considered an enemy to be treated harshly. The thought of what was in store for the prisoner made him shudder. Unless the unfortunate Wascopum gave Gilliam the information he wanted, there was no end to the cruelty the colonel might employ.

Michael Two Feather's thoughts also were on the Wascopum youth. What harm had the boy done? He looked about as warlike as a friendly puppy. He probably had been daydreaming when the confrontation happened, thinking of how he would make the brilliant shot that would down a prize deer, his fellow hunters applauding his unerring aim and strong bow and awarding him the heart and tongue, delicacies that would please his mother. In one brief moment his thoughts of glory would have turned to ones of disgrace. He had been captured and bound like a rabbit caught in a snare. Even if he escaped he would ever afterward be tainted with shame. He had been the rear guard and taken completely unaware. The elders would be reluctant to give him a position of trust again.

The encounter made a variety of impressions on Gilliam's troopers. The idlers and wastrels were not affected greatly. They saw the campaign as a lark. Although they handled the skirmish badly, they were thrilled by the excitement. They had met the enemy. They hadn't spilled blood but they could taste it. The next time the murdering redskins had better watch out. They wouldn't slip up again.

For some volunteers the Wascopum encounter was like a sobering slap in the face. Their inept behavior left them feeling ashamed. They had fired a dozen rounds each and drawn no blood. The youthful prisoner, handled like a piece of baggage, made them uneasy. They tried to avoid looking at him. It was impossible. Each bob of the poor boy's head made them wince. Was this the way Gilliam planned to treat all prisoners? God help them if he did.

Gilliam's sarcastic orders and scolding did not set well either. Soldiering was not their business. They had volunteered to see that justice was done. There was no reason to badger them like unruly kids. If this was a taste of what was to come, they didn't like it. Walsh, the Irish redhead, voiced their thoughts.

"What kind of campaign is Gilliam conducting? This Injun lad is not a murderer. I doubt if he's even a thief."

Hardly had he spoken when the bay carrying the prisoner stumbled. The youth slid from the saddle and flopped head first on the hard surface of the trail. A sergeant seized the horse's bridle and ordered two troopers to pick up the prisoner. They again threw the youth across the saddle like a bag of meal.

Michael Two Feathers, his blue eyes flashing violet, could not contain himself. "He's a human being," he protested. "Treat him like one." He dismounted and tried to make the prisoner comfortable. Gilliam cantered over, his face set in a scowl.

"Easy, lad," Yellow Beard Adams cautioned. "It won't do the prisoner any good to git the colonel riled."

Michael remounted but couldn't keep his eyes off the captured youth. So this was the way Blue Coat soldiers fought. The very thought he was a member of their ranks filled him with loathing. Vomit dribbled from the captured youth's mouth. Michael spurred his mount alongside and lifted the prisoner's head so he wouldn't choke. Yellow Beard Adams came to help.

"Free the lad's feet; let him sit up," Adams ordered.

Colonel Gilliam halted the column. He rode back, his red face twisted in a scowl. "What's going on?" He glared at Michael who remained holding the prisoner's head.

"This man is sick!" Michael's eyes took on the dangerous, unpredictable violet hue. "He should be allowed to sit the saddle like everybody else."

"The lad's right, sir," Adams said. "The prisoner's throwin' up. If he doesn't sit he'll choke on his puke."

"All right!" Gilliam snapped. "Cut his feet free and be quick about it. These damned Indians have already cost us too much time." He glared at Two Feathers. "From now on mind your own business. I don't need any blathering half-breed to tell me how to run my command."

The prisoner was righted. His hands were bound to the saddle horn. Except for a quick glance at his supporter, Michael Two Feathers, the Wascopum looked at no one, keeping his eyes fixed on the horizon.

"What do yuh suppose he's thinkin'?" someone asked.

"If yuh was in his shoes what would yuh be thinkin'?" Adams sarcastically retorted.

DEATH ON THE UMATILLA

III

*I shall die before my heart is soft or I have said anything
unworthy of myself.*

Canonchet, Narragansett

When panic over the Whitman Mission massacre was at
its height, Governor Abernathy had dispatched a force of forty-
six men to The Dalles. In command was Major Henry A. G. Lee.
"Protect local citizenry and keep the Wascopums peaceful," his
orders read. When Major Lee arrived at The Dalles the men
bivouacked on a tract of ground not far from the Methodist mission. To honor his kinsfolk, the famous Virginia Lee family, he
proudly named the camp Fort Lee.

Upon Colonel Gilliam's arrival, the command of the fort
and all men would be transferred to him. After a period of organization and outfitting, the entire troop would take to the field in
search of the Whitman Mission murderers who were thought to
be hiding in the Cayuse homeland.

A strict observer of military etiquette, Lee and his officers met Gilliam's column at the fort entrance. The bugle sounded.
The welcoming riders saluted. Major Lee politely invited Colonel Gilliam to inspect the encampment. Striding along on his
superior's left, he pointed out the carefully erected tents: canvas
stretched tight, wrinkle free; bedrolls and baggage neatly placed;
saddles and bridles gleaming with polish. Rigid and straight as
pokers, tent occupants stood at attention and saluted as the reviewing officers passed.

Gilliam grimly strode along, glancing neither to the right
nor to the left. This young whippersnapper was showing how a
proper camp should look. On the grounds at West Point that was
well and good. Here on the frontier it was fighting that counted.

The troop that arrived with Gilliam was finally invited to
march into the fort grounds. "Break ranks! Fall out! Make camp!"

the arriving noncoms called out, doing their best to demonstrate to the locals they, too, could look sharp.

Nearly frozen after the cold ride, the men dismounted. Thighs, knees and calves were so stiff and cramped they had to hold on to their horses to keep from falling. A thick mist crept up the slopes from the river. A wet film descended to coat everything exposed. Canvas coats, reins, saddles and packs glistened with droplets of moisture. A biting breeze sliced through homespun garments like a knife through soft butter, leaving skin tingling as if pierced with needles.

Those wearing canvas coats and buckskin trousers fared little better. There was no protection against the dampness or the cold. Hunched like crippled old men, the soldiers hobbled around trying to keep warm. Gradually, blood began to circulate. Shelters went up. Fires were built. Horses were led to pasture. The pleasing odors of cooking food filled the air.

The sons of the mountain man, Little Ned, silently went about setting up their tent. Joe Jennings, the eldest, kept a worried watch over his half-blood brother. Marching with soldiers intent on killing Indian people could not be easy for him. Of course, life for Michael Two Feathers never had been easy. While their father attended a trappers' rendezvous, Michael's mother, Raven Wing, ran away with a villainous half-breed mountain man, taking Michael and a little brother along.

For two years the family lived like vagabonds, traveling from one place to another. Then, within a year, both Little Ned and the villainous stepfather had been killed: Little Ned was shot in the back; Francois felled, stabbed by his own hunting knife. Raven Wing believed Michael was the cause of his stepfather's death. Rather than endure his mother's wrath, Michael had fled his Nez Perce homeland. He traveled to Cayuse country where kindly Narcissa and Marcus Whitman had taken him in. For seven years Michael had lived and worked at Whitman's Cayuse mission. He considered it home.

Then came that terrible day when the killing started.

Michael was away on the Umatilla, helpless to protect his bene-factors. When he, along with his brother, Joe Jennings, arrived at the mission it was too late. All they could do was listen to the stories of the terror-stricken massacre survivors. They rode for help but whatever they did was too little, too late. The mission was plundered and destroyed. Kindly Narcissa and Marcus Whitman had been slain. Michael and the survivors of the Whitman's adopted flock were left bereft and homeless.

Joe started to speak. Instead, attuned to his brother's moods, he held his tongue. What could he possibly say to soothe his brother's tortured mind?

Michael's thoughts not only were on the bloody massa-cre, but also on his prized friend and companion, Magpie. Upon leaving Cayuse country the brothers had taken the trail down river that led to the Willamette Valley. Friends at Wascopum Mission in The Dalles had insisted the best route from there to the Willamette Valley was by canoe.

The brothers left their mounts in care of the mission. Shortly after the brothers had started on the water journey raid-ers descended on Wascopum, running off the mission livestock. Among the animals taken was Michael's beloved Magpie, the beautiful horse with the black and white coloring and shiny coat of the talkative scavenger bird so abundantly found on the pla-teau. What made Magpie even more precious was that he had been a gift from Grandfather Lone Wolf. Losing Magpie was like severing Michael's last tie with his Nez Perce homeland.

After inspecting the camp Gilliam selected a ramshackle cabin for his headquarters. The roof had the appearance of a molting reptile. Here and there patches of shakes had blown away. Chinks between the logs had deteriorated, letting in whis-tling spurts of damp, cold air. The floor was warped and ridged like a freshly plowed field. Beneath it came sounds of rodents scurrying to and fro. Wasp nests clung to ceiling rafters. The air was thick with the smell of skunk, but Gilliam claimed the cabin was a more befitting billet for a troop commander than a tent.

"I'll bunk here," Gilliam informed the first sergeant.

"Yes, sir!" The sergeant ordered a party of privates to muck out the place. Buckets of water dowsed the dust but did little to improve the looks or quell the strong skunk smell. In desperation the sergeant had a couple of horse blankets thrown down to cover the worst sections of floor. Then came the construction of a platform for the colonel's bunk. A table, two chairs and a bench completed the furnishings.

"The colonel must plan to stay a good while," one of the privates observed. "I reckoned he'd march straight up country an' have it out with those damned Cayuses."

"Keep your thoughts to yourself," the sergeant growled. "And don't be in such a bloomin' hurry. You'll get a belly full of fighting before we're through. With Colonel Gilliam in command you can count on that."

Hardly did the first group of volunteers make camp when a second, larger detachment appeared. Shivering, swearing and grumbling about the discomfort, the newcomers jostled for what space remained. Major Lee's neat, uniform encampment became an untidy crazy quilt of shelters, baggage, riding equipment and jumbled odds and ends. The early arrivals greeted the newcomers with jeers and belittling comments.

"Hey, yuh poor boobs, yer stumblin' 'round worse'n blind bears in a briar patch," a caustic voice shouted.

"Hell of a time yuh picked to go to war," came an answering shout.

"What kinda place is this, colder'n a well digger's butt and twice as damp."

"Quit complainin'. Kickin' never gets yuh nowhere 'less yer a mule."

Neither Michael nor Joe joined in the repartee. Joe cleaned and reloaded his rifle and hand gun. He had been on the frontier long enough to know weapons could mean the difference between life and death. In this bunch of undisciplined rowdies the enemy could be in the next tent.

Michael was intent on the Wascopum prisoner. Perhaps he knew where to find Magpie. He watched the guards lead the prisoner into the compound where they chained him to a post. The freezing wind flapped the prisoner's skimpy clothing, exposing his bare midriff. Michael shivered. It would not take long before the prisoner would be frozen stiff. He dug into his pack and came up with an extra shirt. When no one watched, he draped it over the youth. The Wascopum remained as still as the post. Only his eyes moved. Michael wanted to ask about Magpie, but now was not the time.

Michael led his mare to the pasture field. He had borrowed the mount at Fort Vancouver from Hudson's Bay. He started to hobble the horse, then changed his mind. It was best to have a look around before dark. He mounted and rode to the heights above The Dalles. From this vantage point he could see up river until it disappeared around a rocky bend. To the west the river was lost in the drizzle and mist that blew in from the Great Water white faces called Pacific Ocean.

Outside of the soldiers in the camp below and the horses in the pasture, there was little movement. The mission, which stood above and to the east of Fort Lee, was surrounded by a cluster of abandoned emigrant wagons. Standing motionless on the hillside above the mission was a small herd of cattle. Michael decided they belonged to emigrants waiting to take Barlow Road across the Cascades and into the Willamette Valley.

In the midst of the cattle he caught a glimpse of a white hide spotted with black. His heart leaped. "Magpie!" He kicked the old Hudson's Bay mare in the ribs. All his fears had been for naught. His dear friend had not been stolen after all.

When he came near the cattle began to stir. The one with the markings of Magpie skittered away from the rest. Suddenly he had a full view of the animal. The beautiful mane had been clipped. The white and black hide was a muddy grey. The head had horns! It was a cow, the kind emigrants called brindle.

Michael reined up and groaned. He must be losing his mind. How could he have mistaken a cow for his beloved Magpie?

A bugle call sounded. The lonely notes drifted up to hang in the air. Michael kicked his mount into a lope and raced for the camp. He would be in trouble if he didn't answer the bugle call. He arrived in time to see the ranks standing stiffly at attention while the color guard lowered the flag. In keeping with his desire to maintain military post discipline, Major Lee had turned the men out for retreat.

"Dismissed!" The order rang over the formation. The men ran for their shelters and the warmth of campfires. Michael trudged toward the pasture to finally stake out his mare. Jasson, Gilliam's orderly, hailed him.

"Where have you been? What kind of soldier are you, missing retreat? The colonel's as mad as a wet hen. He figured you'd deserted."

Jasson's raspy voice was as hard to take as his looks. Besides closely set, shifty eyes, a wart protruded from the side of his nose. A prominent Adam's apple bobbed up and down with every sound he uttered. Michael avoided looking at him. The pale-faced, long-necked man reminded him too much of the pelican bird. He once heard redheaded Walsh refer to him as Pelican Throat.

What does the colonel want with me, Michael wondered. The man had said straight out, he did not need help from a half-breed.

As though reading Michael's thoughts, Pelican sneered. "Don't be so damned suspicious. He needs you as an interpreter. He's goin' to interrogate the prisoner."

A feeling of despair gripped Michael. The poor prisoner! Death was probably preferable to what Gilliam had in store. When he entered the headquarters cabin Michael's spirits plunged even more. A stench attacked his nostrils. The prisoner, tied and bound, had voided his bladder and bowels. Still, the Wascopum youth sat upright, daring his captors to do their worst. Michael was filled with revulsion. Captured animals waiting to be slaughtered received better treatment than this.

Michael steeled himself. Only the violet hue of the eyes revealed his rage. Colonel Gilliam sat on a bench behind the table apparently unmindful of the prisoner's condition or the odious air. In the background stood the officers: Major Lee, Lieutenant Colonel Waters, two captains and the mountain man, Joe Meek. Michael's flashing violet eyes took in each man's face. How could they stand by and watch?

"About time you showed up," Colonel Gilliam growled.

Michael didn't answer. He stood motionless, angry rebellious thoughts racing through his mind. He had to put a stop to this, but what could he do? Nothing. He would have to wait and watch. Perhaps when the interrogation was over . . . .

Colonel Gilliam impatiently banged his quirt on the table top. "Let's begin. Two Feathers, you speak the prisoner's lingo. Ask him where his people are holding the horses and cattle taken from here. Tell him we want them back and damned quick."

Michael glanced at the youth. His anger turned to shame. "Sir, give him a chance to clean up. He won't talk. He's humiliated." There was a murmur of agreement, but Gilliam cut it off. "Do as I say. We're here to render justice, not mollycoddle these thieves. Every single one is guilty as sin. Make this man understand he won't go free until he tells us what we want."

Michael choked back a protest. He drew close to the prisoner until the stench made his nostrils twitch. "This man is like a mad dog," he said to the prisoner in Chinook, the trading language of the region. He knew Joe Meek understood but he didn't care. He continued speaking in slow soothing words. "Throw him a bone and he'll lie down and gnaw. Give him nothing and he'll bite."

Michael went on to ask about the raid and the missing herd. He might as well have spoken to a post. Not a flicker of understanding came to the young man's eyes. In spite of the filth, the prisoner remained erect and defiant. His posture spoke louder than words. "Question all you want. These Blue Coats are not worthy of my answers."

Michael shook his head. "It's no use. He won't speak. He would lose face if he did."

"He'll lose more than face if he doesn't." Gilliam came around the table. He slapped the prisoner with his leather gauntlets. The bound man did not blink. His unseeing eyes remained fixed on the far wall.

"Take him away," Gilliam said in disgust. "We'll give him time to think. By morning he'll be happy to spill his guts."

Michael left quickly. He waited outside and watched the guards curse as they hustled the smelly prisoner away. Joe Meek walked up to stand alongside. "Sorry business. I suppose Gilliam believes stern measures are necessary to bring the guilty parties to justice."

Michael was too furious to speak. Meek had taken Indian women for mates. One of them had given him a beautiful daughter, yet, here he was, speaking of justice, standing by while Gilliam tortured an innocent Indian youth.

"I knew your father," Meek continued. "Good man. I'm sorry Little Ned is gone."

Michael glanced at the bleak bluffs on the far river bank. He knew what Meek wanted. He wanted to hear about his daughter, Helen Mar. Like himself, Helen Mar had been taken in by the Whitmans. Now she was dead. She wasn't killed in the massacre but died afterward while prisoner of the Cayuse.

Meek finally got around to asking. "Helen Mar? I'm sure you know she was my daughter."

Michael nodded. Helen Mar had been only seven-years old, but everyone loved her. Often she and little David Malin came to help in the fields. He remembered them best running up and down the garden rows ringing bells to scare away black birds and crows. Sometimes the two youngsters brought sweets fresh from the oven. They would sit in the shade of the corn and slowly eat the treat, savoring each crumb. Michael glanced at the mountain man. What could he say? There were no words to express how heartsick he felt and how much he, too, missed sweet, loving Helen Mar.

"I know," Meek mumbled. "Some things are too hard to talk about." He stared at the darkening hills, brushed at his eyes and turned away.

Michael untethered the Hudson's Bay mare and led her to pasture. For a long while he stood among the grazing horses, listening to them crop and chew on the dry tufts of grass. Dusk fell into darkness, still he remained on the hillside reviewing the day's terrible events. He remembered a Lapwai medicine man's warning when he was a boy. There were places on Mother Earth where bad spirits gathered. These places were to be avoided. If you stayed there long bad things would happen to you. The bend in the river at The Dalles had to be one of these evil places. It was here he lost Magpie; here his mother and stepfather committed their terrible crime -- here an innocent youth was being tortured.

He could not stifle an anguished moan. The gloomy mist and rushing waters of the river brought back the stark grimness of that night long ago. Like now, dusk had fallen when Francois, his evil stepfather, appeared. Baby Young Wolf was crying. They had eaten nothing that day but a handful of dried salmon. Michael's mother, Raven Wing, expected her mate to return with food. Instead, he stumbled in with nothing, smelling of firewater. Francois had wagered away almost everything they possessed: horses, saddles, bridles, saddlebags and saddle blankets.

"I'll win them all back," he promised. Before Raven Wing could stop him, Francois gathered up their buffalo robes and buckskins. In a few hours he returned empty-handed.

"Your elk skin dress," Francois demanded, reaching for the only pack Raven Wing had been able to save. When she resisted Francois knocked her aside. Michael could stand no more. He went for the knife at Francois' belt but Francois was too quick. He snatched it away. For a moment the blade hung poised above Michael's head. Then out of the darkness a Chinook fisherman appeared. Francois turned on him. One swipe with the knife blade and the fisherman's throat was slit. Michael could still hear the gurgling, whistling sounds as the man drowned in his own blood.

Everything that happened afterward was a blur. In a daze he watched Raven Wing and Francois roll the murdered man's body down the bank and into the river. They hurriedly collected the possessions that remained and fled in the Chinook's canoe. As hard as Michael tried to forget, the horror of that terrible night was imbedded in his mind. His beautiful mother had condoned and taken part in a despicable murder. Never again had he viewed her with loving eyes. Sometimes in his dreams she appeared with blood dripping from her hands.

Michael sadly shook his head. What frightful things some people did in their lifetimes and never gave them a second thought. He left the grazing horses and walked glumly and slowly back to camp. He had a premonition this evil place soon would witness more terrible events. At the tent he found Joe wrapped in blankets snoring softly. Michael sat down on his own bedroll and listened to his brother. After what had occurred today, how could he possibly sleep?

DEATH ON THE UMATILLA

IV

Tell my people I am dead. My bones will be lying beside the road. I wish my people to gather them up and take them home.

Satank, Kiowa

Michael Two Feathers was not the only one to spend a miserable night. The poor Wascopum prisoner, chained to a post and bound hand and foot, had passed beyond feeling terror. Pain was his friend now. He invited it -- the greater the pain the sooner would be the release, he believed. All he wished for now was to see Father Sun rise so he could view his homeland for the last time. Then he was prepared to leave this world for the next.

Although the spirit of death hovered over the Wascopum youth, it was not ready to invite him to the other side just yet. There was more suffering to be done. The thongs that bound him cut deeply into his flesh. Every movement sent pain shooting up his legs and arms. His body stench pained him more than the wounds. Like all Mother Earth's creatures, he had been taught cleanliness. Now, he was coated with filth. The guards couldn't stand the smell either. In the early morning hours they half led and half dragged the prisoner to the creek and pushed him into the freezing water.

Blue Lizard stumbled and fell, his head landed beneath the surface. Taking in huge gulps of water, spluttering and gasping, he struggled to right himself. When it seemed he would drown, the guards tossed their rifles aside, cut the bonds and lifted him to his feet. The ability to move his limbs again gave Blue Lizard hope. He took a deep breath and slowly let it out. He flexed his freed legs and arms, feeling new strength course through his veins. If he acted quickly, he had a chance.

His captors, seeing the transformation, cursed and fell back to retrieve their weapons. Blue Lizard pushed a guard down and splashed water in the other's face. While they cursed and scrambled for their weapons Blue Lizard turned to run. His legs, had been bound too long. They failed him. Frantically, he crawled on hands and knees and made it to the far bank.

Michael, who had rolled out of warm blankets and was pulling on his buckskin leggings, heard the shot. "Halt! Halt!" The loud cry was followed by a second rifle shot, then came an exuberant shout. "Got him!" Michael uttered an anguished groan. Without looking he knew what happened. The prisoner had been shot and killed.

Cursing and mumbling, the men staggered out to stand in formation. "What was the shootin' an' shoutin' all about?" Walsh, the redhead, asked.

"Probably someone saw his shadow an' thought an' Injun was on his tail," Adams replied, combing the tangles out of his yellow stained beard.

As the grousing troopers lined up for roll call they fell quiet. Noisy late arrivals were hushed. In front of the parade ground the dead Indian boy was bound to a post. His head had been propped up, making him appear alive, his blank gaze watching their every move.

"What the hell's Gilliam tryin' to do?" Adams muttered, more to himself than anyone else. "Make us feel like butchers of innocent kids?"

"Quiet in the ranks," the sergeant yelled. When roll call was completed, Gilliam strode purposely out of the ramshackle skunk odoriferous cabin. He took his place in front of the formation and scanned his command. The troopers, ordered to stand at ease, shuffled uncomfortably under his cold stare. A whiff of skunk from the colonel's clothes tainted the crisp, cool air.

"You may well wonder why I put this body on display." Gilliam's voice carried to the far end of the fort. "I did it to get your attention. Our first engagement with the enemy ended in disaster. A small band of Indians made us look like incompetent fools. In the future this is the way I expect you to deal with the enemy." He pointed to the body with its staring eyes.

"You have to be ruthless. You have to learn to take care of yourselves. This sight may sicken you now, but wait until you're face to face with the murdering Cayuse.

"We gave this Wascopum youth an opportunity to clean himself. Once his hands and feet were free, he jumped the guards. Thanks to Private Jasson, he didn't escape. This is a good lesson for all of you. Indians can't be trusted. Turn your back on them, and they'll spring on you quicker than a cat. There's a saying, 'the only good redskin is a dead one.' As far as I'm concerned, it's true." The colonel's searching eyes went down the ranks. The gray-green orbs had the merciless look of a rattlesnake ready to strike.

High on the bluff the band of Wascopum watched. The leader raised his fist in the sign of vengeance. He motioned his men into the trees. They slipped away but not before making mental notes of the Blue Coat campsite and the pasture where their horses grazed.

"Dismiss the men," Gilliam ordered and strode back to the headquarters cabin.

The volunteers fell out and drifted away. Even those eager to engage the enemy were appalled at Gilliam's grim address.

"Damn me! I believe that guy believes what he says," Walsh said. "It's a wonder he didn't hang a medal on that wart-nosed, long-necked pelican, Jasson."

Breakfast did not improve the troopers' outlook. The mess wagons had not arrived. The soldiers had to make do with the provisions they carried. Some possessed none.

"This is a hellava way to run a war," a beanpole of a man complained. "Why weren't we told we had to bring our own grub? My stomach's rubbin' agin me backbone. I declare, this mornin' I heered a rooster crow. Roosters mean hens. Hens mean eggs. I say we do a bit of foragin' an' see what vittles kin be scrounged."

"Yuh cain't do that. That poultry belongs to folks at the Methodist mission. If we start actin' like a pack of thieves we'll be no better than the redskins," Adams protested.

"Save yer sermon fer the Sabbath, brother," ordered a black-bearded man with crooked teeth that seemed much too large for his thin-lipped mouth. "We left good homes to give these folks pertection. It seems fittin' they sacrifice a few eggs an' chickens. What do yuh say, boys? Ol' Gilliam claims we gotta be ruthless an' larn to take care of ourse'ves. 'Peers to me now's the time to begin."

Like a wave of locusts, the foraging troops strode up the hillside toward the mission outbuildings a quarter of a mile away. They plundered the chicken house first. Hens and roosters ran every which way with the men in hot pursuit. A man seized a pitchfork, spearing a hen on the fly. He held the squawking bird up for all to see. "Betcha the old girls got eggs inside," he chortled. "We'll hev a breakfast fit fer kings, 'er mine name ain't Ben, The Chicken Thief."

The scourge of plunderers broke into the hog pens next. The squealing pigs raced around the pen like squirrels on a re-volving wheel, running into each other, knocking down people and squealing like banshees. Here again the pitchfork man tried his luck. He stuck a pig but the pained animal turned on him. The pitchfork wieldier scrambled to get away but the pig was too quick for him. He found himself knocked flat into a sump of pig manure. The pitchfork that had remained stuck in the squealing pig flew into the air, the sharp steel tines coming to rest within inches of the pig tormentor's head.

Across the pen and through the frail fence the pig charged, bursting through the wooden fence boards with the force of a cannon ball. The rest of the pigs followed. Out in the open, squealing loudly, they scattered in all directions. A volunteer with a coil of rope attempted to lasso a shoat. The rope slid off the head, but one leg was caught in the noose.

"Ham on the hoof," he shouted, pulling the squealing porker toward camp. Two young heifers also were roped and led away from the emigrant herd.

Owners of the purloined livestock and poultry ran to save their animals, but the volunteers brushed them off as if they were annoying flies. A white-headed man was knocked down. His womenfolk attacked the troopers with sticks and brooms. Some officers and noncoms made token attempts to stop the pillage. Others joined in. Later, Gilliam, himself, gorged on roasted pig.

Late in the day the first wagon of supplies finally arrived. Still gloating over the successful raid on the emigrant camp, a group of plunderers led by the bearded man with the crooked teeth and thin lips descended on the newly arrived supply wagons. The gang of marauders swelled until half the camp was involved. The corporal and men who accompanied the wagon watched helplessly as coffee, flour, beans, bacon and other edibles went into trooper's pockets, packs and saddlebags.

"This is appalling! It's bloody anarchy! An ant hill has better discipline than this."

Joe burst out of the shelter where he had remained during the raid on the emigrant camp. There was one person only who spoke the King's English so crisply and with such disdain. He thought he had gotten rid of that man. The last time he saw him, he was waiting for a ship to take him back to Great Britain. Joe could see at a glance a body of new troops had arrived. Yes, there he was, the owner of the voice, a handsome erect man in neat buckskins riding a tall, well-groomed bay. In spite of his reluctance, Joe strode toward him.

"Hello, stranger," he greeted. The rider gave him a sharp look of surprise.

"Well, I say, fancy meeting you again, and amongst this rabble. What is the matter with soldiers in this part of the world? Do they not know how to go to war?"

"Yes, it's a bit strange to them. We don't have the long tradition of your people. Perhaps your presence will bring them up to the mark."

"I doubt that," the rider dismounted. "But, it is good to see you are not a member of this mob. As I remember, you attempt to do what is right whether you like it or not."

"Yeah . . . ." Joe fell silent. Yes, he always had tried to do what was right, but some times it was difficult to judge right from wrong. Getting friendly with Macon Laird had been one of those wrong judgements. He had stood by and watched his twin sister, Tildy, who was already pledged to another, fall in love with this handsome foreigner. Did he try and stop it? No, he was too blind. What was this man doing here? He couldn't be hanging around intending to lure Tildy away from her husband, could he?

As Joe wrestled with the problem, another voice startled him. Out of the gaggle of new troops, riding what looked to be a plow horse, was Sandy Sanders, his brother-in-law, the man who had married his sister, Tildy. Joe was almost too stunned to speak.

"Whatever made you join up?" he blurted. "This is a shooting war. You have Tildy and the baby to take care of."

Sandy's freckled face widened in a grin. "I thought you'd put up a fuss, but I couldn't very well sit around and not do my part. Tildy and little John are the reasons I'm here. When a man doesn't protect home and family a sorry fellow is he."

"Well, now that you're here you might as well get settled in. You remember Macon Laird, don't you? He was on the wagon train when we met you at Fort Hall."

"Yes, of course. You were a good friend to Tildy," Sandy said shaking hands. "Never did get a chance to say thanks."

Joe turned away. The irony of the situation made him feel sick. If Sandy only knew how good a friend Macon Laird had been to Tildy he probably would knife him dead on the spot, that is, if he could. To his knowledge, Sandy never had spoken a single word of anger in his life. Joe shook his head. Putting the two of them together was like placing a tiger alongside the crib of an innocent child.

DEATH ON THE UMATILLA

V

We love our country -- it is composed of the bones of our people, and we will not part with it.

Cayuse Spokesman

Michael found himself camped with Joe, Macon Laird and Sandy Sanders. Somehow Joe had brought the group together. In his taciturn way he got along with everybody but selected his friends and companions with care. As far as Michael could tell he had chosen well. Sandy Sanders was married to Joe's twin sister, Tildy. Macon Laird had been a member of the wagon train Joe had helped guide halfway across the continent. But at Fort Hall something had gone wrong. Laird abruptly left the wagon train and traveled from there on his own.

Michael had to keep reminding himself Tildy was also his sister. That made Sandy Sanders related to him by marriage. If Sandy knew of the relationship he never mentioned it. Michael was surprised Joe did not set Sandy straight. After the survivors of the Whitman Mission massacre were rescued, he and Joe had planned to visit Sandy, Tildy and Granddad Jennings in the Willamette Valley. They never got beyond Oregon City where recruiting officials detained them, insisting they join the ranks of volunteers preparing to march on the Cayuse.

Among the four of them crowded together in the single tent, Sandy was the loquacious one. Without any encouragement Sandy spoke at length of his Willamette Valley farm and family. He had homesteaded 640 acres. Much of the land was still in timber, he informed his companions. Forty acres were cleared and fenced. He had a fine home and barn. He raised chickens, pigs, sheep and cattle.

His pride and joy was his baby son. Sandy's freckled face lit up like a candle flame when he spoke of little Baby John. Michael noticed, however, when Tildy or her baby son were

mentioned, Joe never said a word. When the conversation demanded an answer, he merely nodded or shook his head.

Macon Laird acted much the same. Every time Tildy's or
Baby John's name came up the Englishman busied himself with
his pipe, riding equipment or guns. What made the two men act
so strangely? Michael watched them closely. There was something about Tildy and Baby John that made them uneasy. Whatever it was, it didn't bother Sandy. Almost every night he talked
about his family and farm, ignoring the silence of Joe and Macon
Laird.

Anxious to learn more about these folks who came from
Boston country and were related to him, Michael often asked
about Tildy and her baby. He was fascinated by the thought of
having a baby nephew. In his daydreams he had been accepted
into the family. He was the uncle who taught Baby John how to
track, ride, and shoot. He was the one who would show Baby
John the difference between the marks of a bear and those of a
mountain lion. He would take him to the beaver streams to see
the tireless rodents build their lodges. He would teach him to
mimic the calls of Bobwhite, Killdeer and Crow. He would tell
him the legends of Coyote, Badger and Wolf. Most of all he
would teach him there was no difference between dark skin and
white skin. Beneath the skin people were the same, related to
one another by the fact that among the creature world, they walked
on two legs.

Michael knew his hopes of acting the wise and helpful
uncle were slim. He had met Tildy and Granddad Jennings briefly
when their wagon train made a rest stop at Fort Hall. Their manner told him that he could not possibly be related to them. Even
if by chance he was, they had no room for him in their hearts. He
was a savage, like a tamed wild animal that might suddenly re-
vert to its native ways.

Michael did not hold it against them. He would have
been surprised if they had welcomed him with open arms. From
his experience with emigrants who passed through the mission,

he knew white folks did not like half-bloods any better than they did full blooded Indians. They were all "dirty redskins." If Sandy knew he was related to a half-blood would he remain friendly? Would his freckled face light up with pleasure as it did when he spoke of family and farm? Dared he hope this would happen?

Macon Laird was a baffling mystery in himself. What was the Englishman doing marching with American Blue Coats? He was a former British army captain. He had explored in a place called Africa. He had soldiered on the frontiers of a strange country named Afghanistan. Long before the massacre he had appeared at Whitman's Mission. When he announced he was a friend of the Jennings family the Whitmans invited him in. They were impressed by his handsome face, pleasant demeanor and impeccable manners. They were unaccustomed to having polished gentlemen appear at their isolated home among the Cayuse.

Covertly, Michael studied Macon Laird. He liked the British man who always had treated him with respect. For that matter he treated all Indian people in the same pleasant manner he did those of his own race. After the mission massacre he did what he could to relieve the survivors' suffering and bring peace to the plateau. He met with Indian leaders, smoked with them, supped with them and listened patiently to their complaints.

He was an enigma. No one could decide why he was so considerate and sympathetic. He was a complete outsider. He had no one involved in the troubles of the region. Why did he come to this troubled country? What was he after -- what did he have to gain? Michael finally came to the conclusion he was one of those rare individuals who truly was interested in people. He did what he did because he believed suffering inflicted on one people very well could be inflicted on all peoples. He wanted to help shoulder this pain that could befall any of Mother Earth's creatures.

His own brother, Joe, also left Michael perplexed. Since the arrival of Macon Laird and Sandy Sanders he'd barely said a word. His expression was as stern and foreboding as a Blackfeet warrior. Why the sudden change? Before the new arrivals appeared they had joked and laughed. They were truly like two brothers. Had he done something that irked Joe?

For hours Michael laid awake trying to unravel the mysteries surrounding his companions, especially his brother Joe. Then, also there was the matter of finding Magpie. Hardly an hour went by without his four-legged friend coming to mind. He kept hoping they would make a search for the lost mission herd. If Colonel Gilliam did not order one he would have to conduct a search of his own.

##

Michael Two Feathers was not the only one mystified by his tent companions. Sandy Sanders also had difficulty in making sense of their behavior. He thought he knew his brother-in-law, Joe Jennings. Joe and his mountain man companion, Deacon Walton, had spent the previous winter in his Willamette Valley home, recuperating from injuries and frost bite suffered during the 1846 crossing of the plains. Upon their recovery, Joe and Deacon had worked around the homestead, building fences and adding extensions to the small cabin. Along with Tildy, Granddad Jennings and Baby John, they had lived as one happy family. There was no discord. They all were happy to be healthily alive and together.

The thought of campaigning with Joe had brought Sandy to The Dalles. He fully expected a hard campaign. Yet, with Joe along he would be doing his patriotic duty and also have an exciting adventure the family could talk about for years to come. But Joe had turned into a different person. Where before, even in the worst of times, he had been the greatest of companions, there now was a grim intentness about him that made one shy away. Joe never seemed interested in hearing about his twin sister, Tildy, Granddad Jennings or Baby John. Actually, when Tildy's and Baby John's names came up he seemed to freeze as did the Britisher, Macon Laird.

What was it about Tildy and the baby that caused these
two men to act this way? It was as if they didn't want to know
anything about his family and the homestead in the valley. He
could understand Macon Laird. He was English and naturally
reserved. Yet, Laird knew both Tildy and Granddad Jennings.
He had traveled with them, driving one of the Jennings' wagons
from Independence, Missouri to Fort Hall. Agh! The behavior
of these two was shrouded in a mystery too obscure to solve.

Then there was the half-blood, Michael Two Feathers.
Joe treated him with unusual deference. From the way they spoke
they had known each other a good long while. Sandy searched
his memory. During the winter had Joe ever mentioned a special
Indian friend? No, but there was that Indian lad at Fort Hall who
ran with a band of Snakes. Joe and he knew each other. Yes,
actually he brought the youthful Indian over and introduced him
to Tildy and Granddad Jennings. He remembered that clearly
because Tildy had acted shocked and afraid.

Surreptitiously, Sandy glanced at Michael Two Feathers.
It could be the same person. Of course, clad in the dress of the
volunteers it was hard to make a comparison. Michael was just
another dark-faced youth. Yet, there was something about him
that rang a bell.

Sandy stared at the darkened sky overhead and thought
hard about the meeting at Fort Hall. At the time he was so excited over seeing Tildy, his betrothed, he had eyes for nothing
else. On looking back, he did remember a certain strangeness
about the reunion. Tildy greeted him with unusual exuberance,
then immediately broke into tears -- crying for joy, he had thought.
Then it occurred to him she was on edge. Had his sudden appearance upset her or had the presence of the Indian lad and his
band of Snakes cause her unease? No, the Indians were not to
blame. He and Tildy had exchanged greetings before they came.

Sandy closed his eyes. Stop thinking about this, he ordered himself. There was nothing to be gained by dredging up
the past. But the strange happenings at Fort Hall nagged at Sandy

like a sore tooth. Forgotten incidents suddenly came to mind. Tildy had excused herself and gone to the fort trading floor to buy sewing things she needed. He gladly would have gone with her but she insisted she go by herself. Funny thing was, she returned with nothing at all -- not a needle, piece of cloth or spool of thread. When asked about it, she broke into tears.

Shortly afterward Macon Laird packed up and rode away, leaving the wagon train for good. Sandy abruptly got to his feet and strode into the night. He had to stop torturing himself. What happened had happened, and he was powerless to turn the clock back.

##

On the third day in camp, a fourth and fifth contingent of troops arrived. Late into the night grumbling stragglers fumbled around in the darkness, searching for places to bed down. The last to arrive was Captain Tom McKay and his band of French Canadians. They struggled with an ancient nine-pound cannon. Long before it appeared, the big gun's progress could be followed by shouts, curses and cracks of whips that aroused the camp.

"Pull! Haul! Shove! Get behind the wheels. Dammit! No! You're pushing the bloody thing into the river." The shouts came nearer and nearer. Many of the troopers who had turned in gave up trying to sleep. They sat up to smoke and curse as the big gun made its slow way up the muddy slope by lantern light.

"What are yuh goin' to do with that bloody big hunk of iron?" someone wanted to know.

"We're going to blow those murderin' Cayuses to kingdom come, that's what we're going to do," came the answer.

At a dip in the grade the cannon slued to a stop, the wheels mired in mud. A teamster harnessed a pair of horses and went to help. After much cursing and shouting, the wheels pulled free. The cannon rolled up the hill to come to rest at the edge of camp. Captain McKay celebrated their arrival by passing a jug around. "Good work, men," he said, taking the last swig himself.

"Yuh gotta hand it to those fellas," a volunteer remarked.

"I figured they'd never get the big gun beyond the portage at the Cascades. Imagine pushin' an' pullin' it all the way here."

"Tom McKay wouldn't leave it behind," one of McKay's French Canadians confided. "He says one firin' an' it'll scare the bejesus out of those pesky Cayuses. They'll throw down their weapons an' skeddadle fer sure."

"I guess it might," Walsh agreed. "It's worth tryin', anythin' to make 'em come to their senses. Jest the same, I hope they don't ask me to pull an' tug on the bloomin' thing. This long barreled rifle is heavy enuff fer me."

Although it was past midnight, Gilliam had candles lit and received Captain McKay in his smelly headquarters cabin. He did so against his will. McKay was Catholic and the half-blood stepson of John McLoughlin, the former head of the North-west Region for Hudson's Bay. Gilliam had no use for anyone connected with the Catholic Church or Hudson's Bay or people of Indian blood or the French or the damned British.

"Why should I suffer this curse?" Gilliam thought. "Why do I have to be saddled with a rascal who represents all I abhor?"

In Gilliam's opinion Hudson's Bay and the Catholic Church plotted the Whitman Mission massacre. Both organizations wanted to see American missions above the Columbia River closed down. Was Captain McKay a part of this conspiracy? He studied the young captain's shadowed face. He had to admit, McKay's French Canadian contingent probably had more fight in them than all of his volunteers. It was far better to have McKay's troops with him than against him. Gilliam swallowed his pride and motioned to a chair.

"Sit down, Captain. Welcome, glad to have you along."

The arrival of McKay's French Canadians also aroused distrust among the enlisted ranks. "Why do we need these French half-bloods? We can fight our own battles," said Jasson, who had killed the defenseless Wascopum.

"Yeah!" a sarcastic voice answered. "With yuh on our side we hev nothin' to fear. When the Cayuses see yuh comin' fer sure they'll take ta the hills."

"Jest if you want. The colonel's got the right idea. Teach these Injuns a lesson they'll not ferget. If we don't punish the Cayuses, who knows what tribe next will take the bit in its teeth."

"Ah, shut up an' go to sleep," came an angry voice. Someone else cursed and threw a boot. "You galoots make more noise than a roost of settin' hens." Gradually, the camp grew quiet.

The arrival of the cannon bothered Michael. From its looks the big gun could blow a fragile Indian village to bits. The thought of his Cayuse friends facing the monstrous gun made his blood run cold. What defense could war clubs and bows and arrows have against its mighty blasts? He was especially worried about Stickus and his band on the upper Umatilla. Stickus had saved his life. If it hadn't been for Stickus he would have been at the mission when the massacre took place. His enemies, Tamsucky, Tomahas and the half-breed, Joe Lewis, would have made certain he was counted among the dead.

There was ample time to ride ahead and warn Stickus. If the Cayuse leader took his people to the Blue Mountains Gilliam's untrained volunteers would never track them down. He glanced around at the sleeping soldiers. No one stirred. Now was his chance. He started to get up. The mound that was Joe made him pause. It was the first time in three years they had been together for any length of time. If he left would they ever get together again? His thoughts then turned to Magpie. For certain he could not leave while there still was a chance to find and rescue his special four-legged friend.

Michael pulled the blankets up to his chin and closed his eyes, but his mind would not rest: the dead Wascopum; the cannon; Gilliam's grim warnings; Stickus and his fragile village on the upper Umatilla . . . . The tormenting thoughts kept going through his mind. Finally, he fell into troubled sleep. He searched and he searched. He could not find Magpie. He jerked awake in a cold sweat. "Aah!" he groaned. He never should have gone off and left the dearest friend he ever had.

DEATH ON THE UMATILLA

VI

Show respect to all men, but grovel to none . . . .
Tecumseh, Shawnee

Major Lee was up at the crack of dawn. He stepped out
of the tent and walked quickly to keep warm. A cock crowed. A
dog barked. The sounds died away, then returned, echoing back
from the escarpment. They reminded Lee of discordant church
bells, much like the ones that called the family to Sunday wor-
ship when he was a boy.

In front of the headquarters cabin Lee stopped. While he
waited for Gilliam to appear, he inspected the sprawling camp.
It was a disgrace, laid out like a patchwork quilt. A trained blood-
hound couldn't find its way through the hodgepodge of shelters.
Troops quickly called into action would find themselves entangled
in ropes and canvas. The major scowled. What could you expect from an army of volunteers?

Major Henry A. G. Lee was not uppity. He merely liked
discipline and order. He came by it directly. He was a member
of the famous Lees of Virginia. A forefather had taken part in
the First Continental Congress and drafted important sections of
the Constitution. Major Lee's namesake was first governor of
Virginia. He gained fame in the Revolutionary War as the fabled
cavalry leader, "Light Horse Harry Lee." Another member of the
family would later become even more famous: General Robert
E. Lee.

Major Lee was proud of his heritage. Yet, at times he
found it burdensome. Much was expected of him. So far he had
done little to embellish the family name, hopping from one thing
to another. He crossed the plains with Marcus Whitman's 1843
wagon train, spending the winter of 1843-44 helping Reverend
Spalding at the Nez Perce Lapwai Mission school. After learning the rudiments of the native language he traveled on to the

Willamette Valley where he took a job as aide and interpreter to
pompous, irascible Indian Agent Elijah White. He soon left the
post to labor as editor of the *Oregon Spectator*. Then the Whitman
Mission massacre occurred. Men with experience dealing with
the Indian people were needed. He was given a command with
the rank of major and chosen as one of three peace commissioners. His orders as troop commander were to seize and secure
Wascopum Station at The Dalles. As peace commissioner he
was to maintain neutrality among peaceful tribes.

Major Lee considered himself a failure in both duties.
Barely two weeks after arriving at The Dalles a band of Indian
raiders ran off three hundred cattle and horses. He made a desperate attempt to recapture the stock. Several raiders were killed
or wounded in the chase, but the herd was lost. The stolen animals and thieves seemed to have vanished into thin air.

Establishing a military outpost and dealing with hostiles
left Lee little time to seek out and meet leaders of neutral tribes.
Thus, his peace commissioner successes were nil. The future
looked equally bleak. Gilliam's harsh treatment of the Wascopum
made any attempt to gain their good will hopeless.
##
Gilliam sauntered out of the headquarters cabin still buck-
ling his belt. He had not slept well. He had grown accustomed
to the skunk smell, but a dozen rats must have raced back and
forth beneath the floor boards all night. He gave Lee a curt nod
and returned the salute. He inspected the major's impeccable
dress and scowled. "Don't pay to get spruced up. Indian fighting's
a messy business. I should think you'd found that out by now."

Major Lee flushed. Gilliam's snide reference to the disastrous Indian raid struck home. "Yes, sir." He managed to
keep his tone respectful, but had the urge to step away. The skunk
odor emanating from the colonel's clothes was overwhelming.

Gilliam studied the untidy camp and frowned. "The compound isn't large enough to house and train the troops. We'll
expand it to the base of that bluff. Might as well include the

horse pasture. After the raids our boys made on the emigrant camp we need to keep them well apart. To appease the mission people, we'll call the expanded grounds, Fort Wascopum."

"Yes, sir." From the moment he arrived Gilliam had made it clear he was annoyed at being forced to refer to the installation as Fort Lee. The major was surprised the pompous commander didn't name the expanded encampment Fort Gilliam.

After an uneasy pause, Major Lee spoke again. "With your permission, sir, I would like to lead a party to search for the stolen herd. A report has just been received that a band of horses has been seen in the hilly country to the southeast"

Gilliam pulled on his ear lobe and ruminated. He had been reluctant to leave the church congregation in North Luckiamute where he lived and preached, but perhaps it was for the best. The Cayuse campaign gave him the opportunity to teach young fellows like Major Lee the bloody business of Indian fighting. Could this persnickety officer rise to the occasion? He would soon find out whether the Lee reputation was earned or puffery?

"Ah!" Gilliam inwardly gloated. "If only I could have had Lee under my command at the Battle of Bad Ax." Could he have stomached the cold-blooded slaughter of the followers of the Sauk chief, Blackhawk? He thought not. Even hardened border men had puked. It was a scrap that separated men from the boys. They had come upon a thousand or more Sauk and Fox trapped on the shore of the Mississippi. For hours his troop, dug in on the levee, rained shot down on the hapless victims. From the river steamboats raked them with grape and cannon ball. It was like shooting fish in a barrel. That day some three hundred savages had gone to their rewards.

Gilliam studied the youthful major. Lee had let three hundred head of livestock get away. The extra mounts and provisions on the hoof the volunteers needed were gone. The loss meant another delay in the campaign. Lee should be reprimanded severely, but the young man had influential friends in Oregon City. It wouldn't do to upset Governor Abernathy. If Lee failed again .... Yes, that was the answer. Another failure would really put the arrogant young fellow under his thumb. He would either make a soldier out of this man or get rid of him, preferably the latter. He had no use for these people with high breeding who thought themselves better than the normal herd.

"Permission granted. Ask for volunteers. Some of these men are anxious to get their noses bloodied. Might as well accommodate them. Take along that fellow Joe Jennings and the half-breed, Two Feathers. Perhaps you'll find them useful. They should know this country backwards and forwards. We don't want anyone lost, do we?"

"No, sir," Major Lee said stiffly. He saluted the colonel and turned sharply on his heel. Why did Gilliam always make him feel like a plebe being granted permission to relieve himself?

Before most of the troopers finished eating breakfast, Major Lee had a detachment mounted, ready to take to the field. He sent runners to fetch Jennings and Two Feathers. Joe readily agreed. Michael objected.

"Why should I go? Let the colonel find somebody else to track the raiders down." He turned away and began to tidy up the tent. He didn't want to face the Wascopum, not in the company of Gilliam's troops. The thought of the way the prisoner had been treated made him sick to his stomach. He should have done something to save the youth. To his great shame, he had not lifted a finger.

"Major Lee asked especially for you," Joe insisted. "He needs someone who knows the Cayuse language. I expect he thinks you may get a chance to parlay with the raiders. They will listen to you where they wouldn't a regular trooper. If you persuaded them to return the stolen livestock peacefully it would save lives. You'd be a hero."

"Nobody's going to be a hero in this campaign."

"It's an order. Soldiers who don't obey orders are disciplined. No telling what Gilliam might do. He might even have you shot. Besides, what if we stumble onto Magpie? You want to get your pony back, don't you?"

Magpie! Why hadn't he thought of that? Of course he would go. He would do anything to find Magpie, even face the Wascopum. He hurried to saddle his horse. Before he could get mounted, Sandy Sanders, who had been assigned sentry duty, plodded in on his old plow horse. He pulled to a stop in front of Major Lee, a woebegone expression on his freckled face.

"Sir!" Sandy blurted. "A dozen horses have been stolen! The tracks lead into the hills. I would have gone after them but this . . ." He shrugged his shoulders, looking down at the shaggy, ponderous hooves of the big horse.

The commotion brought Gilliam out of his skunky head-quarters cabin. He called Sandy Sanders over and ordered him to dismount. "What kind of soldier are you? Guards are sup-posed to stay alert. When intruders appear you sound the alarm, roust everybody out. What do I have to do? Lead each one of you around by the hand? Major Lee, you have a detachment ready to ride. Get cracking and get after those thieves. We're already short of mounts. And take this idiot with you."

Major Lee accepted the new assignment without com-ment. Perhaps the search would lead to discovery of the first stolen animals. He wheeled his horse around and led the troop-ers out of camp at a gallop. Beyond the pasture grounds he sig-naled for the column to halt.

"Front and center," he shouted to chastened Sandy Sand-ers whose slow mount had him trailing far behind. "Come on! Hurry it up! Show us which way the raiders went."

Sandy urged the big horse forward. His ears still glowed from Gilliam's public scolding. He dismounted and walked a ways, looking perplexed. "I'm all turned around," he confessed. "Everything looks different now."

Major Lee started to upbraid the young farmer, then changed his mind. "All right, trooper. No one should expect a man to become a soldier in a day. Return to your post." He motioned for Michael to come forward. "Perhaps you can find the tracks."

Michael pretended he didn't hear. He hated the way officious Colonel Gilliam had humbled poor Sandy before the whole troop. Sandy had done the best he could. Untrained and riding an old work horse, who among the settler volunteers would have done differently? Besides, the trail was as plain as day. The raiders left tracks an old woman could follow. This was most disturbing. The tracks were too conspicuous. They indicated the raiders either were young men without raiding experience or they were crafty schemers trying to draw pursuers into ambush. He had the distinct feeling it was the latter.

"Looks like they went that way, don't you think?" Joe dryly observed.

Michael nodded. Why should he tell the young officer of the dangers that might lie ahead? He kicked the Hudson's Bay mare into a canter. The major motioned for the detachment to follow. Michael kept a careful watch on the rim of hills where hostiles would first appear. Not only was the trail well marked but it was made up of strange hoofprints -- tracks of unshod ponies, probably the Wascopum horses, others with shod hooves, the stolen animals from the Blue Coats' herd. But among the unshod tracks were two sets with notched hooves. This was the trademark of Buffalo Horn's horses. It was the way the great Cayuse horseman identified his vast lower Umatilla herds.

Michael silently groaned. If these were the mounts of Buffalo Horn riders, it meant these raiders were a long ways from home. What were they doing here? Whoever they were, they were up to no good. How he wished he had remained in camp. Buffalo Horn's riders were certain to recognize him. They would take the word back to Cayuse country. Everyone in the uplands would know he was riding with the enemy, not just riding with them, but guiding them. He would be regarded a traitor and Cayuse warriors had definite ways of dealing with those who betrayed them.

VII

Today is a good day to fight --
Today is a good time to die.

Crazy Horse, Oglala Sioux

Major Lee led his troop of horsemen over a ridge and into the next valley. "Hiya! There the critters are," one of the riders pointed and shouted. Several of the stolen horses grazed on the far hillside.

Michael reined in his mount, and not because of the fear of being recognized by a Cayuse horseman. His native senses warned him of trouble. The situation ahead did not look right. Why were these horses left behind? Where were the raiders? Thieves didn't abandon the bounty they cleverly had garnered. It suddenly came to Michael. He had seen this trick before. It was a trap. The horses were hobbled.

Major Lee rode up at a canter. "What do you make of it?" he asked. He was exuberant. Already he could see the look on Gilliam's face when he brought the stolen animals into camp. That would put a stop to the irascible officer's snide remarks.

"Perhaps we should wait until someone scouts a bit," Joe answered, covering up for Michael's silence. "This looks mighty suspicious."

Lee gave him a sharp glance. "What do you mean, suspicious? There's nothing out of the ordinary for horses to feed on hillsides. The rest of the herd is probably beyond the ridge. Look at them. They're grazing as peaceful as can be." He turned in his saddle and waved his riding crop. "There they are! Go get them, men! Round up those animals. While you're at it, scout the other side of the hill. The rest of the herd may be there."

Led by a sergeant, a squad of soldiers galloped forward. They were almost on the horses when shots rang out. Two troopers fell. Over the crest of the hill galloped a line of warriors.

Yipping and waving weapons, they pulled up to reload rifles and arm their bows and aim their arrows. A shower of the sharp barbed missiles rained down upon the troopers.

"Pull back! Fall back!" Major Lee shouted. The troopers, who had dismounted to give battle, quickly swung into their saddles. The horses started to turn back. One horse stumbled and fell to its knees. The rider scrambled up and attempted to pull the fallen animal to its feet. The watchers groaned as another wave of arrows showered down.

"Take cover! Take cover!" Major Lee shouted.

The rider fell. His hat blew off exposing a thatch of red hair that, in the bright sunlight, flashed like a mirror.

"It's thet blisterin' Irishman, Walsh," someone reported.

"Yep, 'tis Walsh. He'll be safe as rain. A redheaded Irishman's got more lives than a ring-tailed cat."

Adams placed his hands together and raised them above his head. Michael thought he was praying. Instead he swore. "That damned Irishman! I told him to leave that no-good swayback at home. That mare's old enough to be his mother."

"Damn me, damn me," Major Lee kept repeating. No one paid any attention. Every eye was on the downed Irishman.

"He shot his horse. He's fixin' to run. Oh! My gawd! He's fallen. The dirty brutes hev shot him . . . . Now, he's up an' crawlin' . . . ."

Macon Laird reined his big bay around. "I'm riding out there. Who will go with me? Come on Joe. We can't stand by and watch. Those fellows are in trouble."

Joe gave his tall black mount a kick in the ribs, and was away before Macon had finished speaking. Major Lee started to call them back, but the order died in his throat. It was too late. The two horses thundered toward the fallen man. As they came near, another shower of arrows rained down. The watching troopers groaned. The deadly missiles fell short of the riders but bracketed the Irishman who was back on his feet, running for all he was worth. A single arrow struck him in the shoulder. He stumbled, then fell face forward.

The bay arrived first. Before the horses skidded to a halt Macon Laird was on the ground. Behind him came Joe Jennings, firing his hand gun. The line of warriors swerved away. Quickly, the two men had the wounded man on the big bay. Holding the Irishman in the saddle, Laird urged his horse away. Before Joe could mount up, the Indians charged again. An arrow struck his black in the rump. The startled horse jumped and started to run.

"Dammit, soldier, get after that horse," a trooper shouted.

As though he had heard, Joe ran and grabbed for the trailing reins. The black jerked its head and broke away. Joe made another attempt. This time he snared the reins and swung into the saddle. Whipping his mount into a gallop, he barely outdistanced the horde of whooping warriors that raced down the hillside, brandishing war clubs.

"Open fire," Major Lee ordered. The range was too great, but the warriors pulled up. The watchers ran to meet Laird's big bay and carefully lifted the wounded trooper down.

"Yuh old reprobate, what's the matter with yuh, tryin' to win the war all by yerself," Adams admonished his redheaded friend.

"Ah, go soak yer head an' pull this dad-ratted arra outta me back," Walsh retorted. "It tickles like fury."

The detachment retreated, taking refuge in a swale. Lee put a spyglass to his eye and studied the hill. The hobbled horses grazed as if nothing had happened. Not an Indian warrior was to be seen. Should they try and retrieve the downed troopers? Major Lee decided not to try. Already casualties were too high.

"Rest easy," he told the men. He turned to the rider who had been assigned his messenger. "Return to camp," he ordered. "Inform Colonel Gilliam of the situation. Tell him we need more firepower and a wagon for dead and wounded."

The messenger galloped away. Before he topped the far ridge a line of warriors, uttering bloodcurdling whoops, came pouring out of a ravine and up the slope after him.

"My God!" Major Lee uttered. What else could go wrong? Before he could collect his thoughts, another wave of warriors came hooting over the hill. "Take firing positions!" he ordered.

Just out of range the enemy horsemen stopped. Brandishing their weapons, they yelled taunts. "Come get us, Blue Coats. Are you afraid?" one shouted in English. Michael was certain he recognized the voice. The words were spoken in the manner taught by mission school teachers. Another warrior galloped forward, hurling insults. Then, as quickly as they appeared, the warriors vanished, riding back over the ridge.

There was an agonizing wait. Did the messenger get through or was he a casualty, too? Major Lee didn't know whether to stay or leave. Before he could decide, Colonel Gilliam rode up with reinforcements.

"What's all the commotion?" Gilliam demanded. His gimlet eyes took in the situation in one swift glance. "Where the blazes is the enemy?"

The mounted troopers rode to the top of the rise. The hobbled horses continued to graze peacefully on the hillside. The ridge behind the horses was quiet. Gilliam ordered a detachment to gallop east and flank the hillside. The leader of the flanking troops signaled all clear. The Indians had disappeared. The column rode forward to retrieve the hobbled horses and carry away the two dead troopers. Gilliam was furious.

"You see, I told you so. Indians are tricky as sidewinders!" he ranted. "They don't fight like normal people. That half-breed, Two Feathers, did he lead you into this trap? If he did I'll skin him alive."

"No sir, " Major Lee answered. "I'm the one to blame."

"Might have known," Gilliam snapped.

Major Lee bit back an angry retort. What could he say? It was entirely his fault. Jennings had said the situation looked suspicious. In his eagerness to show off he hadn't listened, and again had made an ass of himself.

VIII

Death will come, always out of season. It is the command of
the Great Spirit and all nations and people must obey.

Big Elk, Omaha

"Skirmish at Hobbled-Horse Hill," Colonel Gilliam labeled the encounter in writing up his log. He made his part appear as favorable as possible. He had rescued a besieged detachment. The troop under his command routed an entrenched enemy. A dozen stolen horses were recovered. Casualties, two troopers killed, one wounded.

He barely mentioned Major Lee. No words came to mind that adequately expressed his disgust. The whole affair was a disgrace. If Lee had acted rationally there would have been no loss of life. Actually, Gilliam wasn't satisfied with what he had written. What losses did the enemy suffer? Major Lee did not know, and no enemy bodies were recovered. After much deliberation Colonel Cornelius Gilliam signed his name. He had done what he could to make a bad situation look good.

Gilliam religiously kept a diary. Some day he planned to publish his autobiography -- *Days of an Indian Fighter*. He wrote the title down. He blotted the ink and savored the words. He envisioned the book's cover. In bold colors a uniformed officer was mounted on a rearing stallion. Behind horse and cavalryman, black clouds darkened a menacing sky. Through the darkness a brilliant, jagged lightening bolt exploded above horse and rider. With bridle reins clenched in his teeth, the horseman held a blazing pistol in one hand; the other hand waved a saber. Columns of heavily armed, hideously painted warriors on wild looking horses came charging down from the hills . . . .

"Ah!" Gilliam uttered. Newspapers in the east would love him. Historians would place him on the same level with Zachary Taylor. Gilliam put aside his pen. The bugle had

sounded. The burial party was ready. He closed the diary and
buckled on his saber. For a moment he wished he had the clothes
and youthful figure of Major Lee. He brushed the thought aside.
Compared to him, Major Lee was a pip-squeak. He dug into a
saddlebag and came up with a battered Bible. He straightened
his shoulders and strode out to stand at the head of two freshly
dug graves. Major Lee called the troops to attention, saluted and
upon Gilliam's curt nod, ordered parade rest.

Gilliam thumbed the Bible open to the Book of John.
He started to speak and stopped. He didn't know the dead men's
names. Major Lee sensed this. "Private O'Connor and Private
Timmons," he whispered across the open graves.

"Of course! Of course!" Gilliam growled in reply. "We
are gathered here to say farewell to Private Timmons and Private
O'Connor. These two brave soldiers gave their lives in the line
of duty." Gilliam glibly went on to embellish the characters of
the two men he didn't know.

"Dust thou art, and to dust thou shalt return." Gilliam
nodded to the first sergeant who cast a handful of dirt in each
grave. The bugler sounded taps. The men stared at the two canvas wrapped bundles. This morning they were alive, grousing
and grumbling about the cold. Now they felt nothing. They were
pieces of clay. But for the grace of God they, too, could be lying
there destined to remain forever in this desolate place in the rocky
bend in the Columbia River called The Dalles.

The plaintiff bugle notes went on and on, echoing back
from the hills. Eyes were blinded by tears. One youthful trooper,
a friend of the dead, openly sobbed.

"Ten-shion! Disss-missed!"

The troopers drifted away, their thoughts grim. Rather
than shed the blood of the enemy, it was they who had fallen
instead. Late into the night the volunteers mulled over the tragedy. In the tent next to Michael, Joe, Sandy Sanders and Macon
Laird, a jug of whiskey appeared and made the rounds. Feeling
the effects of alcohol, the men began to quarrel. Strained by the

day's events, Sandy lost his usual placid composure. For the first time ever, Joe saw a side of his brother-in-law he'd never seen before. Sandy strode into the neighboring tent and snatched the jug, just as a trooper raised it to his lips.

"What kind of men are you?" Sandy demanded. "Two of our young men die today, and you see it as an occasion to go on a spree. But for the grace of God you could be one of those lying in that cold, wet dirt. Instead of guzzling booze you should be on your knees thanking the good Lord you're not there too."

"What's the matter with yuh, yuh bunglin' chowderhead?" the trooper snarled. "This ain't a prayer meetin'. If yuh cain't take it, git on thet ol' plug of yers an' go back ta yer farm, an' gimme back thet jug afore I crown yuh with it. Gimme it!" The trooper grabbed for the jug, but Sandy held it out of reach. The trooper's stunned companions came to life. They jumped in to wrestle the jug away and gave Sandy a vicious shove, sending him sprawling.

Sandy picked himself up and dusted off his hands. For a moment it appeared he would renew the attack. Instead, he returned to his tent and wordlessly sat down. He dug into his pack, pulled out a pad and began writing a letter to his wife and family as if nothing had happened.

The uproar in the next tent continued. Quarreling and arguing became more intense. Between pulls at the jug, the carousers staggered out to accost those who passed.

"Lissen! Lissen! The colonel's right. We gotta teach these rascals . . . ." A pimply faced youth tugged at a passing trooper's arm. The trooper shook him off.

"What are you talking about? You should lay off the booze. Before you know it you'll be seeing pink elephants."

"I'm talkin' 'bout the dad-ratted redskins. We oughta rid the country of 'em and sort out the half-bloods while we're at it."

"Shut up! What are you trying to do, pick a fight? If you want trouble, talk to Captain McKay's French Canadians. They'll set you straight on half-bloods." The accosted trooper hurriedly walked away.

The drunk tottered back and forth, looking for someone else to accost. He started for Sandy Sanders, who placidly continued to write his letter, then noticed Michael Two Feathers. "I'm talkin' 'bout yuh, Injun. What're yuh doin' heya, anyways? Don'tcha know yer on the wrong side of the fence?"

"Don't pay any attention to him," Joe said. "He's drunk." He finished cleaning his rifle and tamped down a fresh load.

"Hey! Braids and Feathers, I'm talkin' ta yuh. Don'tcha unnerstan' the English langwich? I'm tellin' yuh yer in the wrong pew. How 'bout a bit of firewater. Thet's it. Join us in a swig. Maybeso, thet'll make a white man outta yuh." Pimple Face thrust the jug at Michael. A shot rang out. The jug blew into pieces. The air became rank as the bottom of a whiskey barrel.

"Sorry fellas, my finger slipped," Joe said, reloading his Hawken.

Pimple Face and his companions lunged across the open space. Michael quickly unsheathed the knife at his belt. Macon Laird cocked the rifle he held across his knees. "Steady on, old chaps," he said in his best British accent. "I think it's time you quiet down and retire for the night."

The attacking troopers clenched their fists and glared. "Injun lovers!" one of them said before retreating.

##

The volunteer army sent to search out and capture the murderers of the Whitman Mission victims was still a hundred miles from the scene of the crime, but, even at that distance, Gilliam's command caused turmoil among camps of the Cayuse. Scouts were sent to keep watch on the volunteers' movements. Criers mounted up and galloped to surrounding tribes, warning of their coming.

The Teninos on the Deschutes River were called into council. A crier, accompanied by Joe Lewis, the half-blood murderer, warned they were in the path of the Blue Coat army; their homes, herds and very lives were at stake. The leader of the Blue Coats was an Indian killer who had slain many of their brothers in the east. All upland tribes should band together -- form an alliance and be prepared to fight.

Cayuse emissaries also went south and west to meet with the Molala, Klamath and Modoc, urging them to stir up trouble among the settlers who already were at their wits end fearing for their lives.

To the north and east of the Cayuse homeland, the Umatilla, Yakama, Spokane, Walla Walla and Nez Perce were urged to take up the fight. The Yakama and Spokane declined. They had no part in the Whitman Mission massacre and were not in the path of the Blue Coat army. However, a number of Nez Perce, Walla Walla, Umatilla and Palouse did join the militant Cayuse. Thus a sizeable force of warriors awaited the arrival of Gilliam's ragtag army of volunteers.

The coming battle inflamed youthful warriors. They saw it as an opportunity to make coups. Organized in small bands, they began a series of hit-and-run raids on the enemy. Hardly did the camp at The Dalles quiet down after the burial of the two men slain at "Hobble-Horse Hill," when one of these small bands of raiders struck. At the first light of dawn they appeared, driving away a dozen horses. It was a bold act. The animals had been brought close to camp for the night. Under the noses of sleepy guards, the raiders swept in and were gone before anyone knew what was happening. One of the stolen horses was the pimply faced youth's mount. When the discovery was made Pimple Face scurried out barefooted, clad in his long johns and ran across the pasture. He returned cursing. He glared at Michael.

"Yer thievin' friends came callin' again," he snarled. "I see yuh had the ol' crowbait yuh ride tied ta yer tent post, must've known those thievin' bustards were comin'. Maybeso, yer in cahoots with 'em. I've a good mind ta take thet swaybacked critter yuh call a horse an' make yuh walk."

"All right! You've had your say, now clear off," Joe ordered. "Save your strength for chasing after those horses. For sure they won't be coming to you on their own."

Fearing Gilliam's rage, the sergeant of the guard did not immediately report the losses. The colonel was far from being in a mood to receive bad news. He had suffered through another sleepless night. He had become accustomed to the racing rats, now it was the odor. He couldn't decide whether a family of skunks had made its home beneath the floor or heat in the cabin made the soggy log walls smell to high heaven. Whatever the case he hardly could breathe. When finally his orderly, Jasson, came to announce the raid, Gilliam was fit to be tied. He came out of the cabin still pulling on his clothes.

"What are you saying? Quit mumbling. A raid! Horses stolen! In the name of Jehoshaphat what is going on? Isn't there one soldier in this whole blinking camp who knows how to stand guard? Dammit! This cannot go on." He stormed back and forth berating the sergeant of the guard. Troopers in the farthest corner of the camp could hear every word.

"Now, get a few men and get after the thieves. They can't have gotten very far." He dismissed the sergeant. Still fuming, he stomped along the line of tents, looking for someone on whom to vent his wrath. He caught Lieutenant Colonel Waters, his second-in-command, trimming his beard.

"Blast and damnation! Is that all you've got to do? What's the matter with this outfit? All the officers think about in this command is their looks. Well, let me tell you something, those Cayuses don't care a snap whether your beard is trimmed or not.

"You and Lee had the men drilling and on the shooting range. What put a stop to that? Did the men do so well you furloughed them? Here, the sun is up and half of them are still flat on their backs. And about this thieving business. How in the hell are we going to give battle to the Cayuse if we lose everything we have to these larcenous Indians before we even get to Cayuse country? I keep telling the ranks to keep alert. They're about as alert as a den of hibernating snakes."

"What can you expect?" Waters retorted. " None of these

men have ever known discipline. The mountain men won't take orders, and the farm lads don't know their left foot from the right. You can't expect to make soldiers out of a bunch of clodhoppers like that."

A detail of men went to search for the horses but to no avail. The trail disappeared in the rocky-ridged escarpment. Two days later a sentry guarding what was left of the herd spotted a cloud of dust rising to the east. "Injuns!" he shouted, galloping into camp.

Colonel Gilliam searched the horizon with a spyglass. "Might be something and might not," he said to Major Lee. "Take a detachment and see what the dust is all about."

An hour's ride gave the answer to the dust. A handful of Indians were driving a herd of horses. "Let's take them by surprise," Lee said. "Keep the troop in formation. Watch out for tricks. We don't want causalities." He didn't dare bungle again or Gilliam would really have his hide.

A lookout saw the volunteers coming. He shouted a warning and rode toward his companions. They galloped away, herding the horses before them. Pushing their mounts to the limit, the troop cut off their escape. Michael riding in the front line, frowned. Something was the matter. This was far too easy. Indian raiders didn't place themselves at risk like this.

"Fire at will," Major Lee gave the order. Shots rang out. A horse stepped in a prairie dog hole and fell, the rider tumbling over and over in the path of the charging horsemen. For a while the volunteers and their foes rode side by side, shooting and hacking at each other.

Michael found himself riding neck to neck with a painted warrior. They were so close he could see the whites of his opponent's eyes. The rider threw up his rifle and fired. Michael's mount veered away just in time. The enemy gave him a mocking grin. He shouted and waved his empty rifle. "You got off easy this time. When we meet again, watch out," he seemed to say.

Another rider pounded alongside. He grabbed for the reins

of Michael's horse. Michael clubbed at him with the rifle barrel. The horses collided. The warrior lost his grip on the reins. He struggled to keep upright on the slick pony's back. Michael seized his long hair and gave him a jerk. Uttering a piercing yell, the warrior went sprawling, disappearing in a cloud of dust. Michael rode on unmindful of the battle. He felt weak and sick. The warrior was a youth no older than himself.

Another, larger party of warriors, came hurtling out of the brush near the river's edge. "Ambush! Ambush!" Major Lee pointed at the wave of hostiles, wheeling his horse away from the approaching riders. The troop followed the major into the protection of a ravine where they dismounted and prepared to give battle. The enemy did not attack. During the lull non-coms counted noses and assessed the damage. All were present and no one was hurt. As near as Major Lee could calculate one enemy warrior had been killed, two others wounded. It wasn't much to show for their efforts.

"Look out! Look out! Landslide!" a sergeant shouted. A cascade of rocks tumbled down the cliff and went scooting through the formation. "It's another one of their blasted tricks. Those damned Injuns won't stop at anything! Let's get out of here."

"Steady," Macon Laird cautioned. "The enemy is trying to flush us out. When we get in the open they will shoot us down. It is a ploy wogs used against the British in Afghanistan."

The attackers rolled stones and hurled rocks until dark, then disappeared into the night. The detachment returned to camp angry and frustrated. The pimply faced youth limped in with an arrowhead buried in his left buttock. He howled as his partner dug it out and sloshed whiskey on the wound.

That night there was little sleep. Sentries who patrolled the perimeter fired at anything that moved, even their own shadows. Macon Laird was appalled. "What is it with these clods? They act like a bunch of grammar school ninnies. The night is young and already they have burned enough powder to celebrate a Chinese New Year."

DEATH ON THE UMATILLA

IX

*The earth is the mother of all people, and all people
should have equal rights upon it.*

Chief Joseph, Nez Perce

Colonel Cornelius Gilliam listened to Major Henry A. G. Lee's report and grimaced. Keerist! This young man was about as worthless as teats on a boar. Couldn't he do anything right?

"Look! I'm getting tired of you blundering around like a ten-year old," he said in exasperation. "I guess I'm going to have to teach you how to handle these redskins. Get the men ready. Tomorrow we'll ride out there, track them down and finish them off like you should have done."

Major Lee walked away with his ears burning. The man was insufferable. Why did he put up with it? Why hadn't he remained in Virginia as his folks wanted?

The following morning Gilliam led a large body of men in search of the Indian encampment. All along the route warriors bobbed into view from behind hills like prairie dogs springing out of their earthen homes. They shot arrows and fired rifles then disappeared. Little damage was done. The range was too great. But every appearance of the hostiles increased Gilliam's ire.

"Get after them. Take scalps," he finally shouted, leading a charge up a hillside after the tormentors. The troopers gained the summit without casualties. The Indians' marksmanship was bad. Shooting downhill, they kept firing over the troopers' heads. Whooping and hollering, the volunteers descended upon the enemy who took to their heels. A two mile chase brought Gilliam's riders upon an Indian camp. The surprised occupants fled, helter-skelter. Squealing children darted away, seeking cover in the brush. Dogs ran in circles snarling and barking. An ancient man sitting on a log sunning blank, unseeing eyes, got run over and trampled by flying hooves. No quarter was given and none expected.

Michael, who found himself in the vanguard, caught a glimpse of a warrior running for his horse. He threw his rifle to his shoulder. He had the brown body in his sights. His finger tightened on the trigger. The warrior desperately struggled to free his mount's halter line. The sights moved to a spot between dark, flashing eyes. A flicker of despair crossed the painted face. The man knew he was about to die. There was something familiar about that face -- those wild eyes . . . . Michael's trigger finger relaxed. The warrior flung himself on the horse, uttered a defiant yell and galloped away to disappear over a sagebrush covered hill.

Joe rode up. He saw his brother take aim at the warrior and then let him escape. Someone he knew, Joe thought. Why else did he let him go? He glanced around. Had anyone noticed? The troopers were busy ransacking the Indian encampment, shooting every living creature, including two scrawny dogs.

When they finished plundering, the volunteers burned the camp. They rounded up the livestock and drove it away. The column straggled back toward Fort Wascopum. The troop looked more like rag pickers and junk dealers than soldiers. The horses were loaded with property scrounged from the Indian camp: pots, pans, baskets, clothes, hides and an old valise. There hardly was room on the horses for the men to ride. Many of the items had been previously stolen from passing emigrant wagons.

Colonel Gilliam didn't object to the pilfering. In fact, he was jubilant. "We're finally getting somewhere," he informed Major Lee. "You see. You have to be ruthless. Roust them out. Shoot them down. Burn their lodges. Take their horses. Sooner or later they'll get the message. Don't mess with Gilliam's Blue Coats."

Joe and Michael rode side by side. Neither one spoke until they returned to camp and were hobbling the horses for the night. "The next time we have the enemy in our sights it will look better if we fire, shoot over their heads," Joe said. "We don't want to give these volunteers the idea we're not on their side."

Michael withheld an angry retort. How would Joe feel if his people were badgered about and shot like mongrel dogs? Every encounter with the Indians made Michael feel worse. This wasn't war; it was extermination.

The ensuing days were even harder for Michael to endure. The successful encounter with the Indians brought a new mood to camp. Soldiers who formerly grumbled about everything, began to swagger around like heroes. To hear them tell it, nearly everyone had made a kill. After one boasting session Adams punched an obnoxious braggart in the nose.

"Yuh're a bunch of fakes. If yer such killers of Injuns where're the bloomin' scalps?"

The incident did not dampen the soldiers' spirits. They had a taste of blood, and they liked it. The redskin foe was not as fearsome as they had believed. Undisciplined troopers became more unruly. They were tired of waiting. They wanted to fight. They looked for targets of opportunity. A friendly Indian tracking horses near camp was shot. Troopers assigned to drive horses to and from pasture, did so with trepidation. The rock strewn hillside with its clusters of dark evergreens and pockets of brush, made it hard to distinguish friendlies from hostiles. Some drink-crazed trooper was apt as not to take any approaching horseman for an enemy raider.

Sandy Sanders, who came in from pasture duty to be challenged by a half-drunken sentry, again lost his composure. "What's the matter with these people?" he blurted, his freckled face red as a beet. "They have no honor -- drunk on duty -- shoot innocent people -- steal, plunder and trample old folks to death. I can't get that blind man out of my mind. These men are worse than the criminals we're after. I volunteered because I thought I was doing good for the country. I was proud of joining up. Now I feel dirty, like I'm caught up in a web of evil." He plunked upon his sleeping pallet and, again, reached for his writing pad.

Gilliam was also disturbed but for other reasons. He was pleased with the raid but it had done nothing to further the campaign against the Cayuse. He stomped around his headquarters cabin talking to himself. The more he thought about the situation the more worked up he became. He was furious at the government, himself and every officer in his command from Lieutenant Colonel Waters on down. The delay at The Dalles was becoming a nightmare. The badly needed supplies and additional men promised by the Provisional Government were yet to arrive. Appropriations had been sanctioned, but that was the last of it. The Provisional Government was bust and its creditability with Hudson's Bay nonexistent.

Of course, he hadn't helped matters by threatening to pull the walls of Fort Vancouver down around the ears of Fort Factor James Douglas. But it was too late to lay blame. The task now was to get things moving. Every day supplies diminished and the men got more restless. He had to take action or his command would become an unruly mob. Spit and polish fancy Dan, Major Lee, was partly to blame. The volunteers didn't take to all that shine your boots and buckles business. They had come to fight the Cayuse, not get spiffed up like blue ribbon show stock.

Gilliam called his officers together. When they gathered in front of the headquarters cabin, he kept them waiting in the chilly breeze that blew through the Columbia River Gorge. When he was satisfied they were chilled to the bone, he marched out in his great coat, rattling his saber. His penetrating, gray-green eyes challenged them to complain.

"It's time to stop shilly-shallying around," he began. "We came to do a job, not lay about like a pack of lazy dogs. Every moment we waste allows those Cayuse cutthroats that much more time to go into hiding. I want the culprits in chains by spring. Most of the men's enlistments are up by then. We've got to get going or we might as well go home now. Give your men their marching orders. We're moving out of here at dawn tomorrow, whether ready or not. Is that clear?"

"We're short of supplies," Lieutenant Colonel Waters reminded. "Even if we had all the supplies needed, there isn't sufficient transport to carry them."

"I see cattle and oxen grazing on the hillsides and serviceable wagons parked around the mission," Gilliam said pointedly.

"Those belong to the settlers. We can't take them."

"Who says we can't?" Gilliam glared around the circle of officers. "This is an emergency. We were sent to safeguard the lives of Americans whether they be Willamette Valley homesteaders or emigrants on the trail. The Legislature expects us to do the job. So, we break a few eggs. Nobody's going to slap our hands."

"Yes, but . . . ."

Gilliam cut the speaker off. "Don't 'yes, but' me. I've been on campaigns like this before. Anything goes. Keep your eye on the important things. If we let these murderers escape, every redskin in the territory will think they're free to kill. Everything we valley folk have worked for will be for naught. Our families will be murdered like the poor souls at Whitman's Mission."

Gilliam's orders were quickly and ruthlessly carried out. The settlers' cattle were rounded up and bunched together in a corral. The wagons and teams of the emigrants waiting to take the Barlow Road across the Cascades were commandeered. When they unloaded the wagons the volunteers pried trunks open and smashed casks and barrels. They raked loose clothing and bedding from wagon beds. Whatever they fancied they took. Fathers, mothers and children looked on aghast as the precious possessions they had guarded over two thousand miles of trail disappeared into saddlebags or were thrown on the ground and trampled by muddied boots.

"This is war," Gilliam told the people who complained. "We need transport and provisions, and we need them now."

"This is highway robbery," a red-faced emigrant protested. "We travel two thousand miles, overcoming every hardship known to man. We fight off the thievin' Injuns, watch our stock starve and die, then come to this. God! What a country. For two cents I'd go back to Kaintuck."

"You can do what you want," Gilliam sarcastically replied. "We're still taking the teams and wagons." Gilliam walked back to the smelly headquarters cabin, chortling to himself. He'd show those puffed up Provisional Legislature people how to get the job done. They were so tight they'd squeeze the beaver off the wooden coins they used for money.

Joe, who twice had accompanied wagon trains across the plains, knew the agonies suffered by the emigrants. They had traveled months protecting their belongings. Now, when they thought they were safe and near the end of the trail, their own kind plundered them like freebooters. Joe couldn't stand to watch. He rode up into the hills. Only after dark did he return.

Macon Laird, who also had not taken part in the Gilliam sanctioned plundering, looked at Joe askance. "Trying to avoid your voracious countrymen, are you? Well, you bloody well should. Compared to these blokes, the Mongols and Tartars who savaged eastern Europe were tame." He waved his pipe toward the next tent. "Witness all the plunder our pimple-faced friend garnered. His arrow wound didn't hinder him one whit."

"Yeah!" Joe agreed grimly. "I guess this is what you call 'a live off the land campaign.'"

Macon fiercely puffed on his pipe. "I don't understand you bloody Americans. You call the red men savages. Yet, you commit the same atrocities and claim you are civilized. Bloody odd reasoning, it seems to me."

DEATH ON THE UMATILLA

*This we know: all things are connected. Whatever befalls the
earth befalls the sons of the earth.*

Hardly had Colonel Cornelius Gilliam made up his mind
to march up river, when another setback occurred. On February
10, 1848 two peace commissioners arrived from Oregon City:
Joel Palmer, Superintendent of Indian Affairs, and Robert "Doc"
Newell, an old trapping partner of Joe Meek. Gilliam greeted
them with a feeling of unease. As representatives of the Provisional Government they had come to give advice which he didn't
need.

"What can I do for you folks?" Gilliam testily asked, impatient at the delay the new arrivals caused. Peace commissioners -- what good were they? Major Lee also had been named a
peace commissioner, and what had he done except make one
blunder after another? If these people were of the same ilk, the
Whitman Mission murderers never would be apprehended.

"Governor Abernathy wants us to precede you up river,"
Joel Palmer said. "Before you and your troops arrive we need to
explain to the uncommitted tribes that the volunteers will not
harm them. Your army's presence is merely a police action. When
the Whitman Mission murderers surrender or are captured the
troops will withdraw."

Gilliam tugged at his ear lobe and raised his eyebrows.
Damn these politicians, he thought. Meddling no-goods, putting
their oar in at the last moment. He had a notion to tell them to
jump into the river. The men were ready to move and in the
mood to fight. If they continued to loiter in camp who could tell
what might happen. The unruly bunch could very well take matters in their own hands, desert, march up river on their own or
just plain raise Cain.

"You can help us by providing an armed escort to the

Walla Walla Valley. That's where we plan to council with plateau tribal leaders," Palmer continued.

Gilliam scowled. "Doesn't make sense to split my command. As it is, I should have twice the number of men."

"If we're successful you won't need them," Palmer argued. "Why don't you speak to your officers. See what you can
do to help us out. After all, we are trying to accomplish the
same thing, to bring these murderers in with as little loss of life
as possible."

Gilliam shot out of his chair. Damn these people telling
him what to do. He paced back and forth, giving his temper time
to cool. "All right! All right! I'll meet with the officers. I'll let
you know what we decide."

The meeting broke up. Gilliam hurriedly ushered the
peace commissioners out. He had no intention of seeking his
officers' advice. He was in command. He, himself, would decide what to do. Whatever happened, he had to keep the troops
fired up. Sitting on their duffs in Fort Wascopum was not the
way to do it.

Gilliam sat down at his table desk and leafed through the
mail the commissioners had delivered. He opened a letter from
home. He was missed by his North Luckiamute family. The old
sow was about to deliver piglets. The wolves had killed a ewe
with unborn lamb. A heifer had got out . . . . Gilliam shoved the
gloomy letter aside. He didn't need any more discouraging news.

A letter from Governor Abernathy caught his attention.
He slit the wax seal and held the page at arm's length. Confound
it! Why didn't the governor learn to write? The blurred words
finally came into focus. Gilliam sat up straight.

By George! What kind of shenanigans were those commissioners trying to pull off? He didn't have to split his command. He read the message aloud. "You are authorized to proceed forthwith to Waiilatpu. If the situation warrants, erect fortifications there to garrison the troops."

"Jasson!" Gilliam shouted. "Ask the officers to kindly

present themselves. And get your things in order. Forthwith, we march up river."

The word quickly swept through camp. Troopers tossed hats in the air. "Whoopee! We break camp! Watch out, redskins, Gilliam's army is on the move."

The news did not cheer Michael. While those around him rejoiced, he quietly slipped away from camp. At the pasture grounds he bridled and saddled the borrowed Hudson's Bay mare. He rode into the hills. He did not look back. He knew Macon Laird and Joe watched. He urged his rough riding mount into a trot. It would do no good to explain. They would only try and stop him. The trip was not sanctioned by Colonel Gilliam, but he was not about to leave Fort Wascopum while there was still a chance his four-footed friend Magpie could be found. Perhaps he also would find answers to the mysterious hoofprints left by Buffalo Horn horses, the taunting call in mission school English and the familiar face he had caught in his sights . . . .

Michael was right. Joe and Macon did watch him leave. "That rascal's riding off," Joe exclaimed. "He didn't say a word. What the devil can he be up to? Where do you suppose he's going? I wonder if we shouldn't trail along?"

"If I were you, I would let him be. The way he acts the chap jolly well wants to be left alone. Can you blame him? Camping with these oafs is enough to drive anyone away."

Joe shook his head. "I still don't like him leaving like this. After Gilliam's raid on the Indian camp there'll be plenty of Indian people out there wanting revenge. If they don't get him, these empty-headed troopers could well shoot him when he returns."

"Perhaps he does not plan to return. Maybe he has had enough of Gilliam's bloody nonsense. I would not blame him. Have you seen how these blokes eye him? Half of them are afraid of him. The other half would like to cut his throat. Our good commander has not helped. He's made it plain half-bloods are about as welcome as venomous snakes."

Joe stared at the spot on the horizon where Michael and the Hudson's Bay mare had disappeared from view. Macon Laird spoke the truth. Michael had good reason to leave and never return. He should have paid more attention to Michael's problems. The poor boy was troubled, and he hardly had given him the time of day.

"Yeah," Joe moodily agreed. "Hey! He didn't take his weapons. He's out there unarmed. He's probably making one last search for his pony, Magpie. Somebody with firearms should be riding with him. I'm going after him. There are too many people around here that would like nothing better than see him dead."

"You better give this careful thought. If you both leave this rabble might get the wrong idea. They are so full of themselves any little thing might set them off. If anyone should go after him, it had better be me."

"Hmm!" Joe grunted. "You're right. We both should sit tight. Perhaps I'm making mountains out of molehills. Michael has been though some rough patches and always landed on his feet. Besides, I wouldn't want either of us to do anything that will get Gilliam any more upset. He's already down on McKay and his Canadians. I don't even understand what keeps you here." Joe studied his companion's face. "You don't like these people. You think we're all a pack of uncivilized ruffians."

"Quite so! Quite so! So far this campaign is a military fiasco, and I doubt it will improve. Look at the commanding officer. He has as much common sense as a hitching post. But I must say, he is full of surprises. This campaign is better than a Shakespearean drama. It is replete with suspense. What disaster will happen next? Watching the plot unfold is what keeps me here. Besides, I have nothing better to do. I cannot leave for England until the next ship arrives at Fort Vancouver."

The two men fell silent. Joe's thoughts were partly on Michael and partly on his companion. Each man worried him. Each one was like a faulty bear trap. One never knew when either would do something unpredictable, bringing chaos down on himself and everybody close to him. He would do his best to protect Michael but Macon Laird . . . ? It was too late to do anything for him. The harm already had been done.

Talk about Shakespearean drama! The Macon Laird - Tildy Jennings affair was a tragedy William Shakespeare would have loved. A handsome British officer and a lovely New England maiden thrown together on the American frontier . . . ! Who could ask for anything more romantic? Across the plains they traveled under each other's spell. Macon was accepted into the Jennings family like an adopted son and brother. He ate with them, spent every evening with them, helped Tildy with the chores and . . .

Ah! The Britisher was a regular Don Juan. His handsome looks, winning ways and attentiveness had befuddled Tildy until she didn't know whether she was coming or going. She threw caution to the winds and fell for him head over heels.

Even so, in spite of what Macon Laird had done, he couldn't but help like the Britisher. When the cards were down he did the right thing. At Fort Hall, where Tildy's fiancee had met the wagon train, Macon Laird rode away and, as far as he knew, never attempted to meet with Tildy again, even though at the time of their parting she was carrying his unborn son.

It must be hell for Macon to sit night after night listening to Sandy Sanders prattle on about Baby John, Joe thought. Yet, Macon kept his and Tildy's indiscretions locked in his heart. He had not given the slightest indication Baby John was anything other than Sandy Sanders' own true-blood son.

Yes, the man had heart. He had proven that. There had been the matter of little David Malin who survived the massacre only to be abandoned when the other survivors were rescued. Hudson's Bay's authorities insisted he was a Canadian citizen, not American. The poor lad stood on the river bank crying his eyes out as his foster family sailed away in the rescuer's flotilla of bateaux. Macon Laird had come to the rescue. He picked up

David Malin and put him in the saddle beside him. Together they rode all the way to Fort Vancouver where he placed him in the care of a kindly widow. It was said he planned to adopt the boy and take him to England.

"Something wrong, old chap?" the Britisher asked. "You are as somber as a hangman."

"I was thinking about Michael," Joe lied. "One of us should keep watch for his return. No telling what these trigger-happy sentries might do."

"Quite so! Quite so!" Macon agreed. "We can spell one another. Who will take first watch?"

##

Michael came to the Deschutes River. Should he ford it and continue east, or should he turn south and search the western bank? He decided on the latter. At this time of year the river was low. Yet, it still carried sufficient water to make it swift and dangerous. He had not ridden the Hudson's Bay mare long enough to know how she would act if forced to swim.

Michael urged the horse around one rocky bend after another. His senses told him he wasn't alone. Curious eyes watched his every move. He made certain the watchers saw that he was unarmed. Warriors did not usually shoot an unarmed man. Instead, they would seize him and hold him prisoner. The coup was more meaningful than killing an enemy in cold blood.

The twang of a bow and sharp whistle of a speeding arrow made the Hudson's Bay mare jump. "Ah," Michael uttered to himself. The watchers had made their move. He had to take care. Death was only an arrow flight away. He pulled on the reins, uttering soothing words until the horse settled down. He sat motionless, resisting the temptation to turn around. There came the clatter of rocks and ring of hooves. In spite of himself, Michael felt the hair on the back of his neck rise. A fish leapt over a riffle and landed with a splash. The Hudson's Bay mare snorted and shook her head, the bridle rattling noisily. From behind a voice spoke in Shahaptian, the language of the Cayuse,

Nez Perce, Palouse, Walla Walla and Umatilla.

"Mission boy! Go back to your Blue Coat friends. This is dangerous territory, no place for unarmed men."

The voice sounded familiar. Where had he heard it before? Ah, yes, it was Cloud Bird, the son of Buffalo Horn, the great Cayuse horseman whose vast herds grazed the pasture lands along the lower Umatilla. So, the tracks with the V shape mark did come from Buffalo Horn horses. Why were Cayuse riders here annoying Gilliam's volunteers? If that was what they came to do, it was dangerous; they were no match for Gilliam's army.

Michael had come in search of his beloved Magpie, but an even more urgent task had suddenly emerged. Here was an opportunity to send a message of warning to his Cayuse friends.

"I am a friend. I come in peace. I bring a message for you and your people," Michael called out.

"Bah!" A new voice spoke. Michael also recognized it. It belonged to Red Calf, Buffalo Horn's second son.

"Why should I place myself in danger unless it is for a good cause? It is true, I ride with the Blue Coats. That is why I have important news."

"What message you bring?" It was Red Calf's scornful voice.

"You must return to your homeland and take your people into the mountains. After next sunrise the Blue Coats start their march up river. When they reach your villages they will destroy them. They have a gun as large as the trunk of a cottonwood tree. The lead it shoots is as big and heavy as that boulder," Michael said, pointing to the hillside. "One firing blows a lodge away. The Blue Coat leader is not an honorable warrior. He shoots women and children. No one is safe. Ask the Wascopum. They know what he does."

"Pouf!" Cloud Bird walked around to stand in front of Michael. "It is the Blue Coats who should flee. Our people will destroy them. The Walla Walla, Palouse, Umatilla and maybe Yakama are dancing war dances. Our warriors are as countless as hairs in a horse's mane. We will stick the Blue Coats with arrows until they are like porcupines. Tell your Blue Coat chief if his warriors lay down their weapons they can return to their lodges in peace. If the Blue Coats march up river . . . ." Cloud Bird took his knife and drew the back of it across his throat.

Michael was not surprised his warning fell on deaf ears. Buffalo Horn's sons had never liked him. He was the mission boy. He had gone to mission schools and learned the ways of the Bostons. Buffalo Horn distrusted missionaries. Right from the first he said they would destroy the tribe and take all it possessed. Most Cayuse did not listen. Now it appeared Buffalo Horn had been right. The tribe was about to lose everything, including its very homeland.

The sons thought like their father. They hated anything connected with Whitman's Mission. They also were skilled thieves. They could have led the raid on Fort Lee. They probably knew exactly where Magpie was hidden. He was about to ask but Red Calf spoke first.

"Enough talk. Get off horse. Renegade walk to Blue Coat camp."

"No. Let him keep his horse. It has mark of Hudson's Bay. We are not at war with Redcoats." Cloud Bird gave Michael's mount a slap on the rump and uttered a shrill war cry. "Yih! Yih! Yih!" The startled mare leaped, nearly unseating its rider.

Michael let the mare run herself out, then jogged to a stop. He grimly reviewed the encounter with Buffalo Horn's sons. They considered him a traitor. Cloud Bird and Red Calf would soon make certain the word got around until every Cayuse in the tribe would know the Whitman Mission boy rode with the Blue Coats. Still, Red Calf had a certain sense of honor. It was Red Calf's face he had in his sights at the village the volunteers pillaged. Buffalo Horn's second son could not bring himself to kill the man who had spared his life.

XI

*Warfare was regarded as sort of a game, undertaken in order
to develop the manly qualities of our youth.*

Ohiyesa, Santee Sioux,

Dusk had begun to fall. An overcast sky painted the evening a dark shade of gray. Pimple Face was standing guard. As usual the cutting wind blew in through the Columbia Gorge. The Fort Wascopum flag flapped straight out. Horses in the pasture huddled together with rumps against the wind. The cold pierced Pimple Face's shabby homespuns. To add to his misery, the arrow wound in his buttock had not healed. Every step he took gave him pain. He wished he had never strayed from home. Out of the gloom emerged a horseman. Pimple Face threw his rifle barrel up and caught the rider in the sights.

"Ah-ha! The half-blood, Michael Two Feathers," Pimple Face muttered to himself. One little tug of the finger and another redskin would bite the dust. With his feathers and dark skin he could say he took him for a raider intent on stealing horses. No one would blame him, least of all Colonel Gilliam. He tracked the Indian youth until he caught the dusky face in the sights.

"Hey! Put that gun down!" Pimple Face pulled the trigger, but the shout threw off his aim. Riding at full gallop, Joe drove his mount straight into the sentry, knocking him to the ground. Before Pimple Face could recover, Joe was on top of him. He jerked the rifle out of his hands and pressed the muzzle between the prostrate sentry's eyes.

"You dumb cluck! Can't you tell friendlies from hostiles?"

"What's the matter with yuh, attacking a sentry?" Pimple Face blustered, struggling to get up, but Joe held him pinned to the ground.

"I asked you a question. Can't you tell friendlies from

hostiles?"

These people are like peas in a pod," Pimple Face whined. "Yuh cain't tell one from the other. Look at him. In those buckskins an' feathers in his hair, he sure enough's got the earmarks of a hostile Injun."

"If you ever even look cross-eyed at Michael Two Feathers again, I promise, I'll kill you." Joe threw the rifle at the prone volunteer and mounted up to meet Michael who had kept stoically jogging toward camp.

The brothers rode to the pasture and staked their mounts. Not a word was spoken until they were back in their shelter and Sandy Sanders served them hot tea. Michael didn't like the stuff but drank it anyway, warming his hands on the cup. He felt like a frozen piece of meat.

"Went in search of Magpie, did you?" Joe quizzed.

Michael nodded. The encounter with the sentry bothered him more than he let on. Pimple Face was right, in the minds of white people all Indians looked alike and were treated the same.

Joe attempted again to draw his silent brother out. "Since you didn't return with Magpie, I assume you didn't find him."

Michael remained silent. He didn't want to talk about his missing friend.

"You must have seen something," Joe persisted. "Did you see any hostiles?"

Michael signaled with his hand that he had.

"For cripe's sake! Don't be so tight-lipped. Tell us what you saw."

"Cloud Bird and Red Calf."

"Hmm!" Joe grunted. "Buffalo Horn's two sons. What are they doing here? This is way off their range. How come they let you go? They hate you. At least they did."

"They gave a message for Colonel Gilliam."

"Oh! What is it? Spit it out. You're making us nervous."

"They said to tell the Blue Coat leader that the troops should lay down their arms and return to the Willamette Valley.

If they march into Cayuse country they will be slain."

"Silly blokes," Macon Laird exclaimed. "Can you see Gilliam ordering the troops to lay down their arms and these bloody volunteers obeying?"

"I don't like the sound of it," Joe said. "These Cayuses may talk big, but it's usually wise to listen. They had good reason to turn Michael loose when they could have held him prisoner. They must have said something else, didn't they?"

"They say Walla Walla, Palouse, Umatilla and maybe Yakama have joined with the Cayuse. More warriors than hairs on a horse's mane wait to fight Gilliam and his Blue Coats."

"Hmm!" Joe grunted. "Do you think it idle talk?"

"Sometimes these people speak with crooked tongues. Sometimes their tongues are straight. Today their tongues are somewhat straight."

"Yes," Joe said thoughtfully. "I wonder if Buffalo Horn is behind this? By delaying us he would have more time to move his herds. Of course, it long has been rumored the Cayuse have gone to all points of the compass seeking allies. If they were successful, a thousand or more warriors could stand between us and the mission at Waiilatpu. I think this is serious enough to take to the colonel."

Jasson, Gilliam's orderly, stood outside the headquarters cabin guarding the entrance. The cold weather left his face pale. The wart on his nose stood out like the small horn of a rhinoceros. "What do you birds want?" he demanded. "The colonel's busy an' ain't seein' nobody."

"Yes, but we have an important message for the colonel," Joe answered, "Leastwise, Michael has."

Jasson gave Michael a disparaging glance. "The colonel can't be disturbed."

"Maybe he's reading or resting. Take a look and see if he can't spare a moment," Joe urged.

"He's not readin' an' he ain't restin'. He's in conference with the peace commissioners," Jasson said hotly. "Now get out of here." The prominent Adam's apple danced up and down in the scrawny neck. Michael suddenly noticed three long black hairs attached to the Adam's apple. They fluttered with each movement like strings of a kite. He smiled to himself. What strange specimens these Blue Coats had in their midst.

"Meeting with the peace commissioners, is he? It's all the more reason he should see Michael. Michael has spoken with a couple of Cayuse. They gave him a message for the colonel. It could affect the campaign," Joe persisted. "I'd hate to be in your shoes when the colonel finds out you kept important military information from him."

"All right! Wait right here. I'll speak to the colonel." Jasson was gone for minutes. Loud voices came from within. "I don't care what message the half-breed brings," Gilliam's strident voice carried through the unchinked walls. "The Cayuses are miles away. They don't dare show their faces around here."

The cabin door opened. The former mountain man, Doc Newell, thrust his head out. "What's this about a message from the Cayuse? Come in. Tell us about it."

Newell pulled Michael inside. Joe followed close behind. Around the table sat Gilliam, Joe Meek, Palmer and Major Lee. Gilliam glowered at Michael. "I ought to have you thrown in the guard house. What business did you have leaving the fort without permission? That's absence without leave, just short of desertion."

"Quit quibbling over details," Newell said testily. "If the young man has important information, we should hear it."

"All right! Spit it out," Gilliam ordered. He raised himself up by the elbows. His neck bulged, turning increasingly reddish by the second. More than ever he resembled a turkey gobbler poised to strut.

Michael had to bite his tongue to keep from laughing. Why did this ridiculous looking, loud-voiced man make him so angry? Every time they met they locked horns. Dislike oozed from the arrogant, red-necked officer like perspiration on a lathered horse.

Joe gave Michael a nudge. "Tell the colonel what the Cayuse brothers said," he urged.

"Cayuse brothers?" Joel Palmer exclaimed. "By all means tell us what they have to say. How bold they are to show up here."

"Poppy cock!" Gilliam snorted. "Can't you people keep your own kind straight? Those had to be Wascopum, not Cayuse."

"Let the young man speak!" It was Joe Meek's turn to snap at Gilliam. "Tell us. Who were these men you spoke to?"

"Cloud Bird and Red Calf, the sons of Buffalo Horn."

"Ah! Yes! Buffalo Horn. He never liked the missionaries. Were he and his sons mixed up in the massacre?"

Michael stared straight ahead. "I don't know."

"You're getting us off track, Meek," Doc Newell admonished. "We want to hear exactly what these Cayuses had to say."

"They told me to tell the Blue Coat chief to stay away from the plateau. The plateau tribes have banded together. They have a thousand or more warriors ready to fight."

"Hogwash!" Gilliam exploded, his red neck taking on a purple cast. "You can't believe what an Indian says. It's another one of their damned tricks. They're trying to keep us away from the plateau. It's as simple as that. Why we sit here and talk about it, is beyond me."

"Nevertheless, perhaps you should wait a while and give us peace commissioners time to meet with tribal leaders. Might save lives if you did," Doc Newell argued.

Gilliam scowled. "I've got my orders." He tapped Governor Abernathy's letter. "They say, 'proceed forthwith to Waiilatpu.' My understanding of 'forthwith' means immediately. That's what I intend to do. If you fellows want to go ahead, I'll wait two days. Then I march."

"You are so generous," Newell retorted sarcastically.

The meeting broke up. Doc Newell left the cabin with

Michael and Joe. He walked down the path with them, grumbling to himself. At the brothers' tent he stopped.

"What made you meet with these Cayuses, anyhow?" he asked.

"Michael's horse was lost in the raid on Fort Lee. He went to look for it," Joe answered for his brother who remained silent. "During the search he ran into the two Cayuse riders."

Newell shook his head. "I'd be mighty careful. Some folks might not understand how you can chat with the enemy and return unharmed." He hesitated. "Take care, lads. During these troubled days it's hard to tell the good people from the bad."

XII

*How easy it is to go from bad to worse, when once we
have started upon a downward course.*

Mark Twain

February 11th was a day of unrest. At daybreak commissioners, Palmer and Newell, left with an armed escort. Colonel
Cornelius Gilliam didn't even get up to see them off.

Aroused early, the troopers ate breakfast in disgruntled
silence. They faced two days of waiting. Already they were
bored stiff. Diligent troopers patched clothes and darned socks.
Bridles and saddles were cleaned and oiled. A few braved the
weather to bathe and wash in the creek. The homesick wrote
letters to loved ones. Others milled about wondering what to do.
A jug was brought out of hiding. It began to make the rounds.
Cards and dice appeared. Rowdy groups gathered in tents and
lean-tos to deal cards and toss dice. A steady bout of drinking
and gambling ensued. The jug of liquor went dry. A half-dozen
drunken soldiers stumbled around in search of more booze.

"There ain't none to be found," a searcher complained.

"It's just as well," his partner replied. "You've had
enough. You're already drunker than a fiddler's clerk."

"Hey!" a voice exclaimed. "A new batch of emigrants
arrived. Maybeso, they have some firewater. It's worth a try."
He pointed up the slope toward the mission buildings where the
recent arrivals had parked their wagons.

The group, gathering strength as it went, strode toward
the emigrants' camp. Children saw them coming and ran shouting to announce their presence. A handful of bushy bearded men
appeared clutching rifles. A rifle report rang out. A trooper uttered a painful shout.

"I'm shot! Dammit! Yuh civilian clods. Yuh don't hev
the sense ta teach chickens ta cluck. Don't yuh bloody well

unnerstan'. We's soldiers, tryin' our best ta save yer bloomin' scalps. We've a right ta everthin' yuh got."

The volunteers rushed the bearded guards. They seized their weapons and swarmed into the campsite. A woman screamed. Dogs raced around in circles, savagely snarling and barking. Children ran pell-mell for cover.

"Corn squeezin's. Anythin' with a leetle kick'll do. Fetch it here an' now," the black bearded man with too many teeth who led the first raid on the emigrant camp, demanded.

"Yeah! A couple of jugs. If'n it don't set right we'll sure be lettin' yuh know," a sallow-faced trooper added.

An emigrant with a flowing white beard armed with a pitchfork, jabbed at the nearest soldier. "Get out of here! We don't have poisonous drink. It's agin our religion."

"Well, maybeso yuh should change yer religion, grandpa," Sallow-Face said. "Now lay down thet pitchfork afore yuh hurt yerself." He grabbed the man by the beard, gave it a yank and wrestled the pitchfork out of his hands. "Search the wagons. Let's find out what these religious crackpots're hidin'," he ordered.

A young mother with a child in her arms blocked Sallow-Face's path. He roughly seized the baby and knocked the mother to the ground. Black beard with all the teeth ripped away her dress. The underclothes went next. The volunteers stopped plundering to watch.

"Look at what we got here. This's better'n whiskey any day. I'm first." Black Beard tossed his hat aside and hurriedly unfastened his belt.

"Like hell! She's mine. I found her." Sallow-Face roughly shoved the bearded man away.

"Fight fer her!" a voice in the crowd yelled.

"Thet's fair enuff. To the winner go the spoils!"

"Stop right where you are!" The words were accompanied by the sharp crack of a rifle shot. The sallow-faced man's hat went flying. An ominous metallic chorus like dull chirping of crickets sounded as a dozen firearms went to full cock. The startled marauders swung around to stare into black holes of rifle muzzles. The cold eyes of Tom McKay and his French Canadians peered over the sights.

"Now, you drunken oafs, march out of here nice and easy. I'd love to have the excuse to put a few holes in your bird brains," McKay said, his voice as steely as the barrel of the Hawken he carried. "Don't be making any false moves. You've had your fun, now it's time to pay the piper."

Later the troop's coarser element jokingly referred to the incident as Emigrant Camp Skirmish. The troopers who participated were awarded garlands of horse dung, but the immediate aftermath was grim. Colonel Gilliam, aroused by the rifle shot, came out in time to see McKay's riflemen march the drunken troopers down the hill and onto the parade grounds to halt them in front of the headquarters cabin.

"What is this all about? Have you lost your senses?" Gilliam exclaimed, his red neck aflame.

"Just a little police action," McKay announced. "Seems your boys can't hold their liquor. They were in the process of raping an emigrant woman."

"Drunk! Rape! I don't believe it."

"We was only funnin'," one of the culprits whined.

The volunteers, feeling safe in Gilliam's presence, lowered their hands and began to protest. "I don't know what the fuss is all about," Black Beard growled. "No one was hurt." A shot rang out. He howled and stared at a bloodied hand. The tip of his little finger was missing.

"You damned Canuck!" He shook his sound fist at McKay. Another shot rang out. The lobe of Black Beard's ear began to spurt blood. A wisp of smoke drifted away from the muzzle of another French Canadian's gun.

"God Almighty!" Gilliam looked wildly around for support. There wasn't any.

"I guess I didn't get the message across," McKay said

dryly. "I'll say it once again. These brave soldiers of yours were about to rape an emigrant woman. That one there, the man with the sallow face, took a baby from the victim's arms. The man bleeding from his hand and ear, ripped off her clothes. Then these two argued who was to take first turn. Maybeso, they think that's funning. I say it's molesting women. I have a dozen witnesses who think the same. If you aren't prepared to mete out justice, my men and I will gladly take the job off your hands."

Gilliam glowered. "This is mutiny!"

"Call it what you like," McKay said calmly. "Someone around here has to keep order. Since you and your officers are busy with other things, we decided to help out."

"Major Lee! Colonel Waters!" Gilliam bawled. "For God's sake take charge. Call these people into formation and put these rapists in irons."

Emigrant Camp Skirmish hung over Gilliam's head like an angry cloud. If he didn't discipline the men McKay's French Canadians would. The last thing he wanted was to let these Frenchies take control of any part of his troop. He was not going to surrender a bit of his authority, certainly not to half bloods. Yet, what was he to do? He couldn't be too hard on the men. They were in an angry mood. It wouldn't take much to start a rebellion. Then where would he be?

The colonel returned to the cabin and grimly reviewed the situation. He sat on a powder keg. "Dammit all," he cursed. It was the fault of those meddling peace commissioners. If they hadn't held him up, the troops would be on the march to Waiilatpu. This idiotic affair never would have happened.

Gilliam called for Jasson. "Tell all officers to meet in the headquarters cabin. We have some sorting out to do."

The officers shuffled in to sit around the headquarters table looking chagrined. Gilliam glared at each officer as though he, individually, was responsible for the turn of events.

"How could this have happened right under your noses?" he finally stormed. "Where was everybody? Don't you keep an eye on the people under your command? You know good and well many of these volunteers are about as unruly as a herd of wild billy goats. But, oh no, you can't be bothered. You're too busy clipping your beards and polishing your boots. Well, I want to tell you something. If we keep this up the Cayuses are going to make us look like silly fools -- dead silly fools."

"Perhaps we can smooth over the emigrant situation with an official apology," Lieutenant Colonel Waters calmly suggested. "These volunteers came to fight. This waiting around has them frustrated. Once on the march they'll straighten out."

Gilliam's neck grew more scarlet by the second. "Dammit! You don't take out your frustrations by raping women, not our own, anyway. We have to punish these men who created this unholy mess. If we don't, there'll be hell to pay. Whether you realize it or not, these French Canadians take matters like this seriously. If we don't shape up, it'd be just like them to turn on us. Then where'll we be? Up a tree. That's where we'll be."

"Court martial the culprits, and send them back to the valley in irons," Major Lee suggested.

"Hell's fire! That's no answer. With the escort we let the peace commissioners have, we're already short of men."

"Take the prisoners with us. Deal with them when we get to Waiilatpu. Cooler heads will prevail by then," Waters advised.

Gilliam shook his head. "I don't like it. One of McKay's men could slip a knife in their ribs along the way."

"Keep the prisoners separate, march them out front. Have the French Canadians bring up the rear. That's where they'll be anyway, dragging that cursed cannon," Waters replied.

Gilliam grunted. He was not satisfied, but no one had a better suggestion. "I guess that's the best we can do. I want each one of you to keep your eyes peeled -- put a stop to foolishness before it begins. And keep the men busy. The old saying is right: 'An idle brain is the devil's workshop.' Any more episodes like this and we might as well call the campaign off."

The Emigrant Camp Skirmish kept tongues wagging late into the night. Some said the French Canadians did right. Others said it was none of their business. The Americans should have dealt with the problem themselves. A few like Adams and Walsh blamed Gilliam and his officers for not keeping the troops occupied with drill and preparations for the coming march. Joe, Macon, Sandy and Michael remained silent and kept to their tent. It was impossible to ignore the conversations. Pimple Face and his companion across the way discussed the event at length.

"Golly! I wished I'd been there," Pimple Face said wistfully. His arrow wound had taken a turn for the worse and kept him tent-bound. "I ain't never seed a nakkid woman, hev you?"

"Of course. Many times," his tent mate boasted. "How come yuh ain't? Yer hitched. Surely yer old woman allows yuh a peek now an' then."

"Naw. She's the nervous type. Her pa brought her up religious. Filled her mind with Bible sayin's. To hear him tell it, lust is the heart of evil even in the marriage bed. 'Flee from fornication. He that fornicates sins against the Lord.' That's the type of thing he preaches."

"What's the matter with him anyways? Layin' with yer wife ain't fornication. Fornication's when yuh bed down some passin' floozie."

"Yeah, well my wife's pa don't know the difference. Anyways, what was thet emigrant gal like? Didja see her nakkid as a jaybird?"

"Ah, yeah. She's somethin' special. Too bad those interferin' Frenchies came along when they did. It was gettin' interestin'."

"Yeah! Those fellas don't have no manners. Why didn't someone stop 'em."

"Are yuh crazy? They had guns. Didja see how those birds kin shoot? Hell, they don't even take aim an' kin knock a freckle off yer nose at a hundred paces. They clipped that guy's finger an' ear lobe off slicker'n if they'd chopped 'em on a butcher's block. Yuh don't go foolin' aroun' with galoots like thet, not if yuh got a noodle in yer brain."

"Yeah! What happened to the nakkid woman?"

"Some ol' graybeard threw a blanket aroun' her an' hustled her outta sight."

Sandy Sanders had heard enough. He thrust his head out of the tent. "Why don't you filthy-minded simpletons shut up? There's Christian folk around here that don't need your filthy talk."

"Yes, reverend," Pimple Face retorted. "We'll sure enuff wash our mouths with lye soap."

Macon Laird knocked out his pipe. "This has been a most extraordinary day," he observed. "It had everything: tragedy, humor, heroes, villains . . . . The backdrop was superb; the glitter of the river on one side and the dark escarpment on the other, gave it exactly the right touch. The plot was realistic and gripping. The actors played their parts to the hilt. The audience was mesmerized. The aftereffect lasting. What more could one ask? It was a performance London's Drury Lane would have been proud to have staged."

Sandy objected. "Humor? It wasn't a bit funny. It was disgusting."

"Ah, my good man. It takes a connoisseur of the arts to appreciate the nuances. Gallows humor they call it -- French housewives knitting while watching the guillotine lop off their countrymen's heads, or Nero fiddling while Rome burns. Can you not see Emperor Cornelius Gilliam strutting about in his nightshirt, red neck glowing, playing the fiddle while his men pillage, kill and rape?"

"Why don't you go back to England?" Sandy retorted in disgust.

"Oh, that would not be playing the game. It would be rude, like leaving after the first act of a three-act play. The players would be most put out. Might even cause them to forget their lines."

"Shut up! It's time we got to sleep." This time it was Joe's testy voice. The tent fell silent.

Michael pulled his sleeping robe up and shivered. A feeling of apprehension gripped him. There was an undercurrent of feeling between Macon Laird and Sandy Sanders that did not bode well. What had happened between them? Joe must have felt the undercurrent, too, otherwise why did he so curtly shut them up?

Michael turned over and stared at a patch of stars that shone through a gap in the tent. What was the Englishman talking about: Drury Lane, connoisseur, nuances, guillotine, Nero, three-act plays? He repeated the words to himself. He suddenly felt terribly ignorant. Teachers at the mission schools never had mentioned such things.

XIII

Half a league, half a league,
Half a league onward . . .
Rode the six hundred.
The Charge of the Light Brigade

On February 14th, the feast day of St. Valentine, Gilliam's troops broke camp. Reveille came early. Grumbling, the troopers rolled out. They stumbled about shivering and swearing. The day they waited for had arrived, but they were not ready. The ever present breeze funneling through the gorge turned into a gale. Tents and wagon covers flapped, dust and sand swirled through passageways. Hats and loose articles went flying. Weeds, dry leaves and camp trash bounced over the parade grounds like fleeing jack rabbits.

Horses brought in from pasture added more confusion. Little used, they shied and crow-hopped, spit out bits and resisted saddles and packs. Reluctant drayage animals were equally maddening. Mule skinners struggled to harness their charges. The stubborn critters laid back their long ears, kicked and bit, hee-hawed and reared, defying their masters.

Finally, a semblance of order was realized. Columns of troopers, four abreast, marched away. Cracking their long snake-like whips, teamsters urged their teams onto the track. Herders hallooing the loose stock, prepared to follow. Wagons, livestock and marching feet raised a cloud of dust that could be seen by Indian scouts on the far bank of the Columbia River.

Like the uncoiling of a snake, the column began to take shape. Buckskin clad scouts led the way. Some distance back rode Gilliam and his officers. Next came the two prisoners and their guards. The Willamette Valley volunteers followed. Tom McKay and the French Canadians brought up the rear. Behind McKay's men rumbled support wagons and a drove of spare horses, mules, and small herd of beef cattle.

As they passed below the mission buildings a scattering of emigrants came out to watch, the men's long beards flowing in the wind. Some cradled rifles, others carried pitchforks, the morning sun glinting menacingly on shiny metal tines. A bevy of dogs snarled down the hillside. A long bearded man shouted and waved his fist. The wind carried away the words, but the gesture delivered the message. They were delighted to see their tormentors leave.

The column weaved its way across the valley and up the slope to the escarpment. To the east, as far as the eye could see, except for low growing bushes, the terrain was bare of vegetation   In the west, at the troopers' rear, the glistening tower of Mount Hood thrust its way into a sky filled with fleecy clouds.

The troop forded the Deschutes and came to the John Day. All along the way Indians on horseback were sighted. Riding out of rifle range, they kept pace with the soldiers. On the hilltops the message was flashed ahead by mirrors. "Sound the alarm! Blue Coats are coming." The presence of hostiles kept the volunteers on edge.

"Those blinkety redskins, they're like a bunch of pesky fleas, hoppin' from one hilltop to the next. Don't the beggars ever rest?" Yellow Beard Adams complained.

"They say a thousand'r more're waitin' on yonder plateau. Guess thet means we'll soon be findin' out how pesky these blinkety redskins kin be," a grizzled trooper announced.

"Golly! A thousand Injuns!" a pale-faced youth exclaimed.

"Could be more. Could be less. Yuh cain't predict redskins. How many turn out depends on how they feel. If they git up feelin' itchy, they'll be wantin' to count coups. Yuh kin count on a bunch of 'em rarin' to go after it. If they git up feelin' a bit puny the number'll be less. They'll be stayin' in their lodges an' takin' a snooze -- jest what I'd like ta be doin'.

"Most people don't unnerstan' how Injuns think. They

don't make war like white folks. They look on fightin' as kind of a game. They keep score, not by dead bodies, but acts of bravery. Fer instance, it don't take no courage to stand off an' shoot somebody dead. It takes a lot of courage to ride up to a foe that's shootin' at yuh an' tap him on the noggin with a coup stick. Yuh don't see any white folks doin' that."

The column stopped on the western banks of the John Day. The frequent sightings of Indian riders made Gilliam cautious. The crossing was a good place for ambush. "We'll camp here until the scouts reconnoiter," Gilliam announced.

It was the first night to bivouac on the trail. The troopers were not accustomed to setting up camp. It was dark before noncoms had the men situated. The prisoners presented a special problem. Was it necessary to tie them hand and foot? Did they require a special guard? Lieutenant Colonel Waters said one thing. Major Lee said something else. Gilliam issued the final order.

"Put them in the center of camp. No need to tie them. We're in Indian territory. They won't escape. If they do, the redskins are waiting. They'll give them a proper how-do-you-do. If they reach The Dalles, you can bet the emigrants will see to it they get their just dues."

Sentries posted on the camp perimeter were drilled on orders of the day. No one, not a soul, was to enter or leave. Sergeant of the guard had the men repeat the orders twice and out loud to make certain they were understood.

Macon Laird found Gilliam's precautions amusing. "If I read the tea leaves right, it'll be another four days before we hit Cayuse country. From the way Gilliam acts you would think behind every bush and rock a hostile was waiting in ambush."

An hour before dawn the sharp crack of a rifle report aroused the camp. Mounted sentries thundered back and forth. "Indians! Get up! Roll out! We're under attack!"

Bleary-eyed troopers grabbed for their rifles. They stumbled over blankets and bedrolls, frantically searching for the enemy. "Where the devil are they, anyway?" a trooper shouted.

"Over there! Look at that son-of-a-gun run." A shot was fired. After a pause there was another shot and another until sporadic rifle fire came from every corner of the camp.

"Ooh, my God! I'm hit," a trooper screamed.

"Hold your fire," Major Lee's voice rose above the uproar. "Everybody fall in! Sergeants take roll! See to the casualties. Make your report."

The first fingers of dawn appeared before order was restored. After counting noses and calling roll, a casualty list was announced: one wounded rifleman, presumably hit by a stray bullet fired by his own troop, two prisoners missing.

"What a way to launch a campaign," Gilliam muttered grimly. On second thought, he was happy the prisoners had escaped. It made one less problem he had to face. The only trouble was that the escapees were armed. The would-be rapists had seized the weapons of their guards.

The scouts crossed the John Day. They found no signs of ambush but did discover a freshly abandoned Indian camp. Whether the occupants were friendly or hostile, the officers couldn't decide. Whoever it was, they had left nothing behind but camp debris. Joe and Michael were called forward to read the signs.

The brothers poked around in the trash. A few strips of rawhide, buffalo hair stuffing from saddle pads, a length of worn-out elkskin tether line, a discarded breechcloth and a broken pot, were among the items found. It was rubbish, but it told Michael enough to identify the campers.

"Tenino, probably twenty families," he reported.

"Are they on the warpath?" Gilliam tersely asked.

Michael shook his head. What a silly question. This was a family camp, and the Tenino were friendly people. He did spot something, though, that was unusual: the remnants of a cow hide. He picked it up and held it out for Gilliam to inspect.

"What am I supposed to read from that?" Gilliam blustered.

"It's cow hide," Joe said. "These Teninos could've been in on that early Fort Lee raid. Either that or they traded for a cow from passing emigrants, or stole it."

"Horse feathers!" Gilliam snapped. "These people never pay for anything they can steal." He motioned to the officers to get the men back in the ranks. "Yah! Ho!" came the shout to move out.

Near dusk the troop made camp on a barren hillside. It was a bad choice. A broad expanse of the river was visible, but a high rocky bank prevented access to the water. Men and animals longingly eyed the stream.

"Gawkin' at the blisterin' thing doesn't wet the whistle," Adams complained, spitting and wiping tobacco drools from his beard. "Best thing is to put yer mind on somethin' else."

"Like what?" Pimple Face asked sarcastically.

"Why on pleasant things, like what're yuh goin' to do when this fracas is over."

"Splendid idea," Macon Laird agreed. "What are you planning to do, Adams?"

"Probably go back to the valley an' sire more kids. That's the most pleasant thing I kin think of right now."

"Hah!" Pimple Face snorted. "How many yuh got?"

"Quite a passel. Last time I called roll came out 'leven, an' that wasn't countin' the one on the way."

"I swear," Pimple Face shook his head. "What in the world're yuh doin' here? With a woman as lovin' as thet, I'd be home takin' care of her needs day an' night."

"Well, maybeso, yuh'd do thet fer a while but wait 'til yuh git a passel of kids. If yuh don't run off inta the mountains or to a tavern yuh'll probably start beatin' yer ol' woman. Besides, yuh don't hev much time fer lovin' with a bunch of kids pesterin'."

Sandy Sanders, who had been half listening, dug into a pack for his portfolio. He withdrew a paper and dipped a pen in ink. Every night he wrote a letter to Tildy. Each one he added to a slow growing packet held together by a strip of rawhide.

"All this talk of kids has me thinking," Sandy said. "I must make plans for Baby John's schooling. Some day I'll send him east to college."

"Good idea." Adams scratched in his yellowed beard. "I got myself edjucated onct. Larned the alpherbet. Could cipher a bit. Two times two equals whatever. Some'ow it all slipped away. Didn't take much schoolin' to plow the fields, milk the cows an' till the corn. Yep, yuh gotta use yer edjucation or it dribbles away like cart wheels in a game of faro. Any more I kin barely count to ten'r writ me name."

Michael, rolled up in his sleeping robe, listened to the languid conversation with half-closed eyes. Adam's words lingered in his mind. He had better use the knowledge he had so laboriously acquired or it would disappear. It was a frightening thought, one he never had considered. But how could he use it? Only white men employed people who could read and write. For sure they wouldn't trust a half-blood to keep their accounts, certainly not one tainted by the Whitman Mission killings.

Two days later the column arrived at Willow Creek Crossing. Joel Palmer and Doc Newell waited on the far creek bank. The peace commissioners just had held council with local tribal leaders. The council was cut short. The approaching army frightened the Indians away. The peace commissioners were curt with Gilliam.

"I wish you had given us more time," Palmer said. "We were meeting with Beardy, the Tenino leader, and a dozen of his tribe. Beardy claims he will not join the Cayuse. He also brought with him cattle and horses taken at The Dalles."

Gilliam swore. "The damned thieves! We ought to get after them -- string them up. I don't see livestock. Where is it?"

They found the animals grazing in a bulrush fringed swale. Michael's hopes soared. Magpie! Was his four-footed friend among the livestock? The cattle looked like walking skeletons. Michael's spirits dropped. The horses were knock-kneed, swaybacked and scarred from many harnessings. He knew what had happened. The raiders separated the good stock from the bad. The good stock they kept. The scrubs they left behind.

Gilliam was furious. "These things are nothing but scarecrows. Leave them. They're not worth the powder and lead it takes to shoot them."

The column proceeded on to Wells Springs. This was Cayuse country. The volunteers marched in silence. The noncoms softened their commands. Every trooper felt hostile eyes watching from the hills. The peaceful journey was over. Any moment the enemy could descend. Over the next rise lay the grasslands where Buffalo Horn, the headman of the lower Umatilla, pastured his vast herds. If Cloud Bird's report was true, the Cayuse would not let them proceed farther.

That night a sense of foreboding hung over camp. The subdued troopers went about their chores with weapons near at hand. In the Jennings brothers' tent Sandy Sanders was the only one who appeared unconcerned. He blithely cleaned up after the evening meal and leaned back to daydream of his Willamette Valley farm.

"Think of it! We'll soon be able to return home. It'll be lambing and calving time. Spring! What a glorious season. Buds break out, grasses spring up, streams start to swell, bees hum and spread pollen; everything has a fresh beginning. It's the best time of the year."

"I say, that is looking on the bright side," Macon commented. "But remember, the buzzing bees you talk about have honey in their mouths and stings in their tails."

"Yep," Joe agreed. "We are not out of the woods by a long shot."

"Ah! The Indians are all bluff. They talk big but don't like to fight. Look! We're in Cayuse country, and no one has tried to stop us yet."

"Son, don't count yer chickens befer they're out of the nest," Adams, who was passing by, warned. "Keep yer powder dry and yer rifle handy. These people who've been trailin' us didn't do it fer their health."

"Good advice," Joe said. "Tomorrow will tell the tale. What do you think, Michael?"

For once the usually quiet Indian youth surprised his companions by speaking at some length. "There will be action of some kind. Hear those sounds? They come from every hilltop for miles around. Those are warrior bands calling each other. They are saying, Blue Coats have come; prepare yourself for battle."

For hours the yipping cries like the call of coyotes kept the camp on the alert. Troopers nervously polished rifles and made certain of their loads. McKay's crew swabbed the cannon and loaded the barrel with shot and powder. Those who were not standing watch turned in but did not sleep well.

Gilliam was equally on edge. Would his unruly troops stand and fight or would they take to their heels? He remained awake until dawn and still did not know the answer.

DEATH ON THE UMATILLA

XIV

I have a rendezvous with death
At some distant barricade.

Alan Seeger

It was February 24, 1848. Colonel Gilliam wrote the date in his journal. He paused and chewed on the pen, listening to the muted sounds of early morning. He knew the volunteers were awake but had not yet begun to stir. Like him, they did not want to face what the day might bring.

No one bothered with a warm meal. It did not matter. The raw volunteers were too nervous to eat. The enemy they disdained had them surrounded. The livestock also faced the day with trepidation. A mule hee-hawed. The cattle began to bawl. They were thirsty. It had been a dry camp.

The tent occupants where Michael and Joe slept were no different than the others. Even cheerful, naive Sandy Sanders felt the tension. The freckles on his pale face stood out like angry warts. The first shot had yet to be fired, but the repelling smell of fear and deadly sense of approaching death filled the air.

Macon's first act upon awakening was to reach for his rifle. After checking the load he looked to his supply of lead and powder. He had no intention of taking part in the killing, but it was wise to be prepared for the worst. Except for Tom McKay's French Canadians, he had little confidence in the fighting ability of Colonel Gilliam's army.

Upon arising Joe also checked his weapons, then strolled to the edge of camp to make certain the horses had made it safely through the night. He spoke to the sleepy herdsmen and counted the herd. It would have been just like youthful Cayuse seeking coups to sneak in during the early morning hours and drive animals away. As far as he could determine no losses had occurred.

Michael also strolled to the edge of camp. His thoughts were on the Cayuse. Who would lead the attack? From which direction would the warriors appear? How could he avoid taking part in the battle that was certain to come? He already was branded a traitor, but he had no intention of shooting his former friends. If he could only leave, but where would he go? His fate was sealed. Whether he liked it or not, he was a member of Gilliam's Blue Coat volunteers.

The setting itself was one of peace. The morning mist that hung close to the land, lifted. For a moment, far to the west, the shiny peak of Mount Hood could be seen. As the sun rose above the horizon, the mountain faded from view as though it did not want to witness the mayhem that was certain to follow. Across the Columbia the purple, sloping plain turned first to bronze and then to gold. Legend had it that plateau people took old horses here to graze in peace until the end of their days. Map makers would one day label the region Horse Heaven Hills.

Michael loved this country. For more than seven years it had been his home. It was rugged open land where on a clear day one could see the distance of a three day ride. It was a land where Mother Earth expected her creatures to work for the gifts she brought forth.

For a moment Michael forgot the events that had placed him here. He sniffed the air and savored his surroundings. Ahead were great pasture fields that bordered the Umatilla River and the rich grasslands along its Butter Creek tributary. To the north flowed the mighty Columbia. To the east rose the dark forested Blue Mountains. South was wild open country filled with game and carpeted with pungent sagebrush. After a rain the air was so invigorating it made one dizzy.

Above the Columbia high flying turkey buzzards circled lazily around and around. The river itself lay hidden behind banks of willow and cottonwood trees. A lone coyote loped across a patch of sand. For a moment it paused with one forepaw uplifted. Its yellow-flecked eyes glanced Michael's way. Then in a quick, furtive move, it disappeared in a thicket of sage. Michael frowned. It was plain as day. By holding one forepaw in the air Coyote had given a sign. What was his message? In the days when animals ruled the land, coyotes were chiefs. They told all other animals what to do. They predicted the coming of humans and planned how they would out live them. The bold appearance of Coyote and the circling buzzards were certainly harbingers of death. Would it be the death of the Cayuse -- Blue Coats, or both?

On a hilltop overlooking the volunteer encampment appeared three armed and painted horsemen. Like stone statues, they remained stationary, outlined against the sky, only the feathers of their war bonnets moved, fluttering softly in the fresh morning breeze.

"What're those people doin'?" a trooper with orange hair hanging nearly to his shoulders asked. "They act like they're out fer a Sunday outin'. Maybeso they've called the war off."

"Don't be figurin' on thet," an old timer who knew the ways of the Indians said. "They're up there lookin' ta see what scalps they fancy, probably yers among 'em. They sure do take ta long, orangish hair. After they take yer scalp, they'll give it a good wash, comb the lice away and hang it in their lodge an' brag whata struggle the poor victim put up when they jerked it off his topknot."

"Ah shet up! They've prob'ly got their eyes on thet scraggly beard of yers, thinkin' it'd come in right handy swishin' flies off horses."

A trigger-happy soldier threw up his rifle and fired. The hilltop watchers did not move. Their stolid stance seemed to say, "Shoot, you stupid Blue Coats! Fritter away your lead and powder. You will have just that much less with which to defend yourselves."

The crack of the rifle brought Gilliam out of his tent. He was still shaving. Lather coated his face. His unfastened suspenders drooped to his knees. "What the tarnation's going on?"

he demanded of his second-in-command. Waters pointed to the horsemen on the hilltop. "We have visitors."

Gilliam wiped the lather from his face, his red neck now the pasty shade of bread dough. He snapped his suspenders in place. "What's new about that?" he growled. "The murdering rascals have pestered us ever since we left The Dalles. Don't be staring at those birds like they're going to eat us alive. Redskins are only people. They pull their pantaloons on one leg at a time. Now, get the men cracking. The way we're dawdling around you'd think we came to enjoy the scenery. By noon, I want us across the Umatilla."

XV

*We do not take up the warpath without a just cause
and honest purpose.*
Pushmataha, Choctaw

The column moved on. The three peace commissioners rode in front carrying white flags. Joel Palmer, especially, hoped to avoid conflict -- get the Cayuse to surrender the murderers through negotiations. As wisps of morning mist melted away clumps of bare cottonwood trees emerged like ghostly wraiths, guarding the approaches to the Umatilla, the river Gilliam was anxious to cross before engaging the Cayuse.

Soon more Indian horsemen appeared riding along the south range of hills. Near mid-morning a cloud of dust rose up on the eastern horizon. Carried on the cool breeze, a sound like rolling drums came nearer and nearer. Over a distant rise in advance of the dust cloud, row after row of bobbing heads came into view. Gilliam quickly thrust up a hand. "Halt!" he yelled. "Make ready your weapons."

"What a silly order," Adams remarked. "My gun has been at ready since leaving Fort Wascopum."

Rising above the thunder of hoofbeats came the chilling high pitch of human voices, yelping, not unlike the chorus of hundreds of coyotes. The enemy was near enough that the troopers could single out each individual warrior, each rifle barrel, lance and war club. There was no doubt the Cayuse were armed to the teeth. The sight so unnerved the man with the shoulder length orange hair, he uttered a squawk like a startled chicken.

"Steady in the ranks!" Major Lee ordered. "These people are no better than you. They walk on two legs like everyone else."

"Thet ain't much comfort," Walsh grumbled. "This ain't no walkin' contest. But if'n its runnin' yer talkin' about, I'm rarin' ta take off. I betcha I kin cross the John Day an' Deschutes an' land in The Dalles a mile ahead of all you galoots."

"Shet up," Adams snapped. "I'm already as nervous as a pig in church. Why'n tarnation're we sittin' here, anyways -- jest bein' perlite, waitin' fer these redskins to invite us to take tea?"

Abruptly the wave of warriors pulled up. The drumming and yelping ceased. The quiet that ensued was even more unsettling than the noise. The war party appeared in no hurry to give battle. The lead horsemen pranced back and forth on their steeds, pointing and chattering as though deciding which Blue Coats to attack first. Then, as though they had been awaiting a signal, on the hilltops lines of women, children and a scattering of more horsemen appeared.

"Now thet they've got an audience, yuh kin 'spect a bit of action," the old timer said. "If I was yuh, I'd put a sack over yer head," he advised the trooper with orange hair. "By now they hev yuh spotted fer certain. 'Twouldn't surprise me none if thet's what they was chattin' 'bout, who'd git first crack at yer scalp."

Gilliam, who had sat motionless on his horse, calmly called for his spyglass. He put it to his eye and studied the line of warriors who blocked the way. He motioned Joe and Michael forward. "What do you make of these people?" He handed Joe the glass. "And what's that bunch doing on the ridge? Do we have to deal with them, too?"

Joe studied the warrior ranks. They were lined up as if on parade: feathered war bonnets, spears with fox tail tassels, horses painted and festooned with banners. It was a magnificent display of color and pageantry.

"Hmm!" Joe grunted. This was obviously no haphazard meeting. It had been thoughtfully planned. He attempted to single out people he knew. In war dress the horsemen all looked alike. He did recognize the shaman, Gray Eagle, and chief of all Cayuse, Five Crows. Other riders appeared familiar but he couldn't give them names. He handed the spyglass to Michael.

Michael pushed it away. It was bad enough to stand out front with the Blue Coat leader. Using a spyglass on his former

friends would label him even more of a traitor. Besides, he didn't
need it. He could tell most of the warriors by the way they sat
their horses. Five Crows and Gray Eagle of the Umatilla Cayuse
were out front. A cluster from the Waiilatpu band was next:
Tamsucky, Tomahas, Tiloukaikt and his sons . . . . He didn't see
Joe Lewis, but most of the other Whitman Mission murderers
were there. What a coup for Gilliam if he could capture them
now. It would be best for everybody. The Blue Coats would go
home. The Cayuse could put their lives back together.

Michael turned his attention to the hilltop observers.
Stickus, the single feather cocked on the side of his head, was the
first he recognized. Behind him his mate, Kio-noo, stood with
folded arms. Around her shoulders was the blanket she always
wore like an oversized shawl. Close by were other members of
the upper Umatilla band. Michael's spirits lifted. His friend,
Stickus, had kept his people peaceful. Instead of facing a thousand warriors it was more like four or five hundred in the war
party.

"What do you think, Michael?" Joe asked. "It looks like
only part of the Cayuse tribe is prepared to fight. I don't see the
Umatilla, Palouse or Walla Walla, either. There may be a few
but not in the numbers Buffalo Horn's sons claimed."

Gilliam grunted. "Just as I thought. The great army of
warriors you predicted was a lot of hot air." He gave Michael a
cold stare.

"This doesn't mean the Umatilla, Walla Walla and Palouse
won't join the Cayuse," Joe cautioned. "They may wait to see
how the battle goes before they decide."

The warriors began to move. Remaining a good distance
away, they formed a circle around the Blue Coat column. "Bunch
up! Dismount! Horses to the rear!" Officers went back and
forth snapping orders, preparing for the impending attack.

In unison the enemy horsemen cantered forward, then
wheeled to ride in single file around and around the troopers,
shouting and waving their weapons. Slowly the circle became

smaller until the dust the pounding hooves raised sent a cloud of gray over the surrounded Blue Coats.

"What the tarnation're they tryin' to do? Yuh cain't see an yuh cain't breathe. Are they tryin' to make us dizzy-headed or suffocate us to death?" Walsh asked petulantly.

The old timer who knew the ways of Indians, spat and wiped his whiskers. "Yuh see, I told yuh Injuns're different. Before fightin' they like ta show off a bit. Kinda like bulls pawin' an' snortin', showin' how fierce an' mean they is. Maybeso, it's a way ta see if we'll cut an' run or maybe we'll get so flustered it'll throw off our aim. Don't get impatient. Soon as these preliminaries're outta the way they'll come at us like a swarm of angry bees."

In a surprisingly military manner, the Cayuse horsemen pulled to a halt, forming two ranks. The leader rode toward the volunteers and shouted.

"Who is that and what does he have to say?" Gilliam asked Michael.

"It's Five Crows, the Cayuse leader. Says his warriors will never allow the Blue Coats to enter the Cayuse homeland. If we do not leave, all Blue Coats will die here in these sandy hollows. He says when this happens his warriors will ride to the Willamette Valley and take the soldiers' women, their children and all their possessions."

"Hmmp!" Gilliam grunted. "Talks big, doesn't he?"

Gray Eagle, the shaman, also rode forward. His painted Appaloosa pranced back and forth in a little dance. A breeze whipped up sending the feathers of the rider's war bonnet fluttering. Gray Eagle raised his arms skyward. In a loud voice he called on his guardian spirit for protection, then reined his mount toward the troopers.

"Shoot your iron sticks," he shouted. "I will swallow your lead. Your bullets will do me no more harm than a shower of rain."

Not to be out done, Five Crows reined up alongside the

shaman and shouted that he, too, was immune to Blue Coat bullets. The two horsemen pressed forward into the no man's land separating the combatants. The hollow grew quiet. The dull click of hammers drawn back sounded as loud as pistol shots. A mongrel dog darted out from the trooper ranks to bark. Gray Eagle, holding his rifle with one hand, shot the canine dead.

"My gawd!" an awed trooper muttered. "That galoot could shoot the eye outta a hummin' bird."

Shouting and whipping their horses forward, the Cayuse ranks charged. Just as it appeared they would overrun the front line of volunteers, the main body of warriors turned back. Only Five Crows and Gray Eagle kept coming. Tom McKay swung his rifle up. There was a report like the bark of the dead dog. The shaman slid from the saddle. His body pitched into the sand.

"Swallow that lead," McKay shouted.

A half-breed named Dorien ran out and jumped up and down on the fallen shaman's head. "You invincible braggart, you're dead. Dead! Dead!"

Another French Canadian, also named McKay, took aim at Five Crows. The bullet struck him in the shoulder. He remained in the saddle but rode away, barely keeping his seat. Gilliam waved his saber and shouted. "Good shooting!" He was elated. His men might be unruly, but they could fight. In the first attack both Cayuse leaders had been put out of action.

Trained in Indian fighting by the legendary Buck Stone, Joe quickly prepared for a lengthy, tedious battle. He threw the bedroll forward, placed the saddle on top and laid flat behind the simple barricade. Using the saddle as a gun rest, he sighted his rifle and waited.

The violence stunned Sandy Sanders. He sat frozen, his eyes as large as half-dollars. Never before had he witnessed such savagery. Yet, death was not unknown to him. In crossing the Oregon desert in '45 he watched people sicken and die. On the Applegate Trail Digger Indians had rained down arrows from canyon heights. But this was different. Everyone had suddenly gone mad, killing each other like the end of the world was at hand. Only when Joe scrambled up to take him by the arm did he move.

"Get back! Take cover!" Joe shouted.

Groping his way like a blind man, Sandy let Joe guide him to a hollow in the sand.

"Look!" Joe said, "it's best we work as a team. You stay here, right behind me. When I fire I'll pass you my rifle to re-load. You hand your loaded gun to me. Understand? That way we will always have an armed gun on the enemy."

Sandy nodded numbly. "Is Indian fighting always like this?"

"Yep," Joe answered. "I suppose it is. Not pleasant, is it?"

When the shooting started Michael went to help with the livestock. He calmed the old mare he had ridden from Fort Vancouver and did his best to keep the rest of the animals tightly corralled. He was glad to be away from the front line action. He had no desire to witness the death of former friends and could not bring himself to shoot them.

The tempo of fighting increased. Tom McKay's gunners wheeled the nine-pounder into the front line. "Fire!" the bom-bardier shouted. The cannon ball whistled through the air. The shot did little physical harm, but the explosion frightened the charging horses. They veered away in panic. Riders frantically pulled and jerked on the reins in vain.

"Ho! Ho!" the bombardier chortled. "Raise the angle. Next time we'll blast 'em into kingdom come."

After the initial charge, except for the scream of a wounded horse, the battlefield fell silent. One of the French Canadians shot the horse. Afterward, only the murmur of hushed voices and the click and rustle of reloading rifles, could be heard. The dust and rifle smoke drifted away. The air was so filled with tension one could cut it with a knife.

The Cayuse, in shock by the loss of their leaders, fell back to collect themselves. The Blue Coats were a more formidable foe than they first had thought. But they could not stop now. The spirits of the dead warriors would haunt them forever if they did not take revenge. After milling about, they formed a line with their best warriors out front. This time they would succeed. A sharp cry came from the new leader. They pounded toward the volunteers in an attack more ferocious than the first. This time Gilliam's troopers did not go unscathed. A youthful warrior rode his horse over the front line. He fired point blank into the ranks. Lieutenant Colonel Waters fell to the ground.

"Yip! Yip! Yip!" the warrior shouted in glee. To kill a Blue Coat officer was a great coup.

Joe swung his long barreled Hawken around and shot without taking aim. The horse reared and fell, pinning the rider to the ground. The trapped youth uttered a war cry. It was the last sound he ever made. A French Canadian bullet caught him between the eyes.

Joe went to give aid to the wounded colonel. Waters waved him away. "Get back to your post. I'll manage."

The ferocity of the struggle left the troopers shaken. Besides Waters, two other soldiers lay wounded. Gilliam saw the fear in the men's eyes. He had to do something drastic or the volunteers would fold. He jumped to his feet and waved his saber. "We've got them on the run. Reload and give them hell!"

Tom McKay also saw the volunteers waver. He signaled the bombardier. "Fire again," he yelled. A second cannon ball went whistling across no man's land but this time the warriors were ready. They were not frightened. The big gun made a lot of noise but did little damage.

Sensing they had the enemy unnerved, the Cayuse gathered for another assault. The warriors threw caution to the wind. Pell-mell, they galloped into the Blue Coat ranks. Joe brought down another rider. He quickly handed the discharged rifle back for Sandy to reload. When he didn't take it, Joe turned around. Sandy sat hunched over like a man in prayer. Joe shook him by the arm. Sandy toppled backward, his glazed eyes stared unseeing at the turkey buzzards circling the cloud-scudded sky. As long as he lived Joe would never forget Sandy's perplexed expression which seemed to ask, "Why did this happen to me who has so many things left undone?"

The deadly hiss of arrows and angry buzz of lead continued. A bullet sent a stinging spray of sand into Joe's face, jerking him back into the battle. He snatched up the rifle Sandy had loaded, the last act of his short life, and swung the barrel up to catch a warrior in the sights. He pulled the trigger, but the rifle misfired. The warrior, his life spared, uttered a defiant yelp, wheeled his mount to disappear in a cloud of dust and smoke. Joe reached for lead and powder. Blindly he attempted to reload. Tears rolled down his cheeks like droplets of hot rain.

"Sandy! Oh! Sandy," he moaned. "Why didn't I watch over you? From the very first, I let you down."

Overwhelmed by grief and self-condemnation, Joe threw the rifle aside. He lowered his head onto Sandy's blood stained chest and cried. Poor Sandy, he had not been treated fairly, and now it was too late to do anything about it.

DEATH ON THE UMATILLA

XVI

There were no war songs nor dances, as wont after a battle, but a strange silence reigned.

Ohiyesa, Santee Sioux

The Battle of Sand Hollows, as historians later called it, continued into a second hour. The Cayuse were dismayed. Their medicine was not strong. Some thought it deserted them when Gray Eagle was killed. Instead of Gray Eagle swallowing the Blue Coats' lead, it swallowed him. The battlefield which the Cayuse had chosen as a favorable place to fight had turned into a field of death. Brown mounds of dead and wounded lay scattered in the low growing sage. Spooked by the noise and smell of blood and powder, riderless horses galloped madly back and forth, finally to disappear over the ridge that hid the Columbia River from view. Several, holding their heads to one side to avoid stepping on trailing reins, ran toward the war party, creating confusion as the warriors attempted to catch the half-crazed creatures or clear a path for them to pass.

On both sides the warring factions were stunned by what had happened. The warriors were disappointed to find their bravery and head-on charges resulted in few coups. The dire fact was beginning to sink in; this was no ordinary foe and no ordinary war where you dashed in, knocked off an enemy or two, then rode safely out of range again.

Look at these people. They do not stand and fight as normal warriors do, they bury themselves in the dirt. Like sidewinders, they remain hidden in the sand until threatened and then uncoil to strike with deadly hot lead. To win this battle the warriors had to smash them in their gopher-like holes and trample the life out of them; it was not a noble way to make war.

Gilliam's ragtag troopers saw the conflict from a different point of view. The reckless charges into their ranks and insatiable desire of the enemy to make coups, left the unexperienced men in a state of shock. Although casualties were light, the dead body of Sandy Sanders, wounded Lieutenant Colonel Waters and others bleeding from lance slashes, flying lead and arrow heads, brought home to them their own mortality. This business of war was lethal. In the blink of an eye lives could be snuffed out here in the sand of Sand Hollows.

The holes the volunteers had dug in the sand did not give as much protection as they had hoped. If the warriors on their horses made a sustained charge they easily could be overrun, shot in their holes where they lay or trampled under the hooves of the thundering horses -- not a good way to die.

The nine pound cannon that was supposed to blow the enemy to smithereens, was as worthless as a pile of junk. The troopers eyed it and the gun handlers with disgust. They had been foolish to place any faith in it.

The cannon crew was desperate. After tugging and hauling the big gun all the way from Fort Vancouver and bragging on the chaos it would cause, to find the prized weapon was worthless was a bitter pill to swallow. The cannon balls that were supposed to knock down horses and send the enemy running for cover barely had ruffled a war bonnet feather. Derisive comments came from every side.

"When're yuh fellas gonna larn to shoot thet blitherin' thing, anyway?" Walsh queried. "Yuh shoulda traded it in on a scatter gun, least then yuh could bring down some birds."

"Tug an' haul thet hunk of iron two hundred miles an' all yuh get is a double hernia," someone else grumbled.

Yet, the battle was not over. Again the warriors regrouped and again they mounted a charge. This time they made a feint toward the volunteers' front line and then veered to attack the column from the rear where the wagons and livestock waited. The Blue Coat troop was thrown into confusion.

"Watch your backs. Guard the horses and wagons. Get that big gun swung around," Gilliam shouted.

Still stinging from the criticism the gun crew had received, the bombardier in turn shouted at his men. "Yuh heard the colonel. Set the sights on those redskins. Double the powder. Leave out the ball. Throw in bolts, chain an' shot. Get a move on! Cram thet blinkin' barrel with everything yuh've got. Set the fuse. We'll show what this bloody thing kin do."

The ensuing explosion reverberated from the far bank of the Columbia. From the trees that fringed the Umatilla a swarm of crows flapped up to darken the sky. The gun crew lay flattened. The bombardier's hat sat askew on his head. He glared from powder scorched eyes to see the gun's barrel split in two.

The blast sent warrior horses shying and jerking their heads against the taut reins that held them in place. The warriors, unaware the big gun had been rendered useless, were awestruck. It was a sound as loud as the loudest thunder Father Sky made when preparing Mother Earth for a storm. They retreated, uncertain how to deal with this monstrous noise making thing.

On the ridge overlooking the battleground the shock wave struck like the crack of doom. Stickus, leader of the upper Umatilla Cayuse, turned away. He had warned his people fighting the Blue Coats was fruitless. A few Blue Coats killed today would bring that many more tomorrow. These hairy faced invaders were as countless as hairs on a dog and had frightening weapons that cut down man and beast as easily as their scythes felled swaths of wheat. Fighting them with rifles and bows and arrows was like taking handfuls of pebbles to down big horn sheep. Missionary Whitman, who spoke with a straight tongue, had said nothing would stem the flow of these people. Only fools like Five Crows and Gray Eagle believed the Cayuse could sweep the white man from the surface of Mother Earth.

At the bottom of the ridge, where hilltop watchers had tethered their horses, Stickus helped Kio-noo onto her mare. He mounted his gelding. Together they rode toward their Butter Creek camp. Stickus urged the horses into a lope. He knew from the tired way the warriors sat their horses the end of the battle was near. The riders did not have the strength to continue the fight and neither did their mounts. They soon would be coming. They would be furious, frustrated and ashamed of their lack of success. It was best to keep out of their way.

Stickus' reasoning was correct. After three hours of conflict the weary attackers had had enough. They collected what dead and wounded they could and left the bloodstained earth of Sand Hollows behind. They followed the same trail Stickus had taken. Upon arriving on Butter Creek, Five Crows, whose wound tortured him, called a halt. They would stay the night alongside Stickus and his band of noncombatants. The Cayuse chief detested Stickus and his peaceful followers, but their campsite was good.

Stickus watched the defeated warriors make camp. Their presence made him uneasy. They might take out their frustrations on anyone who crossed their path. To protect his people from harm Stickus walked around camp and posted armed guards. Before he finished two horsemen rode out of the dusk. An alert sentry threw up his rifle.

"Wait!" Stickus called out. The riders came from the enemy camp, but Stickus had no desire to spill more blood. The riders reined to a stop, holding their hands up in the sign of peace. Stickus silently studied the newcomers. They appeared familiar -- a white face and a dusky one.

"Ah, yes," Stickus said to himself. He knew them both. The white man had been a friend of the missionaries. The dusky one was the white man's half-blood Nez Perce younger brother. The latter had lived and worked at Whitman's mission and attended the mission school; Two Feathers, he was called.

What were they doing in the enemy camp? They had taken part in the battle. The white brother was in the Blue Coat front line. The Nez Perce youth had tended the Blue Coat livestock. Stickus felt no enmity. He liked the two young men, especially the half-blood, Two Feathers. He and this young man had something in common; they both had attempted to save Missionary Whitman's life. Boston Joe, the other was called. Unlike most hairy faces, he respected the natives and got along with them well.

In the past the brothers often visited the Stickus lodge on the upper Umatilla. During these visits he learned much about them. Neither young man had a place he could call home. Their mountain man father was dead, shot in the back by a Crow arrow. The Boston mother died when the white brother was born. Two Feathers' Nez Perce mother might as well be dead. She had banished her son from her lodge. Now that Whitman's Mission was destroyed he probably had no where to go. For years the Nez Perce and Cayuse had lived side by side in peace. They spoke a similar language and frequently intermarried. Did the Nez Perce youth plan to join his band? Surely not. To come from the enemy camp and expect to be taken in made no sense.

Stickus nodded to the brothers. "Are you lost?" he asked. "This is enemy territory. The lodge of Five Crows is less than an arrow flight away."

Joe understood the Cayuse leader's concern. "We come in peace," he answered in stumbling Shahaptian and sign language, although he knew Stickus understood English fairly well. "We are sick of killing. It is not good to fight friends."

"Hmm!" Stickus grunted. Even if the young men came in peace they presented a problem. Their lives were in danger and their presence threatened him. The Boston brother had killed Cayuse warriors. Two Feathers hadn't fired a shot, but just being with the Blue Coats marked him a traitor.

Stickus turned his weathered countenance away to stare at the glow left by the setting sun. What was he to do? If he allowed the two men to continue on their way they were likely to stumble into a hostile camp. If he took them into his lodge Five Crows and his followers could descend and murder them and the people who gave them protection. Members of his own band could not be trusted. Youths anxious to count coups had joined with Five Crows to fight the Blue Coats. With the battle going against them, they, too, would be thirsting for revenge.

The glow of the setting sun was nearly gone, still Stickus could not make up his mind. He had a notion to turn his back on the brothers -- order them to leave and let them fend for themselves. Better still, turn them over to Five Crows and his followers. It would appease Five Crows, possibly make them friends again. Yet, Stickus prided himself on being a Christian. He had promised his murdered friend, Missionary Whitman, he would follow the teachings of the one called Jesus. The Christian god would not turn away from these young men; neither could he.

"Give me your weapons and follow me," he ordered in Shahaptian, knowing Two Feathers would understand. "Should anyone ask, you are prisoners. Leave your horses. We walk. Looks better."

The brothers did as they were told. Joe followed closely behind Stickus. Michael brought up the rear. All three men walked along in silence, troubled at the way fate had thrown them together.

Joe was furious with himself. He had had no intention of deserting Gilliam's army, but here he was in the camp of the Cayuse. The death of Sandy Sanders had shaken him so badly he couldn't think straight. He had been the cause of Sandy's death. His accurate shooting had made Sandy, who was close behind him, a prime target. The two bullets lodged in Sandy's chest were meant for him. He had been protected by the saddle and bedroll barricade, leaving Sandy exposed.

As if fate wanted to punish him, after Sandy's death nothing went right. Sick with grief, he and Macon Laird had prepared Sandy's grave. While he wrapped Sandy in a blanket shroud Macon went to get the chaplain. The chaplain was not to be found. Then, while they were laying Sandy's body in the grave, Gilliam gave the order to mount up and give chase to the retreating Cayuse. He called Joe and Michael forward to act as scouts. Ironically, Macon Laird was left to finish filling and marking Sandy's grave.

After a few dusty miles tracking the enemy, Gilliam had changed his mind and called a halt. He ordered the troopers to return to the battle site encampment. Riding out front in the fast darkening dusk, it was a while before Joe and Michael discovered Gilliam's change of plans. When they looked around to check on the column only a cloud of dust hung in the hollow where the troopers had been.

"Look! We're out here all alone," Joe exclaimed. "Gilliam must have decided against attacking the Cayuse tonight. That's probably the best decision he's made all trip. Can't you see our brave troopers making war in the dark. Likely as not they would shoot as many of themselves as the enemy. I guess we'd better turn back. I don't fancy running into Five Crows' gang by ourselves."

Michael studied the distant horizon. The dark mound that was the Blue Mountains beckoned. Beyond them was the Nez Perce homeland. It would be good to see his people again. He glanced at Joe and smiled. "Why do we not go on?"

Joe started to argue, but Michael's eager expression and the thought of returning to the site of Sandy's death kept him silent. His brother was homesick for his Nez Perce homeland. Why shouldn't he ride with Michael for a while? It would be so pleasant to have a few moments of peace away from Gilliam and his obstreperous volunteers.

"Why not?" he answered. Without another word they reined their mounts toward the distant Blue Mountains.

##

Michael had more reason than Joe to upbraid himself. It was all his fault they had stumbled into the Cayuse camp. He was so anxious to get away from Gilliam and the rapacious volunteers he hadn't thought of the consequences. It was such relief to be away from the terrible battlefield he could think of nothing else but the wonderful peace -- no cannons, no rifles, no bloodshed. But he should have known the Cayuse would not travel far. The grasslands of Butter Creek were a natural place for them to regroup. If he had used his head and taken a circuitous route around Butter Creek they would not be in this fix. Now the least misstep could cost them their lives.

The three men walked in silence, then Stickus held up his hand. "Walk careful," he whispered. "Many people angry. Many people grieve. A bad day for the Cayuse. A bad day for everybody."

They passed near silent lodges and avoided those where moans and cries of anguish could be heard. Finally, in front of a large white tipi, Stickus held up his hand and told Michael and Joe to wait. In a moment Stickus returned, opened the tipi flaps and ushered his prisoner guests inside. Near the center of the lodge a low fire gave off a little heat and a flare of light that sent ghostly shadows flickering against the tipi covering.

"Speak softly or make signs," Stickus warned.

Joe nodded. He didn't need or want to speak. He needed to think. Now that they had blundered into the Cayuse camp they had to find a way out. He laid on a buffalo robe covered pallet and turned his face to the wall. If someone stumbled in and discovered his white skin it could be the end for them all.

It was wise that Joe had taken the precaution. A moment later one of the men guarding the camp appeared at the tipi entrance. Before Stickus could stop him, the guard burst in. "Two strange horses graze nearby," he hurriedly said in Cayuse. "One has the mark of . . . ." As he caught sight of the two strangers he stopped in mid-sentence to stare.

The guard took a step back and swung the rifle barrel up to cover the brothers. Joe remained frozen, his face buried in the sleeping robes. His heart pounded as if it would burst. What he feared would happen had come to pass. They had been discovered -- unmasked in the camp of the Cayuse.

XVII

*You will die like the rabbits when the hungry wolves hunt
them down in the Hard Moon.*

Little Crow, Santee Sioux

For a second the tipi lodge fell so silent Michael could
hear his heart beat. The sharp metallic click, as the guard thumbed
the hammer back, cocking the rifle, sent chills racing up his spine.
One shot, one cry of alarm and the whole camp could erupt and
descend on the lodge of Stickus

The families who had men engaged in the battle were
unnerved. The families without members in the conflict were
under an equally great strain. Not only were they afraid of the
Blue Coat enemy but also of neighbors who had chosen to defend their homeland against the invading Blue Coats. It was impossible to imagine what would happen if either group caught a
glimpse of Joe's white face in their midst.

If Stickus felt the tension, he did not reveal it. In his
unhurried, deliberate way, he placed a piece of sagebrush wood
on the fire. The flame flared up to light the lodge. Stickus took
the sentry's rifle. He released the hammer so it was on safe, gave
it back to the man, uttering words of approval.

"It is good to have alert guards," he said. "Makes camp
safe." He glanced at Michael.

"It is good," Michael replied quickly. He got to his feet
and extended his hand, then quickly drew it back. He had been
with white folks too long. The Cayuse did not welcome the touch
of a stranger. He hoped the action did not make the guard suspicious, but the Cayuse man did not appear alarmed.

"Two Feathers," Stickus said by way of introduction,
motioning with his lips to Michael. "His weary brother lies
asleep." He waved a hand at Boston Joe's prone body. Joe buried his head deeper in the sleeping robe and began to snore softly.

The sentry studied Michael. "You Nez Perce storyteller who tells of giant killer."

Michael nodded. He had met this youth before. Once on a visit to the upper Umatilla he entertained people with stories learned at the mission school. The Bible story of how youthful David had slain giant Goliath with a pebble and slingshot had been a favorite. For days afterward this young man, along with most of the other youthful listeners, fashioned slingshots and practiced the art of slinging stones. No one was safe from the flying objects.

Michael inwardly smiled at the thought of soft-spoken, stoic Stickus furious with him and the slingshooters. He had ordered them out of camp and into the hills where the errant missiles would do no harm.

"Did you become skilled with the weapon that kills giants?" Michael asked.

The guard, who had stood stiffly like a soldier waiting to be dismissed, abruptly relaxed. "My shooting is not good. I need you to teach me."

"No more talk," Stickus said. With a motion of his head and lips, Stickus dismissed the young man. When the guard had gone Stickus closed the tipi flaps and tied them shut. He glanced at Michael, then cast his eyes downward as if to say that was a close call.

Joe turned over and sat up. "Do you suppose he's suspicious? Will he cause trouble?" he asked in a whisper.

Michael held up warning fingers. Someone was trying to untie the tipi flaps. Joe flopped back onto the pallet and covered his face. Stickus stood back to let his mate, Kio-noo, enter. She kept her head lowered, barely giving the brothers a glance. Stickus motioned with a hand to his mouth, asking her to prepare something to eat. Kio-noo busied herself with bags of dried meat and sacks of meal. Each man, wrapped in his own thoughts, silently watched her swift, deft hands.

Joe was the first to break the silence. "I am the one who

brings danger," he whispered to Michael. "These people will accept your presence but not mine. They will recognize me as one who killed their warriors. Tell your friend, Stickus, I must leave. If he will guide me to the edge of camp, I'll slip away and be gone before anyone is wiser."

Michael didn't need to interpret. Stickus nodded. "Boston Joe speaks wisely," he said. He sat by the fire, staring into the coals. He had been foolish in bringing the youths to his lodge. The youth with the white face would draw attention like a bull buffalo running amuck in camp. He had thought it his Christian duty to take the youths in but by doing so he endangered all of his people, especially his family. They could get through the night, but in the brightness of day a white face would be impossible to conceal. Tomorrow the camp would be on the move. Five Crows' warriors would break camp, too. His band of warriors would be bitter, angry and revengeful. Finding an enemy in their midst would set them off like a prairie fire. No one, not even Five Crows, would be able to keep them under control.

Stickus thrust a stick in the fire and watched the tongues of flame run up its length. His mind remained a blank. Who could he trust? No one. Whatever had to be done, he had to do himself. Should he send Boston Joe back to the Blue Coats' camp? No, that would not do. It was said they shot soldiers who left their ranks and went over to the enemy. He would not be able to live with himself if he caused the boy's death.

Michael was as distressed as Stickus. He was the one who had led them into the Cayuse camp. He should be the one to get them safely away. "We will both leave and take the trail to Lapwai," he said to Joe. "The Nez Perce are not at war. We will be safe there."

Joe shook his head. "The guard recognized you. If you leave he will ask questions. He will tell others. People will be suspicious of Stickus. If you stay you can explain your presence by saying you hate the Blue Coats. You went with them against your will. At the first opportunity you deserted. You will be able to make these people believe it because you'll be telling the truth."

Michael stared into the fire. His brother's words were true. He had hated every minute of his march with the troopers. All that kept him going was the hope that he would be able to find Magpie. As soon as they crossed the John Day, that hope had disappeared. By now the herd the Wascopum had stolen would be scattered all over the plateau, and Joe was right. They had to think of Stickus. Their presence not only endangered Stickus but his people, too. He would never forgive himself if harm came to his old friend.

Michael scowled. Now that he and his brother had started to know one another, he hated to be separated from him. But there was no other way out, the guard was certain to be suspicious if he was not there in the morning. The solution was not at all to his liking. If they parted now he might never see his brother again. The dream he had of becoming a member of the Jennings family would fade into nothingness like the morning mist. What if Joe didn't get away? What if he was discovered and killed?

"How can you leave?" Michael abruptly asked. "You also have been seen by the guard. How can we explain your absence?"

"Tell him I'm helping with the herd," Joe quickly replied. "Believe me, there will be plenty of confusion tomorrow. Everyone will be thinking about Gilliam and his army of volunteers who are certain to be on the trail like hounds after a fox."

Kio-noo placed bowls of food near the fire and withdrew into the shadows. Stickus motioned with his chin for his guests to come close. When they were seated, Stickus folded his hands. "Let us pray," he said in English, words learned from Missionary Whitman. He glanced up at the smoke hole and began to whisper a blessing of thanksgiving, also in English. Although he spoke barely above a whisper, his voice reflected a reverence Joe never had witnessed. Stickus truly meant what he said. As the Cayuse leader lowered his hands Joe thought he saw tears glistening in the dark eyes.

Only after eating and politely belching did Stickus speak

again. "Plan good," he said to Joe. "Walk horses to pasture. I make talk with guards. Boston Joe rides to Lapwai."

From a distant corner of the Indian encampment came an ear-splitting scream. It was so filled with anguish it sent cold shivers down the listeners' spines. Kio-noo swayed back and forth, an animal like answering cry came from deep within her throat. Joe turned over, his face whiter than white. Michael shifted uneasily. Even a flicker of concern momentarily crossed Stickus' impassive features. Everyone knew without speaking, one of the wounded warriors had died. What if it was Five Crows? By morning every voice in the camp would be wailing in grief.

Gradually, the moans and shrieks died away. Dogs ceased to howl. An uneasy quiet fell over the camp. Stickus ran a hand over his furrowed brow. "War no good. Now we sleep. Lapwai long ride." With that the Cayuse leader pulled a robe around himself and stretched out by the fire, closed his eyes and began to snore softly.

The brothers also laid down near the fire but unlike their host, could not sleep. The shrieking cries of grief were like daggers in Joe's heart. He suffered along with the mourning family. Sandy's body, hunched over as if in prayer, flashed before his eyes. Would he ever be able to live down the horror of that moment? Sandy, who had so much to live for, his beloved family and beloved farm -- Sandy who never had harmed a soul, lay lifeless in a battlefield grave. Oh, Tildy! What an awful burden you will have to bear. Sandy only came to Oregon because of you. The trip west had started so happily, took so many sad turns and now has ended like this.

Joe turned over to wipe the wetness from his eyes. Nothing was gained by tears. He should make plans. He told Michael he would go to Lapwai but what would he do there -- hide like a coward? But where else could he go? He had no desire to rejoin Gilliam's army and kill more Cayuse. Besides, by now Gilliam would have discovered his absence. It would be just like him to claim Joe Jennings a deserter and order him shot on sight.

One thing he could do was travel to the Willamette Valley and break the sad news of Sandy's death to Tildy and help on the farm. But was he ready to face going to the Valley? What excuse could he give for deserting Gilliam's army? Then there was Bithiah, the one he had planned to marry who had thrown him over for that Olafson scarecrow. Could he face seeing Bithiah and her flock of Olafson kids? Never! Ah, he inwardly groaned; he was as homeless as his brother Michael.

Michael also lay awake. The stark shrieks of grief had shaken him to the marrow of his bones. He had the awful feeling the dead warrior was Five Crows. If so, his followers would be in a frenzy. Vengeance would be uppermost on their minds. If they turned their wrath upon Stickus and his people who had refused to join in the battle . . . ! He tried not to think of the consequences.

Through half-closed eyes he watched Kio-noo glide about cleaning up after the meal. She then filled a buckskin pouch with provisions for Joe to take along. Michael turned away. What was the matter with him? When Joe left he had to go with him. It would be cowardly to desert him. He had led him into this trap. He should do his best to get him out. How he wished he never had thought of leaving the Blue Coat camp. Michael finally slept only to be jerked awake.

"It is time to see your brother away," Stickus whispered.

"I go, too," Michael also said in a whisper.

Stickus made a sharp motion with his hand. "No good! You stay. Boston brother leave," he tersely replied.

The three men stumbled around in the dark. The fire had gone out. The chill of the February morning penetrated buckskin garments like needles of ice. With benumbed fingers they fumbled with strings and laces. Before leaving the lodge Stickus inspected each brother's head with his hands. He removed Joe's wide-brimmed hat and replaced it with a fur trimmed cap from which dangled a feather. He took ashes from the fire pit and rubbed them on Joe's face.

"Make you Indian," he explained. Kio-noo came to give Joe the bag of provisions. Joe pressed her hand to express his thanks. No sooner did they stumble outside before they were challenged. It was the slingshooter guard. Stickus quietly told him they were on the way to make the rounds of the sentries. The guard started to speak, but Stickus quickly moved away, pulling the brothers after him.

On the eastern edge of the camp they came upon another guard. Stickus snorted in disgust. The sentry lay slumped on the ground asleep. He jerked the rifle from his hands and awakened the youth with a rap in the ribs.

"What kind of guard are you?" Stickus scolded. "Go to your lodge. New sentry takes your post."

Stickus handed the rifle to Michael. The chastened guard stumbled toward his lodge, muttering to himself. Stickus glanced at the sky. "It is good. Sister Moon watches to light path," he said. He motioned to Joe. "I show Lapwai Trail."

Joe and Michael looked at each other and grasped hands. Then, in a rare display of emotion, they threw their arms around each other in an awkward hug. Joe abruptly turned to walk away. Michael took up the rifle and began to pace the sentry's post, his heart heavy with dread. Something told him Joe never would arrive in Lapwai. Along the trail some unexpected peril lay waiting to engulf him in its grip.

The first light of dawn appeared in the eastern sky. Still Stickus did not return. A feeling of apprehension made Michael's steps quicken. He marched back and forth, stopping every few steps to listen. Suddenly Stickus appeared, stepping out of the sagebrush so silently Michael was taken by surprise. He started to speak, but Stickus put three fingers to his lips.

For a while they stood together, waiting and listening. A coyote howled. A camp dog gave an answering bark. A rodent rustled in the brush. A night bird took off, its wings whirring as it gained height. Then came the sounds they feared, shouts of herders and the pounding of galloping hooves. Michael groaned inwardly. Joe had been discovered.

The clamor of the chase grew fainter and fainter until it faded away. The deathly silence that followed was more disturbing than the noise of the chase. Did Joe get away or was he captured or killed? The light of morning became brighter. The moon slid behind a ridge. The gray sage lost its ghostly glow to be swallowed by dark shadows. The eerie change made Michael shiver. Was it a good omen or bad? He could not decide.

They waited until the first rays of Father Sun appeared to turn hilltops to shiny peaks of gold. Stickus raised his hands, silently thanking the Creator for bringing forth a fresh new day. Michael, joined in the ceremony by repeating a long remembered prayer taught him by his grandfather, Lone Wolf. He added a plea for the safety of his brother. Stickus glanced at him approvingly. "Boston brother need plenty-plenty help," he said in English learned in trading sessions at Fort Walla Walla.

XVIII

Death will come, always out of season.
It is the command of the Great Spirit . . . .
Big Elk, Omaha

Early risers already were up and about when Michael and Stickus returned to the Butter Creek camp. There was an ominous feel in the air. Chores were done in silence. A mother cut off the whimper of her child with a sharp look and hand signal. A dog barked and was quieted with a snap of a quirt. After a quick meal women and children scurried to dismantle lodges. Men brought pack animals in from the pasture.

Like phantoms gliding about in the cold morning gloom, the people grimly went about breaking camp. The campsite that had been good to them in the past, forever would be linked to the deadly, tragic Battle of Sand Hollows.

The slain warrior was wrapped in a blanket. Making low crooning sounds, family members bound the body to a travois. It was the fallen man's wish his remains be taken across the Umatilla and laid to rest with the bones of his ancestors. A woman and two children draped in blankets huddled together. Uttering mournful moans, they clung to the travois. Their eyes, filled with pain, were fixed on the body that so recently had been a vigorous husband and father. Stickus stopped to say words of prayer. The dead man was one of his band who, against his orders, had joined the war party. Five Crows was still alive.

Although the men stood aside while the women and children struggled with lodge poles and tipi coverings, Michael readily helped Kio-noo. Work freed his mind from worry over Joe's fate, yet, at the same time his industrious presence attracted attention, something he desperately wished to avoid. In the rush to get on the trail, he spilled a bag of jerky. Hungry camp dogs, snapping and snarling, pounced on the fallen scraps. Kio-noo seized a blanket and slapped them away. Out rolled Joe's wide-brimmed hat. The startled dogs began to growl and sniff it. One snapped it up and started to scamper away. A passerby grabbed at the hat, jerking it out of the dog's mouth. The rescuer started to hand the hat to Kio-noo then turned it over in his hand.

"This is a white man's hat -- the hat of a Blue Coat," he exclaimed. His eyes bored into Kio-noo and then into Michael. The cold stare sent a chill up Michael's spine. The man was Tamsucky, the murderer. He long had been a troublemaker and was one of the leaders in the bloody massacre. It was said when the mission killings began Tamsucky promised to lead already wounded Narcissa Whitman to safety. Convinced Tamsucky was telling the truth, Narcissa left the protection of her bedroom only to be shot down shortly afterward in her kitchen.

Kio-noo paid the man no attention. She scolded the barking dogs, sending them scurrying. She plucked the hat from Tamsucky's hand and clapped it on her head. She went back to packing as if he was not there. Tamsucky made no attempt to leave. Kio-noo waved a hand in an impatient gesture in the same manner as she had in shooing the meddlesome dogs. When Tamsucky did not move, she gave him a shove.

"Why do you stand like a stump? Are you asleep? Do you not know there is need for hurry?"

Embolden by Kio-noo's spirited actions, Michael turned on Tamsucky, too. "Do as the woman asks, stand back."

Tamsucky took a step forward. "I know you. You are the mission boy." He reached for the knife at his belt. He saw Stickus approach and turned away but not before giving Michael an insolent glare.

Stickus, who saw the byplay, scowled. "Watch out for this man. He is evil. He does not like himself nor anyone else."

Michael felt terrible. The worst possible thing he could have done was make an enemy of a man like Tamsucky. His friends were murderers like himself -- Tomahas and the Delaware half-blood, Joe Lewis. Tamsucky believed the hat suspicious and would not forget it. He and his murderous companions were certain to keep close watch on the lodge of Stickus.

Michael kept busy helping Kio-noo pack and break camp, but the knowledge his presence placed his friends in great danger made him physically ill. He should have insisted on going with his Boston brother. But where was Joe? Had he stumbled into a camp of hostiles and been killed or perhaps caught and held prisoner? If that had happened it wouldn't take Five Crows' warriors long to link the two of them together -- discover there was a traitor in their midst. Michael shuddered. The consequences were too frightening to consider.

Finished with the packing, Kio-noo tied the load fast with woven rawhide rope and glanced around the campsite. Satisfied she had left nothing behind, she took the pack mare's halter line and led the animal into the fleeing throng.

Michael glanced around for his own mount, the borrowed Hudson's Bay mare. She was not to be seen. Then he remembered his and Joe's horses had been left for the guard to attend. He questioned the slingshooter who Michael remembered had the name Willakin.

"Man with hard eyes take horse to pasture," Willakin motioned with his chin toward the edge of camp.

A man with hard eyes! Did Stickus have a follower like that? Michael didn't ask. He must not do anything that would arouse suspicion. He thanked Willakin and started in the direction the guard pointed. He kept his head down and walked fast. He didn't need to take precautions. No one paid him any attention. As Joe had said, everyone was concerned with escape. He merely was another harried individual trying to hurry away before Gilliam's army of Blue Coats appeared.

Yet, as he strode toward the pasture grounds Michael sensed there was more than fear of the Blue Coats that had people unnerved. Riders going past were muttering angrily to themselves. Their mounts appeared equally disturbed, jerking their heads, snorting and looking about. Cautiously, Michael moved on. The air became thick with the sweet, sickening smell of fresh blood. On the far side of the trail lay a dead horse, a man busily butchering the carcass. He straightened up. In one hand he held a skinning knife, the other held a piece of dripping hide.

Bile rose in Michael's throat. The poor animal's neck had been slashed; the head lay in a thick pool of blood. The rump was a raw patch of bare, bleeding flesh. Horrified, Michael stopped; a blinding rage surged through his veins. The butcherer was cutting on the carcass of his black mare. It was Tamsucky! The patch of hide the murderer held in his hand carried the brand of Hudson's Bay.

"How do you like that, Mission Boy?" Tamsucky taunted. "This will teach you to wear Blue Coat hat and ride Redcoat horse in Cayuse camp." Tamsucky wiped the blood from the knife blade on the dead horse's hide. "Mission Boy, you are in big bad trouble. Your missionary family and friends are dead. Their God, Jesus, did nothing to save them and will do nothing to save you."

Michael clenched his fists. How he wished for his rifle. For the first time ever, he would have shot a man dead in cold blood.

"What is this, killing a good horse?" a hoarse voice rasped.

Michael spun around. A tall man riding a dappled gray stallion had reined to a stop. The long morning shadows hid his features but not the outline of the hooked nose nor the light of the piercing eyes. Michael took a step back. Here was another man he had hoped to avoid -- Buffalo Horn, the father of Cloud Bird and Red Calf, all three longtime enemies of the Whitman Mission.

"I teach Mission Boy lesson," Tamsucky said proudly. "If he lives with Cayuse he must shed his mission ways."

"What does that have to do with killing and butchering a good horse?" Buffalo Horn demanded.

"Cayuse have no need for horse with mark of the Redcoats of Hudson's Bay. I cut mark away." He waved the piece of bloody hide.

Buffalo Horn uttered a word of disgust. "Kill unarmed missionaries . . . kill good horses . . . . You are a mad dog. You and your kind are the cause of all our trouble." The rider raised his quirt. For a moment Michael thought he would bring it down on Tamsucky's head.

Tamsucky threw the bloody patch of hide on the ground and backed away. He mounted up and wheeled his horse around, nearly knocking Michael down.

"Never mind him," Buffalo Horn said. "He is sick in the head. Come!" He beckoned to Michael. "Follow me."

Michael stared at the famed horseman. It was said Buffalo Horn owned more horses than the entire Nez Perce tribe and here he was speaking to him, the mission boy, taking his side.

Seeing Michael hesitate, Buffalo Horn motioned him on. "Small walk," he said, pointing with his quirt.

Michael had to stretch his legs to keep pace with Buffalo Horn's stallion. What was going on? Buffalo Horn had hated the mission, yet he here he was, almost friendly. The Cayuse horseman pulled up near a group of horses tethered in a draw; among these was a black and white pony saddled and bridled ready to ride. The horse lifted its muzzle and whinnied.

"Magpie!" Michael cried out in surprise. He looked again to make certain his eyes hadn't betrayed him. The pony bobbed its head and whinnied again. There was no mistake. It was his beloved four-legged friend. Michael glanced at Buffalo Horn. Was this a cruel joke? Buffalo Horn, whose herds ranged over miles of grasslands on the lower Umatilla, was not known as a kind man. When a horse strayed on his land, he claimed it for his own and never gave it up unless he received full measure in return.

"Is that not your pony?" Buffalo Horn asked, a slight smile lighting up his dark eyes.

"Yes, Magpie, I call him."

"Why don't you take Magpie before someone else decides to ride him."

Michael did not hesitate. Whatever trick Buffalo Horn was playing, he still could say hello to his old friend. He ran and threw his arms around Magpie's neck. The horse's muzzle came up to nibble at his shirt. Michael choked, trying to swallow the lump in his throat. He glanced up at Buffalo Horn who waited alongside. To have the great horseman give up a horse made no sense at all. "Why do you do this?" he asked, fearful Buffalo Horn would change his mind.

"I pay my debts," the horseman said. "You had my son, Red Calf, in your sights but did not shoot." He wheeled the dappled gray stallion about and was away before Michael recovered from his surprise.

XIX

*Every struggle, whether won or lost, strengthens
us for the next to come.*

Victorio, Mimbres Apache

For the first time in a long while, Buffalo Horn was satisfied with himself. He had turned a bad situation into a good one. When Cloud Bird and Red Calf had appeared with the animals raided at The Dalles, he was furious. They had implicated him and his band in the stupid war with the Blue Coats, something he had hoped to avoid. The most damaging evidence of all was the black and white pony that belonged to the mission boy.

"You have the brains of a flea," he had stormed. "Bringing this pony into our herd is like sending up a smoke signal that we have joined Gray Eagle and Five Crows. What are you trying to do, get us all killed?"

That was when his two sons told him of the mission boy's presence in the Blue Coat camp and of the battle in which Two Feathers caught Red Calf in his sights. The mission youth could have killed Second Son, but he didn't. Why didn't he do it? Cloud Bird, Red Calf and even himself had treated the mission boy worse than they would a scurvy camp dog.

For many long nights afterward the thought of the Nez Perce mission boy sparing his son's life nagged at Buffalo Horn's mind like a coyote worrying with a cornered rabbit. At first it pleased him. The boy had been so in fear of Buffalo Horn and his sons, he did not dare harm a member of the Buffalo Horn family. But he knew better. This lad was fearless. More than once he had proved his courage in protecting his mission friends.

Finally, Buffalo Horn had decided the boy had done it because of his mission training. Like Stickus on the upper Umatilla, he followed the teachings of Christian God, Jesus. Love for fellow man was stronger than his desire to count coups. The thought was staggering. Buffalo Horn, who had hated all things about Whitman's Mission, pulled the dappled gray up so short the animal snorted. Perhaps he had been wrong about the white man's religion. Had he been blind to the good things it offered? Did the near death of his son, Red Calf, open his eyes to something he should have seen when the missionaries first arrived?

Buffalo Horn's gaze roved over his prized herd that dotted the grasslands and into sagebrush. Usually, the sight brought him great pleasure, but not today. His precious horses were in grave danger, and all because of his stupidity. If he had befriended the missionaries there would have been no killing. The Blue Coats would not have come. He spit in disgust.

Soon after sunup every lodge in the Cayuse encampment on Butter Creek had disappeared. The destination of the campers was Umatilla Crossing. Stickus, Buffalo Horn and other Cayuse leaders cantered back and forth keeping an eye on stragglers, urging them to move faster. "Stay together and keep up," they shouted. It would be disastrous to be caught on the west bank of the river. They would be trapped. The Blue Coats would cut them down as easily as netting salmon coming home to spawn.

On either side of the fleeing column herds of horses raised clouds of dust. A band of horsemen trailed, making certain neither animal nor human was left behind. Scouts ranged far to the south and north. No one knew when or where the enemy might next appear. There was the fearsome thought Gilliam's Blue Coats might have marched through the night and seized the crossing on the Umatilla. If that happened, they were finished. Burdened with women and children, it would be impossible to escape.

It was said during the Black Hawk War the Blue Coat commander had taken part in decimating the Sauk and Fox, shooting old men, women, children, horses, even camp dogs. There was no reason to believe he would not use these same tactics in dealing with the Cayuse.

Michael's sharp eyes took in every detail of the retreat, keeping a special watch on those around him. He did not want to encounter Tamsucky again or meet with any of the murderer's friends. From time to time he recognized people who had come to have their grain ground at the mission gristmill where he had worked. He did not speak to them nor did they pay attention to him.

At times the trail took them through sagebrush lined ravines. The column was forced to slow. People crowded into the narrow space, rubbing elbows and jostling each other. Michael, walking along leading Magpie, bumped into a slender figure with a large bundle on her head.

"Pardon me," he said in English before realizing it. The bearer of the head load balanced the burden with her hands and glanced up. A round face with dancing eyes and an impish grin appeared below the bundle. Michael gasped. "Little Fox!" The name popped out of his mouth in surprise. The meeting was so unexpected he couldn't think of another word to say. This was his dream maiden. Although she was destined to be the mate of Edward Tiloukaikt, son of the Waiilatpu Cayuse band leader, he had long worshipped her from afar.

"Where did you come from, Mission Boy?" she asked, her voice as merry as her eyes. She continued to stride along, shyly looking up from time to time. For the first time ever, Michael didn't mind being called Mission Boy. He glanced down to see a short round nose and cheeks pink from exertion. Her hair, what of it he could see, was dark and glossy as a blackbird's wing. From the very first moment he saw her, it was her voice that had captivated him. He loved to hear her speak, but after the first outburst she said no more. He tried to think of things to say, but suddenly his tongue refused to move.

At the end of the ravine leaders of the column were waiting, urging the travelers to hurry. The pace quickened. The dust thickened. The column spread out. In the flurry of activity Michael lost sight of his dream maiden. He searched for her. She had vanished as suddenly as she had appeared. Silently Michael upbraided himself. Why did he allow her to excite him so? She was spoken for. He didn't stand a chance in seeking her hand.

During the remainder of the journey Michael remained at the side of Kio-noo who plodded by the pack mare dragging the travois. He rode along enjoying Magpie's effortless gait. From time to time he dismounted and walked alongside the pony, talking quietly and patting his neck and sides. When he did not speak or pat, the soft muzzle swung around to give him a nudge. Kio-noo noticed and smiled.

"You make him feel good. He is spoiled as a first child."

Kio-noo's remark pleased Michael. He felt honored, for she seldom spoke. He watched her walk along indifferent to the noise and dust. Joe's big black hat had slid down to cover her forehead. The wide brim made her appear thick and squat. She reminded him of his Nez Perce grandmother, Quiet Woman. The methodical manner in which the two women labored, and their stoic acceptance of hardship were the same. Dependable and durable, they weathered any and all travails.

Michael's thoughts were interrupted by a shout. A galloping horse thundered up in a cloud of dust. The rider skidded to a stop in front of Stickus. His lathered horse looked ready to collapse.

"The Blue Coats have broken camp. They come this way. By sundown they will be on the banks of the Umatilla."

Up and down the column the urgent call was taken up. "Hurry, hurry, Blue Coats are coming! We must get across the Umatilla before they arrive!"

DEATH ON THE UMATILLA

XX

I think all the old things will soon be dead . . . .
Things will never be the same as before.

Wood Fire, Kiowa

After parting with Michael and Stickus, Joe Jennings reined his horse toward a bright star in the east. When he thought he was safely away from the Indian camp, he urged his mount into a lope. There was no time to waste. Stickus had warned he would not be safe until he crossed the Umatilla.

For a while he made good time. Then everything went awry. A ghostly shadow slid through the sage. The horse shied. Joe grabbed for the saddle horn. His heart popped into his mouth and fell back again. It was only a coyote on a nocturnal hunt. The shapes of more bodies, huge bodies, came at him. Horses! "Ah!" He had run into one of the Cayuse herds.

Joe soothed his mount and again took aim on the bright eastern star. He topped a low ridge. The horse slid to a stop. It was all Joe could do to keep his seat. Joe jerked at the reins and urged his horse away. Behind the ridge a group of herders sat huddled around a small fire. A herder uttered a sharp command. A bow twanged. An arrow hissed. Joe bent low in the saddle, urging his mount faster. Another herder hailed him. He veered into the grazing horses, weaving a path through the herd. The animals snorted and scattered in all directions. Shouting wildly, the mounted herders gave chase.

The patches of brush became thicker and higher. Joe's mount dodged hither and thither attempting to avoid them. It was like racing through an erratic gauntlet. Just as it appeared he was about to break into the open, the horse stumbled. In righting itself it fell to its knees. Joe leapt down to pull it to its feet. The animal struggled up only to nearly fall again; a leg had been twisted or sprained. Hurriedly, Joe pulled off the saddle and bridle.

Barely able to put its weight on a foreleg, the horse struggled away to mingle with the Cayuse ponies. Momentarily, the pursuers paused, trying to locate their prey. Dragging the saddle behind him, Joe slid into a thick patch of brush. Picking up the sound, his pursuers came pounding toward his hideout. They crashed by so near the dust they stirred up nearly suffocated Joe. It was all he could do to stifle a sneeze.

Spooked by the commotion, a band of grazing animals skittered away, hightailing it toward the east. "Yip! Yip! Yip!" the herders shouted, flogging their mounts, charging after the runaways.

This was the break Joe needed, but he had to be quick. Soon the Cayuse horsemen would be back. He took the bridle and began to search for another mount but the herd had taken flight. The only animal left behind was a docile old mare, so tame she lifted her muzzle to nibble at Joe's outstretched hand. He slid the bridle over her ears and led her to where he had hidden the saddle. The mare was slow with a rolling gait but it was better than walking. Joe's plan was to circle the Cayuse herds, ford the Umatilla and turn up river guided by the North Star. After a mile or two, the mare's swaying motion lulled him into a half doze. For a long while he let her lead him where she would.

"What am I doing?" he finally muttered, jerking himself awake. How long had he been drifting along half asleep? He scanned the horizon, trying to orient himself. Daylight had arrived, revealing a great expanse of low growing sagebrush. He had no idea where he was. He kicked the mare into a slow lope. She lumbered along, her heavy hooves raising a trail of dust. Suddenly, out of the morning gloom came a shout.

"Halt!" The order was followed by the click of a rifle hammer pulled back.

Joe groaned. He knew the voice. It was that sharp, whiny croak of Pimple Face. In the attempt to avoid the Cayuse herds, he had become twisted around. He was nearly back at Sand Hollows where the volunteers were encamped. He did not attempt to make a run for it. The mare was too slow. Besides, Pimple Face was a believer in Gilliam's philosophy of shoot first and ask questions afterward.

"Dismount an' be slow an' keerful," Pimple Face ordered. "I'm jest itchin' ta plug a redskin."

Joe remained mounted. "You're making a mistake. I'm Joe Jennings returning from scouting patrol," he said, snapping out the first plausible explanation that came to mind.

"Come forward an' show yerself. An' don't make any false moves. Yuh don't look like Joe Jennings." The rifle muzzle wavered to point at the fur cap with the dangling feather Stickus had insisted Joe wear.

"Scouting camouflage," Joe explained, realizing his face and hands were coated with the ashes Stickus had rubbed on to hide his white skin.

"Yuh sound like Jennings, but yuh look Injun. I told yuh ta git down. Now, do as I say. Nothin'd please me more than shoot an Injun afore breakfast."

Pimple Face came close and jabbed Joe in the ribs with the rifle muzzle. Joe flinched. "Let the hammer down on that thing! It's liable to go off," he protested.

"Shut yer trap. My orders're ta stop anyone suspicious. In thet Injun getup yer suspicious as all get-out." Pimple Face jerked on the dangling feather, pulling the cap off. "Hmm! So it is Joe Jennings. What're yuh doin', sneakin' in like this? Everybody figured yuh'd deserted, yuh an' that half-breed, Two Feathers. Where the hell is he?" Pimple Face swung around, scanning the sagebrush.

"Hidin' in the shadows, is he? Tell him ta get out here, an' no monkey business or I'll fill yer belly full of lead."

"Quit acting stupid. Nobody is hiding. Now let me go. I need to report to the colonel."

"Yuh bet yer life, yer goin' ta report to the colonel. He'll probably tie yuh ta a post like he did thet Wascopum Injun. After the boys hev seen what a dirty deserter looks like, he'll shoot yuh dead as a side of beef."

Joe gave a deep sigh. He had jumped from the frying pan into the fire. The only way out was to stick to the story he'd given Pimple Face. He had been scouting the enemy. Even so, since Gilliam hadn't sanctioned it, he probably would accuse him of desertion anyway.

Jasson met them at the headquarters tent. "What have yuh got there?" he querulously asked. "Ah! The deserter! Turn him over to the sergeant of the guard. We don't want him here. The colonel's still asleep."

"Jasson! What's going on out there?" Gilliam's rasping voice demanded.

"Damnation! Yuh woke him up," Jasson muttered. "Sir! The sentry's brought in a prisoner. It's the trooper, Jennings, sir. He was lurkin' outside camp. I'm puttin' him under guard."

"Well, don't be so noisy about it. Did you say, Jennings? Hold him right there."

Joe could hear Gilliam's cot creak as he threw back the blankets. The colonel angrily muttered as he struggled into his clothes. This was turning out worse than he thought. Gilliam probably had been stewing over Michael's and his disappearance all night. Minutes ticked by. Rays of the early morning sun began to paint the tips of Horse Heaven Hills a brilliant shade of gold.

"Damn! I wish he'd hurry up," Pimple Face muttered. "I've got ta pee."

"Serves you right," Joe said. "I hope you wet your pants."

"Send Jennings in," the colonel finally ordered.

Joe stepped inside the tent. He tossed the colonel a half salute. "Jennings reporting, sir." He stood at attention as Gilliam insisted his men do when making a report.

"Jennings! Explain yourself," Gilliam demanded. "I recall the troops and for some reason you continue on as if you hadn't heard. This is enemy country. Before I clap you in irons I want to hear what you've been up to. You're too damned knowledgeable about this country to say you strayed off and got lost. What's on your face? You need a good wash-up. You look like a cockeyed chimney sweep."

"Yes sir!" Joe put a hand to his cheek. His finger tips came away a blackish gray. For a moment he had forgotten the ashes Stickus had rubbed on his face. He cleaned away the dirt the best he could with his sleeve. "Camouflage, sir."

"So, you were out scouting, were you?" Gilliam's steely eyes scanned him as thoroughly as if he was standing inspection.

"Yes, sir. Otherwise I would not come in looking like this."

"All right! All right! Where have you been? Out with it. After being gone all night you should have learned something."

He might as well be as truthful as possible, Joe decided. Reporting the Butter Creek camp wouldn't cause the Cayuse any more trouble than they already had. Gilliam would trail them there anyway, and Stickus said at daylight the Cayuse would break camp and head for the Umatilla. By now they should have left. "I've been in the camp of the Cayuse."

"The hell you say? I suppose that half-blood, Two Feathers, went with you. He's bloody well not here."

Joe nodded. "He's still there."

"Why? Did he go over to the enemy?"

"No, he's a captive." It was not too big a fib. Stickus had said he and Michael were his prisoners.

"Good riddance. I hope those murdering Cayuses burn him at the stake. I didn't trust him for a minute, toadying up to the Wascopum and all that talk about the Indians joining together to kill us off. It was all a trick to save his Cayuse friends. I should have run him out of camp or better still shot him as an example to the men. Tell me about the Cayuses. Where are they and what are the no-good rascals up to, anyhow?"

Gilliam drew a sketchy map from a dispatch case. "Now, let's see. We are about here." He pointed to a blank space bordered on the north by the Columbia and the Umatilla on the east.

"Now, whereabouts are these dim-witted Cayuse?"

Joe put a finger at the point where the Umatilla emptied into the Columbia. His finger followed the wavy line that marked the Umatilla to the confluence of Butter Creek. The Cayuse had camped about half a dozen miles up the creek. "What a dummy I am," Joe muttered to himself. The greenest greenhorn could have made it across the Umatilla, but not him. When he lost his horse he must have lost his bearings.

"All right! I didn't tell you to memorize the damned thing," Gilliam said impatiently. "Where is the bloody enemy?"

Joe pointed to a curve in the thin line representing Butter Creek. "The Cayuse camp is about there, I'd say."

"Hmm!" Gilliam grunted. "For certain they'll not be waiting like sitting ducks. Where do you suppose they'll go from there?"

Joe hesitated, should he reveal what Stickus had said about their retreat? He didn't have to. Gilliam answered the question himself.

"They'll retreat across the Umatilla. They're sure to do it here." He pointed to the site emigrants traveling the Oregon Trail had given the name, Umatilla Crossing.

The colonel jumped to his feet. "Hell's fire! We're wasting time." He stepped outside and bellowed for Jasson. "Tell the bugler to sound reveille," he ordered. "Maybe we can catch the cutthroats before they cross the Umatilla. Bring in the horses. We're breaking camp. Get a move on. No time for breakfast. Issue jerky. We'll eat on the run." Gilliam shouted one order after another. He turned on Joe. "Hurry up and get ready. You're going to lead us to the Cayuse. In case they haven't left yet, we'll start at their Butter Creek camp."

Joe walked through the encampment searching for Macon Laird. The Britisher didn't seem surprised to see him. Macon handed him a couple of pieces of jerky and hardtack. "Sorry, old man. That is the best I can do. Like old Mother Hubbard, the commissary cupboard is pretty bare."

Joe nodded and munched on the tasteless fare. The hustle and bustle of breaking camp left him feeling sick to his stomach. Why had he revealed the location of the Cayuse? He assumed they would be across the Umatilla before Gilliam and his troops could get there, but what if they weren't able to make it? The ruthless volunteers would descend on them like vultures. It would be the Black Hawk massacre at Bad Ax all over again.

The bugle sounded. "Mount up!" came the order. "Form column of twos. Fall in line. We ain't got all day!"

Joe swung into the saddle. The old mare's sad eyes gave him a worried glance.

"Where'd yuh pick up that nag?" Adams barked as he fell into formation. "The poor thing's big as a house. Take it from an' ol' farmer, that critter's 'bout to foal."

Joe was chagrined. He had his first good daylight look at the old mare. No wonder she hardly could move. Adams was right. She was as pregnant as could be.

"Give the old girl a break," Macon Laird said. "She'll be lucky to make it over the first hill. Why not take Sandy's mount? And where's your hat and rifle?" The Britisher looked at him as though he were half dressed.

"I left them in the enemy camp."

"The devil, you say. Well, you can't go into battle un-armed. Take Sandy's rifle. Take his hat, too. He doesn't need them any more."

"No, poor Sandy doesn't need any worldly possessions any more, does he?" Joe answered dryly.

"Right! What bloody bad luck. It should have been me instead of Sandy. By the by, where is Michael? Did you leave him in the Cayuse camp along with your hat and rifle?"

"Yep."

Macon gave Joe a critical glance. "Will he be all right?"

"I hope so."

Major Lee rode up to cut off the conversation. "Jennings, the colonel wants you up front."

The column of volunteers wended its way over one range of hills after another. Joe's feeling of dread increased with each passing mile. He sighted the line of trees that marked Butter Creek. He searched the banks for signs of the camp. He breathed easier. Not a tipi or horse was to be seen. When the troop arrived at Butter Creek only a few scraps of debris and deposits of human and animal waste marked their brief stay.

Macon Laird was the first to stumble over the dead horse. "My word! These bloody Cayuse have taken to murdering and savaging animals. Look at it! The poor creature's throat is cut and hide carved off the flank. What do you suppose that's all about? Is it some kind of maniacal ritual?"

Joe dismounted and examined the carcass. "This is Michael's!" The relief he felt when they found the camp deserted left him, turning into alarm. He and Macon exchanged uneasy glances.

"You suppose something happened to Michael?" Macon asked.

"I don't know," Joe answered. He tried to ignore the pain that gnawed at the pit of his stomach. Only someone filled with hate could commit a dastardly deed like this -- one of Michael's enemies. If he killed and mutilated Michael's horse what would he have done to Michael? The imagined atrocities that might have befallen his half brother tormented Joe for days to come.

DEATH ON THE UMATILLA

XXI

The army has taken possession of the country,
and expect to fortify at the mission station, Waiilatpu.
H. H. Spalding, letter to S. Prentiss, April, 1848

The vacated Butter Creek Indian camp infuriated Gilliam. He knew he had blundered. If he had marched straight for Umatilla Crossing he could have trapped the Cayuse on the west bank of the river. What a hero he would have been. Tamsucky, Tomahas, probably the half-breed Joe Lewis -- three of the most notorious killers -- would have been bagged in one fell swoop. The thought of the lost opportunity made Gilliam grind his teeth.

He walked around silently cursing, snapping a quirt against his boot top. He glared around at his command until his gaze fell on Joe Jennings. There was something about his scouting report that did not ring true -- remaining all night in an hostile camp and coming back looking like a rag picker. Besides, he was not the type of person who would abandon a scouting partner, leaving him hostage in the hands of the enemy. Both young fellows knew the land and people. What kind of monkey business were the whippersnappers up to?

"Where are these blistering Cayuses? I thought you said they were here," he said, accosting Joe. "Are you trying to throw me off their trail like your friend Two Feathers attempted to do?"

"Sir, that's unfair," Major Lee spoke up. "You can't expect the enemy to wait for us. It's obvious they were here. It's up to us to catch up with them. Perhaps, we can still cut them off before they reach the Umatilla."

"Hmmp!" Gilliam grunted, but for once took the advice of his subordinate and placed him in command of the advance party of troopers.

The trail of the Cayuse was not hard to follow. From the banks of Butter Creek it went almost directly east, straight for

Umatilla Crossing. The column hadn't progressed far before a black horse was spotted grazing on a hillside. Major Lee, remembering Skirmish at Hobbled Horse Hill, held up his hand. "This may be a trap," he cautioned.

Gilliam put the spyglass to his eye. "That nag looks familiar. I've seen it someplace before -- seems to be lame."

"Isn't thet yer broomtail, Jennings?" Adams asked. "Looks like the one yuh rode afore yuh took on thet big bellied mare."

"Yep, it's old Blackie. The poor horse fell and sprained a leg," Joe confessed.

"What kind of scouting trip did you take?" Gilliam demanded, the skin above his shirt collar taking on its turkey gobbler hue. "That was Two Feather's dead mare back there. Now here's your nag wandering around like a clubfooted dog. What kind of funny business went on last night, anyhow?"

Before Joe could answer an advance scout interrupted with a shout. "Ho! Enemy in sight!" On the horizon a cloud of dust spiraled skyward.

Gilliam stood in the stirrups and whipped out a spyglass. "Isn't much to see, but it has to be them. Major Lee, get A company after them, and don't be taking any prisoners. It's time we put an end to this ridiculous campaign!"

"Come on, Jennings." Major Lee motioned to Joe. "I want you with me." The company spurred out. A line of trees marking the Umatilla came into view. Major Lee urged the men on. The heavily breathing horses arrived at the bank of the river. A discarded travois, bundle of luggage and hundreds of hoof prints were the only signs of human passage.

"They went that way!" A trooper pointed a finger to a spiral of dust on the far river bank that lingered above a thick stand of locust trees barren of leaves. The riders spurred their mounts through the shallow stream and up a steep slope. They galloped along a well traveled trail that cut through the locust trees. When they came to a bend where the trail curved between a brace of hills, Major Lee reined in his mount.

"This is stupid," he said. "Our mounts are bushed. We are outnumbered. What if the Cayuse should turn on us? They would shoot us down like sitting ducks. I don't need another blot on my record, that's for certain."

That night the volunteers bivouacked on the eastern bank of the Umatilla, waiting for the supply wagons to catch up. After hobbling and rubbing down the horses, Macon and Joe selected a flat area to lay out their bedrolls. They gathered dry locust branches and made a small fire. It seemed strange to make camp for only two. Always in the past Sandy had cooked and Michael had taken care of the fire.

"Shall we toss a coin to see who cooks?" Macon asked. "I am not particularly fond of it myself."

"I'll do it," Joe volunteered. They went through their packs in search of foodstuffs and cooking utensils. There was neither food nor pots and pans.

Macon swore. "I packed them with Sandy's things. They are in the supply wagon."

"Well, that's that!" Joe picked up the pouch of food Kionoo had prepared. "We won't starve." He pulled out some dried meat and a handful of pressed berry cakes.

"Jolly good!" Macon exclaimed. "Where did you get it?"

"Oh, I have friends."

"Little wonder Gilliam is all over you like a wet blanket. You are as blooming forthcoming as a deaf-mute. What mischief were you two blokes up to last night?"

"It's a long story. Much too tedious to go into tonight."

Macon thoughtfully puffed on his pipe. "All right, old chap, but both of you are sailing frightfully close to the wind. When you did not show up last night, the good colonel was fit to be tied. I tried to cover up, but he would not listen, called me a damned interfering limey."

Joe shook his head. "I must say, it was silly of us to do what we did. Gilliam has every right to be mad."

Macon puffed away in silence. "In case you suddenly decide to leave again I have something to give you." Macon dug in a saddlebag and brought out Sandy's journal and packet of letters. "I took the liberty of keeping these out of Sandy's things. Letters and journals coming from the dead can sometimes wreak havoc with those who receive them."

"Mighty thoughtful." Joe gingerly took the journal and letters. He didn't trust himself to look Macon in the face. What could have gone through the Britisher's mind as he searched through Sandy's belongings, the dead husband of the woman whose child the Britisher had fathered? Absently, Joe opened Sandy's journal. Sandy had started a letter.

"Dearest Tildy, Baby John and Granddad, we are in Cayuse country. Perhaps tomorrow we will accomplish the things we came to do. You are in my thoughts every hour . . . ."

Joe closed the journal and put it aside. He had been taught not to read other people's mail. Now he knew why. It was like peeking into the heart of a defenseless soul. He idly leafed through the letters. Each one was numbered. One, two, three, four, five, six, seven, eight . . . . Sandy had been writing letter number nine when he was killed. Joe counted back. They left The Dalles on February fifteenth. The battle of Sand Hollows was on the twenty-fourth. Yep, each day Sandy had written a letter, although he hadn't finished the last one, the one he started the night before he was killed. Joe wound the thong around the letters and tightly tied it. What should he do with them? Was it fair to give them to Tildy? He glanced at Macon Laird. He found no answer there.

During the night the supply wagons rolled to a stop on the west river bank. The next morning, with much swearing and snapping of whips, the teamsters guided them across the river and up the far side. When the teams had rested, the column continued the march into Cayuse land. From every ridge and hilltop the volunteers could feel Indian eyes upon them. In late afternoon a party of horsemen waving a flag approached. Scouts riding in front halted the marchers. Gilliam rode up to see what the holdup was all about. He recognized them as Indians and swore.

"Keep going," he ordered. "It's a trick to slow us down. If they don't move, fire on them; let these murdering Cayuses know we mean business."

Tom McKay, who sat a horse nearby, shaded his eyes against the sun. "Those aren't Cayuse, they're Nez Perce. They come in peace. Might be wise to palaver with them. Perhaps they can tell us where to find the murderers. Besides, there is nothing to be gained by making enemies when there's no need."

"I'm fed up with the lot of them. If these pesky rascals want to powwow they can wait until we reach Waiilatpu," Gilliam retorted. "They can palaver on the bloody grounds where they can see the havoc they caused and smell the blood they spilled."

Gilliam spoke with authority, yet was racked with uncertainty. He had the Cayuse in his grasp but should he try and run them down now or wait for a better time? His troop was weary from the long march from The Dalles and shaken by the encounter at Sand Hollows. Were they up to a long chase -- one that might take days? On the other hand, Governor Abernathy's orders were to proceed forthwith to Waiilatpu. It would not be wise to disobey. Gilliam made his decision.

"Our orders are to establish fortifications on the old mission grounds at Waiilatpu. From there we will carry out the campaign against the Cayuse," Gilliam informed the officers.

McKay was appalled. Didn't these bloody Americans know anything about military tactics? The enemy was in disarray. It was time to attack, not retreat. "Shouldn't you find out what these Nez Perce have to say, before you decide?" McKay tactfully suggested. "They might give us important information."

"I don't give a damn. Far as I'm concerned they're all guilty. The trouble with these Indians is they've been coddled too long by Hudson's Bay."

McKay flushed and started to retort. Instead, he turned away. "You could reason better with a runaway pig," he muttered to one of his lieutenants. "This dimwit is going to fool around and make enemies of every tribe in the Northwest."

The column brushed by the Indian delegation and continued the march east. Away from the Umatilla River groves of trees and valley pasture lands came sagebrush country dotted with rocky outcroppings. Long eared jack rabbits dashed madly back and forth along trails worn deep over the ages. A pair of coyotes loped from a patch of sage. Two troopers gave chase. One of the horses put a foot in a badger hole and broke its leg. Gilliam was furious.

"Idiots! Quit acting like schoolboys. I've a good notion to take the worth of that horse out of your pay," he raved.

"Pay? What's pay? We ain't been given a wooden nickel durin' the whole campaign," Adams complained.

"Quit bellyachin'," Walsh retorted. "What've yuh done ta earn pay? Walkin' with a rifle on yer shoulder ain't work."

The following day after leaving Umatilla Crossing, just before sunset, the troopers caught sight of the waters of the broad Columbia. Soon Joe, who was riding out front, could hear the great river's complainings as it squeezed into the gash it had cut through strata after strata of lava flow, leaving giant stair steps on the walls of the chasm. Wallula Gap, some traveler had named it. At the upper end of the gap stood Fort Walla Walla.

Joe pulled his mount to a halt to watch the sun slide behind the rugged, ageless bluffs. For a moment he caught sight of the shadowy figures of the Cayuse maidens who Trickster Coyote had turned into stone. "Ah!" he thought, if their mission and the recent past were not so grim it would be like coming home. He first had passed this way after the last fur trappers' rendezvous in 1840. From then on he traveled this way often to visit Michael at Whitman's Waiilatpu mission. How exciting and pleasant those times had been. The Whitmans always greeted him with warmth and great hospitality. Like Michael, he came to think of himself as a member of their large adopted family.

Archibald McKinlay, a Presbyterian from the Highlands of Scotland, a hospitable, good friend had been Fort Walla Walla factor then. Under his regime Fort Walla Walla welcomed all who passed through the fort gates: Indian, fur trapper, missionary, homesteaders; all comers were the same to Archibald McKinlay -- friends and customers. His policy of treating all fairly and honestly did much to keep peace in the region. Unfortunately for the missionaries, in 1846 McKinlay had left Fort Walla Walla. The peace that reigned seemed to leave with him. A year later the terrible massacre had occurred.

"Ah!" Joe blinked to clear his sight. The fact the Whitmans were gone, and the way they had died continued to bring a lump to his throat and tears to his eyes. A shout went up from the column's lead riders. Joe abruptly was forced to jerk his mind to the present and turned back. Gilliam had decided to make camp.

It was a restless night for Joe. Besides distressing thoughts over the loss of his Waiilatpu friends, the mystery of Michael's dead mare haunted him. What kind of maniac would cut the throat of a horse and then carve off a slab of the rump and leave the rest? It was not the Cayuse way to do something like this. They loved horses almost as much as they did children. It had to be someone filled with hate -- someone who had no feeling for man nor beast. What was a more horrendous thought was that the horse killer was intent on doing harm to Michael. He would not stop by merely slaying his mount.

Weary and bleary-eyed, Joe rolled out of the blankets at dawn to be told to scout ahead. Gilliam did not want to stumble into an ambush on the approaches to the Hudson's Bay trading post, Fort Walla Walla. Joe, who had exchanged Sandy's old plodder for a swifter mount, broke out of the sagebrush to follow a juniper lined ravine that led to the well marked trail on the south bank of the Columbia.

There was no sign of hostiles so Joe proceeded to ride on. He forded the shallow Walla Walla River and pushed through a row of willows onto the far bank's whitish clay and gravel surface. Almost before he realized it, the palisaded fort loomed up before him. He stopped to allow the column to catch up. Gilliam might take it amiss if he rode in by himself.

He dismounted and walked around to keep warm. A cutting breeze whistled in from the gorge. The Hudson's Bay flag blew nearly straight out, making the beaver emblem dance up and down like a jack-in-a-box. Below the fort a small flotilla of bateaux were anchored.

The bateaux were grim reminders of Joe's last visit to the Hudson's Bay trading post. Macon, Michael and he had stood on the bank watching survivors of the Whitman Mission massacre leave. The air, with flurries of snow, had been even more brisk than it was today. The rescue bateaux had bounced on the endless whitecaps whipped up by a gusty breeze. But the survivors did not mind. They boarded the bouncing craft happy to be alive.

Joe still could see their cheery faces. Even solemn Henry Spalding, the missionary from Lapwai, cracked a smile. Where were these good people now? Matilda, Elizabeth and Catherine Sager, the Osborns, Saunders, Canfields -- more than forty of them had set off down the Great River to be scattered to the winds. They were the lucky ones. Tomorrow or the next day Gilliam and his volunteers would be in Waiilatpu viewing the graves and devastation the survivors had left behind. The thought of what they would find sent a shiver up Joe's spine.

The volunteers made camp outside the fort walls while Gilliam went inside to meet with the fort factor, William McBean, Archibald McKinlay's replacement. He found him closeted with two Catholic priests. Gilliam's aversion to Catholics made him see red. He didn't wait to talk to McBean. In high temper he stomped straight back to camp. He stopped by Lieutenant Colonel Waters' tent where Waters was tending the wounds he suffered at Sand Hollows.

"I was right," Gilliam declared. "Hudson's Bay and the Catholic missionaries are in cahoots. It wouldn't surprise me if they didn't plot with the Cayuse to wipe Whitman's Mission off the map."

Before the troopers broke camp more Indians appeared seeking audience with the Blue Coat leader. The Walla Walla chief, Yellow Serpent (Peu-peu-mox-mox), brought along a gift of beef on the hoof to offer as a token of his desire for peace. This time it was Tom McKay who argued against talking.

"The wily old boy is no good. He has a thousand or more horses he wants to keep from falling into our hands. Take his beef but watch him like a hawk. He has no love for white folks. His boy, Elijah Hedding, was killed at Sutter's Fort. He never got over the fact the killer was white and is still on the loose."

The next evening the advance detachment of volunteers arrived at the Whitman Mission site in Waiilatpu. Those who had visited there before were appalled. The neat mission buildings surrounded by well tended fields, were in ruins. Only the old gristmill remained intact. Fences were torn down, burnt timbers marked where buildings had stood and rags and bones lay like scattered offal over the mission grounds.

Although he had prepared himself, Joe still was shocked by the carnage. Survivors of the massacre had related the grim events that took place following the tragedy. Wednesday morning, after the Monday killings, Catholic Father Brouillet appeared and was entreated to give the dead a Christian burial. The French Canadian, Joe Stanfield, who later was accused of taking part in the massacre, dug a shallow grave and washed the bodies before they were wrapped in shrouds a Mrs. Saunders and other women had made of sheets. Stanfield and Father Brouillet then placed the bodies in an ox drawn wagon.

On the way to the mission cemetery the oxen bolted, upsetting the wagon, dumping the bodies on the ground. The oxen were caught, the bodies reloaded and the funeral procession continued on its soul-searing way. The body of Narcissa Whitman was placed in the grave first, then, one by one, the other bodies were laid by her side. Father Brouillet then presided over the burial ceremony. No one understood, for he spoke in Latin. At the end of the service Joe Stanfield began to cover the dead. It was dusk before he finished. That night wolves came to dig through the shallow covering, gnawing on buried flesh and bones.

The troopers, unaware of the first burial details, stumbled around in a daze. They were ordered to properly rebury the massacre victims, but where did they begin? Body parts lay scattered like windblown leaves. Putting them together to make whole bodies was not only heartbreaking but almost impossible. Body parts could not be found. At first count five skulls were missing. The body of Marcus Whitman was discovered partially decomposed but whole. Perrin Whitman, Marcus' nephew, who had accompanied the volunteers from The Dalles, identified his uncle by the missionary's dental work. Narcissa Whitman's head had been severed. Her long hair still clung to the skull that lay some yards from her torso.

Joe Meek combed the mission area until he uncovered his daughter's body. The skeletal remains were so pitiful the tough old mountain man wept. "Oh, Helen Mar, what have they done?" he cried.

Gilliam silently inspected the mission grounds. Dolefully, he shook his head. He had done horrifying things and viewed many battlefields but nothing he had seen or done moved him like this. He ordered the troopers to unload one of the wagons. The wagon box was removed from the chassis and used as a huge coffin. The remains of the victims were placed inside and lowered into the ground. Gilliam got out his battered Bible, prepared to conduct the burial service. Joe Meek brushed him aside.

"These are my people," he said, his voice choked with emotion. "It's proper I be the one to say the final good-byes."

At the end of the brief ceremony, Meek dropped to his knees, folded his hands and prayed. He rose, dusted off his trousers and packed his belongings. "In the morning I leave for Washington," the former mountain man announced. "I will not quit the capital building in Washington until the Federal Government promises to send us troops. It is a national disgrace for our citizens to be at the mercy of people like these murderin' Cayuse."

XXII

*He counted many coups and exhibited
his bravery again and again . . . .*
Ohiyesa, Santee Sioux, OLD INDIAN DAYS

The Cayuse were on the run. The Blue Coats nearly caught them at Umatilla Crossing, but they had slipped safely away into the hills. Unaware Gilliam's army had temporarily abandoned the pursuit, the Cayuse continued to flee. Word had drifted up from the Wascopum how cruel and ruthless these hairy faced men could be. Fear of this rapacious army kept the Cayuse going as fast as they could travel.

Indian leaders were stunned to hear that the volunteer army had quit the chase and instead marched toward Fort Walla Walla. With victory so close, why had the Blue Coats turned away to break a trail through the sagebrush almost in the opposite direction? Surely, it had to be a trick. The Blue Coat leader was a cruel, implacable Indian fighter. He did not give quarter and expected none in return. What was he up to? Did he have another column circling around to entrap them in ambush? Some warriors thought this was so and warned to keep alert; danger lurked behind every hill and in every hollow. Wounded Five Crows was in too much pain to think clearly. His main desire was to get away, gather his strength to fight another day.

Michael was as anxious about Gilliam's movements as any of those on the run. If the colonel caught up with the Cayuse and he was discovered among them, the Indian hater would deal with him in much the same manner as he would the murderers. But Michael's greatest worry was about Joe. Did his brother escape, or did he lay dead or wounded in the rolling grasslands between Butter Creek and the Umatilla, or perhaps Five Crows' men captured him and held him prisoner? He wanted to ask Stickus if he had news of Joe, but the Cayuse leader was much too concerned over the fate of his flock to give any thought to a missing white face named Joe.

The retreat continued well into the night before the Cayuse leaders called a halt. A bright moon slid out from a bank of clouds. Its light helped the weary travelers find space to bed down. Even the tiniest of babies slept in the open. With the enemy so near there was no time to set up and take down shelters. Making fires was ruled out. They would be like beacons announcing their presence. Although worn to a frazzle, few got any sleep. Fear hung over the temporary camp like a dark shroud. Babies cried, and the freezing cold made those who did lie down get up and stomp about to keep warm.

The end of the journey found Michael as nervous as any Cayuse. All day he had the uneasy feeling he was being watched. It would be just like Hard Eyes Tamsucky to sneak up behind him and plunge a knife in his back. After helping Kio-noo make camp, Michael made his own preparations for spending the night, taking special precautions to choose a place that would be easy to defend and difficult for intruders to approach. He discovered a protected hollow with a supply of dry bunch grass. He fashioned a lengthy line out of halter ropes and tethered Magpie to a willow tree. He took off the bridle and saddle and carefully rubbed his four-footed friend down.

"There," he said when he finished, "have a good sleep."

Michael returned to the main camp to eat the evening meal with Stickus. He found his taciturn friend beside a low fire. Stickus motioned for him to sit. For a long while they remained silent. Except for the pop and crackle of the fire, soft rustle of breeze through the dry grass, and the occasional cry of a baby, the camp was deathly still. The people were so exhausted they didn't have strength enough to speak.

"This is not good," Stickus finally said. "No one knows what to do or where to go. Our people are like birds without nests. We flit here and flit there. How long will it be before we can rest? The Blue Coats have quit the chase, but they have not given up. They came to capture the murderers and won't stop until they have them in their hands. Joe Lewis, Tomahas and Tamsucky are in camp. If the Blue Coats find them with us, we are lost. The Blue Coats will say we all are guilty and must suffer the same fate as the killers.

"Scouts who kept watch on the Blue Coats at Wascopum tell us this man called Gilliam is a cold, heartless warrior. He took a young Wascopum prisoner, tortured him and then shot him to death. You know these things. You were there. You saw the terrible deeds he did. You know the kind of man we face. He knows no mercy. If he finds we are guilty of hiding these murders in our midst -- men, women, children, all of us, young and old, will die like the Wascopum youth."

Stickus took a blanket wrapped bundle and handed it to Michael. "Your weapons," he said. "Take them. Who knows how soon you will need them."

Kio-noo glanced at Stickus and frowned. "Do not make such talk. You must get these missionary killers to give themselves up. You must make them see the trouble they cause our people."

Stickus gave his mate a bleak glance. Joe Lewis, Tomahas and Tamsucky were like vipers filled with deadly venom. No one dared approach them for fear they would strike out. They had killed innocent people and would have no compunction about killing again. Joe Lewis, the Delaware half-breed, was the deadliest of them all. In the near future he would slice the throats of his Cayuse friends and steal all they possessed.

Michael returned to the hollow where he'd left Magpie. He unrolled the blankets Stickus had given him and placed the rifle within easy reach. He laid down and looked up at the stars. In the clear, cold air the sky was a silver blue blanket so near it was like a giant tipi covering, the twinkling lights so bright they resembled distant campfires.

His uncle, Vision Seeker, said each star was the light of a person who, after passing to the other side, was taken to live with

Father Sky. Was his other uncle, Many Horses, who had frozen to death on the plains of buffalo country, one of the bright lights? And how about his mountain man father? Did they allow non-Indian people to have lodges up there? Michael closed his eyes. Thoughts of the dead always made him sad. Perhaps that was why his people never mentioned the names of those on the other side. It made them feel too badly.

Michael thought over every hour of the day. Only this morning Stickus and he had accompanied Joe to the edge of the Butter Creek camp. It seemed a lifetime since Stickus had blackened his brother's face and set him on the trail to Lapwai. Michael's stomach still ached from the tense parting, the waiting to make certain Joe had safely escaped and then the awful sounds of pursuers on his brother's trail.

Michael uttered a low groan. It was all his fault. To escape from Gilliam's terrible army he had deliberately led Joe astray. Was Joe now a prisoner or worse, lying dead in the rocky fields of sagebrush surrounding the Butter Creek camp? He had half a notion to saddle up Magpie and ride back, but it was too late. Until daylight broke he never would find the way. He had been so busy keeping an eye out for Tamsucky he didn't watch where they were going.

Suddenly, a brilliant thought struck Michael. Perhaps Joe had turned back to join Gilliam's volunteers. No! That would be the worst thing he could do. In his irascible mood Gilliam could easily label him a traitor and make an example of him as he did the Wascopum youth.

The lonely sounds of the night did little to soothe Michael's anguished thoughts. "Who-who." The mournful hoot of an owl came from a tree bare of leaves. In the small pasture Magpie's busy jaws champed away with the measured beat of a funeral drum. The owl left its perch on the nightly search for prey. The passing wings gave off a ghostly whisper. A coyote uttered a doleful cry. Camp dogs answered with a chorus of alarmed barks. Michael pulled the blankets up to ward off the cold, damp breeze. In spite of his vow to keep awake and stand guard over Magpie, his eyes closed. He fell fast asleep.

It was the alarmed "who-who" hoot of the owl that jarred him awake. For a moment he thought he was back in the Blue Coat camp. The champing horse and two men silhouetted against the star-studded sky gave the illusion it was the changing of the guard.

Michael sat up and rubbed his eyes free of sleep. These were no soldiers. One wore a feather in his hair. Perhaps they were herders or on guard. No! Herders would be mounted and sentries would not stand together. They would be walking back and forth. The men turned to face Michael. A ray of moonlight danced on the shiny surface of a naked knife blade. The second man carried a war club. Michael started to rise, then remained still. The men were walking toward him. Michael's heart pounded. Beads of cold perspiration made his skin crawl. These men meant to kill him!

Michael reached for his rifle, then drew his hand back. Shooting wouldn't do. He would get only one of them. Besides, with the nervous state the people were in, a rifle report could create panic. Also it would signal the enemy, if it was anywhere near, bringing disaster down on the entire camp.

For a moment the approaching men paused. The man with the knife whispered to the other. The man with the war club appeared to agree. Again, they relentlessly moved toward him. Michael slipped out of his blankets and bunched them up to make a little mound, then quickly slid back into the shadows. The two men dropped to their knees and began to crawl. The man with the war club came first, pushing the weapon before him.

Nearer and nearer they came until Michael could hear them slither over the nearly frozen turf. The crisp, cold air turned their breath into vapor which drifted over their faces and above their heads like little puffs of steam. A few steps from the mound of blankets the man with the war club paused. He rose up into a crouch and then, leaping to his feet, he raised the club high over his head and brought it crashing down on the blankets.

The attack was so vicious, Michael winced. The sight of the cruel grin as the man raised the cub again, made Michael see red. It was the crafty face of the half-blood Joe Lewis, the most bloodthirsty of all the Whitman Massacre killers. Michael lunged out of the shadows. He swung the rifle butt into Lewis' midriff with such force he thought it would break.

"Ooof!" The breath exploded from Joe Lewis like the firing of the French Canadians' monstrous gun. The war club went flying. Michael gave the downed man a kick and threw a handful of dirt into his face. The second man was upon him. The knife flashed in the moonlight. Michael stepped inside the swinging blade, butting the man with his head. The knife swished harmlessly through the air.

The knife wieldier quickly recovered. He swung again. Michael ducked and jabbed him in the ribs. For a moment they grappled, the knife blade slicing through the sleeve of Michael's shirt, drawing blood. He drove a knee into the attacker's groin. The would-be assassin doubled over. Michael seized the war club and brought it down on the knife wieldier's head. The man refused to go down. The knife's shiny blade made another swipe. Michael pounded the attacker again, striking his arm. The knife flew harmlessly away.

Michael turned to face the first attacker. Lewis stood, clawing at the dirt in his eyes. Michael drove the heavy war club into his chin, knocking him off his feet. Breathing heavily, Michael leaned on the war club and surveyed the battlefield. He hadn't felt so bruised and beaten since the day a wild mustang pitched him and dragged him through a field of rocks. His face felt wet and hot. He put up a hand. It came away sticky, thick with blood. A patch of hair had been torn out by the roots and a feather was missing. The second attacker, who lay flat, had the feather and a lock of his hair in his hand. Michael gave the fingers a tap with the war club. The fingers opened. He took the feather, brushed it off and fastened it above the bare bloodied spot where his hair had been torn away.

Joe Lewis, who had attacked first, groaned and struggled to get up. Michael seized the knife and yanked his head back by a single braid. With a slash of the sharp knife blade he sliced the braid off close to the scalp. Lewis uttered a squeal. Michael took the other braid and cut it off, too. The second attacker, who lay prone on his belly, started to turn over. Michael also seized him by the hair. Pulling his head up, he pressed the sharp edge of the knife blade against the man's throat.

"Get out of here!" he ordered Joe Lewis. "One wrong move and I'll hand you the head of your friend." Michael gave the hair a jerk and applied more pressure on the knife. Blood began to drip down his hand and onto the victim's hunting shirt.

"Go! Go!" the downed man gurgled.

Joe Lewis, the deadly Delaware half-breed, scurried away on hands and knees. Michael grimaced. The man who at first had appeared so terrifying looked more like a scuttling crawfish than a death-dealing human being.

Michael pulled the downed man's head around until they were face to face. Tamsucky's terror-stricken eyes stared back.

"Ah! The Cayuse brave who murders women, children and mares." Michael drew the knife blade across the bared throat, lightly, but with enough force to make the blood spurt.

"That is for the mare," he said. Michael took the knife point and pressed it into Tamsucky's forehead. In two quick slashes, he carved a crude Christian cross in the quivering skin. "That is for the dead at Whitman's mission. If I find you sneaking up on me again, I'll slice off your manhood. That I will do for fun."

Michael wiped the knife blade on Tamsucky's shirt front and released him. The murderer scrambled to his feet. He turned and ran so quickly he tripped and stumbled. He righted himself to go crashing through a bank of brambles.

Michael brushed himself off and went back to his blankets. For the first time he noticed the figure standing in the shadows. It was Stickus, a rifle in his hands. "Your visitors left in a hurry," the Cayuse leader observed.

Michael grinned. "They didn't enjoy their visit much, did they?"

"No, they get big surprise. They came to tame a cub and ran into a grizzly."

Long after Stickus left, Michael sat on the buffalo robe savoring the experience. Stickus had been impressed. The Cayuse leader had feared for his young friend's life, but then saw he could take care of himself. Michael glanced up at the twinkling lights in Father Sky and grinned. If his uncle, Many Horses, was up there looking on, he had seen his nephew come of age. He was a full-fledged warrior. He had faced a foe single-handed. The odds had been against him, but he had triumphed.

Yet, Michael's jubilation was short-lived. With enemies like Tamsucky and Joe Lewis, he could well end up with an arrow in his back as did his father, Little Ned.

XXIII

*In the Moon of Black Cherries the scattering of our people
began, because now we learned that the soldiers
were coming again.*

Black Elk, Oglala Sioux, BLACK ELK SPEAKS

The fleeing Cayuse were confused. Scouts reported
Gilliam's volunteers had reburied the dead at Waiilatpu and were
constructing a fortification from remains of the old mission buildings. Instead of finding the news encouraging, Cayuse elders
were more troubled than ever. The behavior of the Blue Coats
was unbelievably strange -- far different than the Cayuse expected.

However, one thing was clear. The fortification the invaders were erecting meant they were planning a long campaign.
Rumors were rife that more Blue Coats would soon appear, perhaps down the Oregon Trail from the east. This indeed would be
an unwelcome turn of events. An army marching through the
Blue Mountains would cut off the principal escape route the Cayuse had intended to use.

The uncertainty of what was to come kept everyone in
the Cayuse encampment on edge. Children were scolded for the
slightest breach of discipline. Parents quarreled for no reason at
all. Families who had lived side by side for years avoided speaking. The friction stemmed from fear and anxiety. An enemy
foreign to their nature occupied their homeland and no one knew
when they would leave. Would the Cayuse people ever be able
to return and lead normal lives? No one had the answers.

Evenings were the worst. Sharp words led to quarrels.
Quarrels led to tantrums and sometimes fights. The uneasy state
of affairs got on Michael's nerves. He chose to roll out his sleeping robes away from the others. Stickus warned it was not safe.
Tamsucky and his murderous friend, Joe Lewis, were still in their
midst, furious at the indignities they had suffered and would not

rest until they had taken revenge.

One evening a late arriving family set up camp next to the spot Michael had chosen to spend the night. He started to pick up his robe and bed down somewhere else but was too weary to make the effort. It was a family of five. Dusk had fallen. Michael idly listened to the head of the family assign the chores.

"Straight Arrow, help your mother unpack. Black Fox, start the fire. Little Fox, fetch water. I'll tend the horses."

Instantly, Michael became alert. Little Fox! Was this her family? Michael sat up and strained to see though the deepening shadows, his heart beating like a village drum. A slender maiden carrying a pot emerged from the gloom. She went to the creek near where Magpie was tethered. The girl paused for a moment to wash her hands. She filled the pot and walked up the bank. The dim light hid her features. Yet, Michael could see the white glint of her eyes. She walked straight toward him.

"Mission Boy!" she called out. "Your black and white pony tells me you are here."

Michael scrambled to his feet. For certain, it was Little Fox, the girl with the impish grin and merry eyes, and she was coming to him! He took a step forward to meet her but he was suddenly struck dumb. He wanted to speak but his tongue refused to move.

"Are you not pleased to see me?" she asked, her smile an intriguing flash of white in the darkening dusk.

Michael finally found his voice. "I am much too surprised to speak." He took the pot from her, slopping a little water on himself as he did.

"You are humble enough to do the work of women. That is good," she said. "But I must go. Father will be angry. He will soon finish with the horses and will want his meal."

Before Michael realized what was happening, she had taken the pot of water from him. She uttered a little laugh and glided away. Michael watched her disappear into the shadows, disgusted with himself. He had acted like a man with no brains.

Why hadn't he asked to carry her pot and walk with her? Late into the night he kept reliving their brief meeting and berating himself. Yet, he was happy. Little Fox was only a stone's throw away.

The next day Five Crows called his warriors together. "The Blue Coat fort at Waiilatpu is like an arrow pointed at our hearts," he grimly announced. "It tells us these Blue Coat invaders are here to stay. The plan of these people is to take over the Cayuse homeland. If our land goes, next will be that of the Walla Walla, the Umatilla, Palouse, Nez Perce -- the homelands of all of us will fall. We must not let this happen. We must join together and fight -- destroy these Blue Coats before they steal everything we have."

Five Crows' followers took his words to heart. Emissaries rode away to enlist the support of every plateau tribe. "Take up arms against the Blue Coat intruders. Everything about them is bad. They kill our people with disease, shoot us with fire sticks as big as tree trunks and now build a war lodge in our midst. If we do not drive these Blue Coat invaders away we will lose our lands and everything we possess." This was the essence of the message Five Crows' envoys carried from encampment to encampment.

The Cayuse leaders desiring peace were equally energetic and determined. Day and night Stickus met with influential tribal members and spokesmen from outside tribes. Often he sat in council late into the night discussing ways of bringing peace to the plateau. Sometimes Michael sat in on these meetings. At other times he was excluded. People did not trust him. He had ridden with the enemy.

A band of peaceful Nez Perce came to visit. After a lengthy council meeting it was decided Stickus, Cayuse Young Chief and the Nez Perce leader should attempt to meet with the Blue Coats. The Nez Perce leader was Michael's uncle, Vision Seeker.

Michael was delighted to know of the wise man's arrival.

It was a good sign. Vision Seeker's advice was the best anyone could have. In the past Vision Seeker frequently had given Michael wise counsel when he faced a problem he could not solve.

Upon learning of Vision Seeker's presence, Michael immediately sought him out. But Vision Seeker, who was with Stickus, Young Chief and other Cayuse leaders, greeted him with a negative motion of his hand. "Not now," his signal said. Michael did not get to speak to his uncle until the next day when the delegation to meet with the Blue Coats was preparing to leave. Certain that he would be welcome, Michael had saddled Magpie, ready to ride along. When Vision Seeker saw him, he drew Michael to one side.

"It is best you stay in camp. You rode with the Blue Coats. Now you ride with the Cayuse. The Blue Coats do not like people who ride with them, then turn about and ride with the enemy."

"I know how the Blue Coats think and speak," Michael protested.

"Then you know I am right," Vision Seeker brusquely answered.

All morning and late into the afternoon Michael paced back and forth. Would Gilliam respect the white flag? If he did, would he meet with the emissaries? It was said at Umatilla Crossing the Blue Coat leader refused to speak to a Nez Perce peace delegation and ordered them shot if they got in the way.

Hours passed. Each moment Michael became more concerned. He was on the verge of following the trail the peace delegation had taken when he spotted them returning. He could tell by the way they sat their saddles they had failed. He galloped to meet them. When he pulled up to ride beside Vision Seeker his uncle held up his hand.

"It did not go well." He said no more.

Only that night did Vision Seeker tell him he had seen his brother, Joe. "Is he well? Are they holding him prisoner? What did he say?" The questions tumbled out one after another, not giving Vision Seeker time to answer.

"I do not know," Vision Seeker said. " There was no chance to speak. The Blue Coats' welcome was as cold as the Season of Falling Snow."

Gilliam and his troops had good reason to give the Indian delegation a cool reception. They had not recovered from the gruesome task of collecting and reburying the savaged, dismembered bodies of the massacre victims. The ghoulish labor left the entire encampment depressed and outraged. They were in no mood to sit down and calmly talk with anybody, least of all members of the tribe who had committed the horrible crimes.

"Now I know what it's like workin' in a charnel house," Adams declared. "I go to sleep an' there I am shovelin' bones an' skulls. I wonder if I'll ever again sleep free of nightmares."

Joe Jennings was as depressed as everyone else. Everything about the destroyed mission compound was a grim reminder of the Whitmans and their adopted family. The faces of the Sager orphans: John, Francis and sweet Hannah Louise, rose up to haunt him -- innocent children slain for no reason at all, their body parts scattered about like dried leaves after a storm. Only mad men carried out such scurrilous deeds. The useless destruction of the mission also appalled Joe. Even the young fruit trees Marcus Whitman so carefully had guarded across the plains and meticulously planted, were destroyed.

Joe walked around the former mission compound trying to accept the horrific carnage and piece together the events that occurred that fateful day. Survivors had commented on the dark, dreary weather and the scourge of measles that decimated the Cayuse village next door.

On November 29, the day of the massacre, eight members of the mission family were sick. An Indian funeral was held that morning with Dr. Whitman conducting the services. A beef was killed and butchered in the meadow. Several men staying at the mission helped with the butchering. A group of Cayuse villagers, wrapped in blankets, gathered to watch.

At the mission house two other blanket-clad Indians appeared asking for medicine. Village members were ill, they said. Dr. Whitman, who had returned after performing the burial service, went to the medicine closet. While his back was turned, one of the blanketed men drew a tomahawk and buried it in the doctor's skull. John Sager, who was in the room, reached for a pistol. The Indians shot him in his tracks.

The shots signaled the start of a wholesale killing. Watchers at the butchering grounds whipped out weapons from beneath their blankets. Jacob Hoffman, a visiting settler, fought back with an ax. It did him no good. The Indians killed him with thrusts of a lance. Another butcher, Nathan Kimball, was shot in the arm. The next day he was killed fetching water for his five sick children. A third butcher, Canfield, escaped to the blacksmith shop where he hid until fleeing to seek help at Spalding's Lapwai Mission.

At the gristmill the miller, Walter Marsh, was slain. A man running for the mission house was overtaken by a mounted Indian who killed him and hacked off his head. Then came the most villainous treachery of all. People barricaded in the mission house were assured the killing was over; they would be safe. When they came out carrying the already wounded Narcissa Whitman, they were shot down. Narcissa's body was dumped in the mud. A Cayuse man lifted her head by the hair and struck her across the face. The schoolteacher, Rodgers, died at her side.

When they identified the headless remains of Narcissa Whitman, Joe could take no more. He climbed the hill that overlooked the valley and wept. Emotionally drained, he tried to think of something else, anything but the headless cadaver that had been beautiful Narcissa Whitman. He thought back to the last time he saw her. It had been a cool fall day. She came out of the mission house to bid him what was their last good-bye. She glanced at the haze that hid the Blue Mountains and shivered.

"Fall depresses me," she said. "It is a time of death and

decay." Through the years he remembered her exact words. Joe audibly groaned. Did she foresee her death? Did she know one fall day she would be slain and her body left to the coyotes and wolves?

In addition to the grievous business at the mission grounds, Joe had other burdens to bear. The role he had played in the senseless death of Sandy Sanders nagged at him like an aching tooth. He laboriously wrote a short letter to Tildy to send with a volunteer whose enlistment had expired and who was returning to the Willamette Valley. After he had the letter written, he tore it to shreds. It wasn't right to send such tragic news by mail.

He glanced helplessly at Macon Laird, who sat smoking his pipe. "You're the one who should deliver this news. You still love Tildy, don't you? If you don't love her, you should. She's the mother of your child . . . !" There, he had said it. He could have bitten off his tongue. He had promised Tildy he never would reveal to anyone who had fathered her son.

Macon Laird stared at him, then methodically knocked the ashes from his pipe. "Who told you that?"

Joe took a deep breath. He should have kept his mouth shut. The truth lay before them as cold and unresponsive as Sandy Sanders' corpse. The words seemed to have little effect on Macon Laird. Of course, Joe thought. The Britisher always did what was correct. Macon had done the honorable thing by keeping the damaging knowledge secret. But Blabbermouth, Joe Jennings, had to let the world know -- his sister had done the unforgivable, had a baby by someone other than her husband. And he, in one sentence, had destroyed her reputation.

Joe glanced around. Actually, the only one who could have heard was Adams. Yellow Beard appeared half asleep. He was not likely to go around blurting gossip. Ah! He had to forget about things he could do nothing about. Now that he had brought up the matter of apprising Tildy of Sandy's death, he had to settle it once and for all.

"I still say, you are the logical person to deliver this news,"

Joe persisted.

The Britisher shook his head. "It would be bad form. "People might get the wrong idea -- think I had a hand in his death."

Macon's British sense of properness outraged Joe. "Bad form! This isn't an English dancing class we're talking about. We have a tragic situation on our hands, and you talk about social niceties. This is not Great Britain where everything has to follow tradition. We're on the American frontier. People don't have etiquette rules that have to be followed. When something has to be done, they do it, no matter what."

"Quite so!" Macon replied. "And look at the bloody mess you blokes are in."

The exchange with Joe had a far greater impact upon Macon Laird than he'd let on. At first he was furious. If he had been home he might even call him out. Indirectly, Joe had be-smirched the name of the one he loved. Although the accusation was true, it was not up to the lady's brother to expose her sin to the world. Yet, in a way, he was glad the matter had come to a head. No more secrets -- no more trying to pretend.

No one ever would know how much he had suffered these past weeks, listening to Sandy Sanders go on and on about his Baby John, the plans he made for his son's rearing, his education -- a son who was not his. How often he almost had to physically restrain himself from shouting to the tree tops, "Baby John is not your son, he's mine!" Now he was asked to go hat in hand and report Sandy Sanders' death to Tildy. It was a cruelty he did not deserve.

##

With the onerous task of reburying the massacre victims completed, the volunteers were eager for action. The usually complacent Adams was even hankering to do battle.

"Let's quit sittin' on our duffs an' bloody a few noses," he said. "What the hell's goin' on yonder?" He poked a gnarled thumb at the headquarters tent where Colonel Gilliam held court.

Facing Gilliam sat Lieutenant Colonel Waters, Tom McKay and the two peace commissioners, Doc Newell and Joel Palmer.

"They're nattering over how to deal with the Cayuse. An Indian delegation seeking peace is expected tomorrow," Macon Laird explained.

"What's there to discuss?" Adams growled. "Run down those blinkin' murderers. That's what needs to be done. What are we wastin' time for, anyway?"

"From what I hear, things have come to an impasse," Macon Laird replied. "Suddenly Gilliam is anxious to wind things up. He says if the Cayuse turn over five murderers he'll return to the valley and call it quits. He's in a bind. Supplies are short. There is no money to pay the men. The volunteers' enlistments are running out. Besides, I think the colonel sees the handwriting on the wall. This is going to be a long and difficult campaign. The Cayuse are a more elusive foe than anyone realized. Gilliam apparently wants to do what he can and leave. The peace commissioners want him to stay until every one of the guilty parties surrenders. They insist on hanging the whole kit and caboodle."

"For once I'm in agreement with the colonel," Joe said. "It's going to take a long time to smoke out the criminals. By now they're scattered all over the plateau and into the Blue Mountains."

The next day the Cayuse peace delegation appeared carrying a white flag and an American flag announcing their peaceful intentions. Alongside Stickus rode Young Chief and the Nez Perce wise man, Vision Seeker. Gilliam sent a messenger to request Joe's presence.

"You've been a party of sorts to this monkey business, I'll wager. Why else would this Stickus fellow show up?" Gilliam queried. "I want you to let them know under no conditions will we talk peace until they hand over the varmints who killed the missionaries."

It was an uncomfortable meeting. Gilliam refused to take

part in the customary ceremonial smoke. Joe stumbled through the statement the colonel had prepared until Vision Seeker abruptly interrupted.

"Please read in English. We understand," he ordered. At the end of the reading silence fell over both groups. The Indians stared straight ahead, expressionless. The peace commissioners, Doc Newell and Joel Palmer, were just as cool. Joe sat waiting nervously. Since neither party would speak he had nothing to do but watch. The only greeting he was able to give Stickus was a nod and a smile.

When the Indian delegation turned to leave, Joe hurried after them. "Tell me, please, what has happened to Michael?" he asked Stickus.

The Indian leader's stoic expression did not change. "Your brother well. He make big coups." Stickus abruptly turned away. He did not know what to think of Boston Joe. He sent him off on the trail to Lapwai and here he was back with the Blue Coats, the voice of their chief.

Joe glanced at Vision Seeker. The tall Nez Perce looked through him. He knew nothing of Stickus' thoughts or of Michael's coups. Nevertheless, Joe was delighted. Michael was alive and well. That was one bothersome worry he could discard.

XXIV

*Only his own best deeds, only the worst deeds of the Indians,
has the white man told.*

Yellow Wolf, Nez Perce

The meeting with Stickus and the Indian delegation's quick departure sent rumors buzzing through Fort Waters, the name given to the Blue Coat encampment at Waiilatpu: Gilliam had declared war on both the Cayuse and the Nez Perce and sent their emissaries packing; the peace commissioners and Gilliam had a falling out; hundreds of Nez Perce warriors were on the march to Waiilatpu; the Cayuse had asked Gilliam to surrender; Red Neck Gilliam had told the Indian leaders to go to hell.

"Latrine gossip," a sergeant declared. "These dummies sit on the crapper and think up nonsense. I oughta boot 'em in their rear ends and knock some sense into 'em. That's where they keep what little brains they have."

Shortly after the meeting with the Indian delegation Gilliam issued orders to complete the Waiilatpu fortifications with all possible speed. He sent Jasson galloping off to Fort Walla Walla with a list of needed items. The troops were turned out to scavenge among the mission ruins for additional building blocks. A detachment was sent to recover a cache of boards near the mission's vacated Blue Mountain sawmill.

The renewed building activity initiated another set of rumors: something big was in the wind; the plateau tribes had banded together; the volunteer army was badly outnumbered and in for a siege; Jasson was on his way to the valley for reinforcements. This time the noncoms did not scoff. They, too, reckoned Gilliam was preparing for the worst.

Joe, who had sat in on the meeting with the Indian delegation, was badgered with questions. "What the heck's goin' on?" Pimple Face asked. "Didja talk to the Injuns? What did they say? Are they goin' on the warpath? For God's sake, don't leave us in the dark."

"Actually, there wasn't much said. Gilliam wouldn't talk, demanded the Cayuse turn over the murderers first."

"Then what're yuh lookin' so smug about? Yuh look like the cat that swallowed the canary. Are we goin' ta be attacked or not?"

"Who knows. I can't read tea leaves."

"Blast yuh! A man'd learn more talkin' ta a mule. Should've shot yuh when I had the chance." Pimple Face angrily stomped away.

Macon Laird was also inquisitive. "You seem extraordinarily cheerful after the tête-à-tête with your Indian friends. Was there a breakthrough or did Gilliam send them away with a flea in the ear as usual?"

"I fear it was a flea in the ear, but they brought good news. Michael is alive and well. His uncle, Vision Seeker, was present. We didn't have a chance to visit, but I expect Michael will return with him to Nez Perce country."

"Indeed, those are jolly good tidings." Macon glanced speculatively at Joe as if he wished to say more. Instead, he remained quiet until after a meal of beans, bacon and sour dough biscuits, raw on one side and tough as shoe leather on the other. "I say, a bit of home cooking would brighten one's life."

"Are you complaining about my cooking?" Joe sharply asked.

"Of course not, old man. This simple fare reminds me of the culinary efforts we enjoyed at the start of the trip west. We had so much more to work with then."

"Yeah, Tildy did out do herself." Joe glanced at Macon. What was the smooth talking Britisher leading up to?

"I was just thinking." Macon paused to light his pipe.

He took so long Joe became impatient. "Thinking about what?"

"Well, you see, with Michael safe and you coming and

going as easy as you please, there is no reason why you shouldn't travel to the valley and break the news to Tildy. It is the only kind thing to do."

"Yeah!" Joe said testily. "If anyone goes it should be you."

"Well, we might go together."

"Out of the question!" Joe said sharply. He poked at the campfire, sending sparks flying. He didn't want to return to the valley. It only would bring back the past. Bithiah! Why did the thought of her still torture him? Was it injured pride? No, it was more that. She had captured his heart like no one ever had or would. The image of her living and sleeping with that oaf, Luke Olafson, set his mind on fire. Already a baby had arrived. Perhaps another one was on the way.

Joe gave the campfire another vicious stab. Damn! Why did Demon Jealousy eat at him day and night? He hadn't seen Bithiah in nearly two years. Yet, he remembered their parting like it was yesterday. He got up so abruptly he kicked dirt onto Macon's boots. "I'm going to see to the horses," he said and strode toward the pasture.

Macon stared after his departing companion dumbfounded. What possibly could he have said to cause such aggravation?

##

The Indians who sought peace did not give up. Small and large delegations arrived at Fort Waters seeking audience with Gilliam. Yellow Serpent and a few of his followers again appeared. The Walla Walla leader still harbored hopes of saving his vast herds. Joe, who rode guard on the camp perimeter, met the Walla Walla delegation a half mile from camp.

"We come to see Blue Coat chief," Yellow Serpent tersely announced. "When people visit our homeland it is our custom to greet them. How else can we become friends?"

Joe nodded. He understood. He politely asked the Walla Walla leader to wait while he reported his presence to Gilliam.

Once again the colonel refused to sit in council with Indians.

"You know better than to ask," Gilliam growled. "As I said before, we'll talk peace when these people give up the Whitman Mission murderers, not a day before. Also, they'd better bring back every item they stole. What they didn't destroy they ran away with, the blasted scavengers."

"These people are Walla Walla. They had nothing to do with the massacre and plunder of the mission," Joe protested.

"I don't care if they're the Twelve Apostles. I'm not giving them the time of day. All they're trying to do is whitewash the murderous crimes that were committed here. They can swear on a stack of Bibles and I still wouldn't believe them." Gilliam turned away. Joe glanced at peace commissioners, Doc Newell and Joel Palmer. They shrugged as if to say, "What else can you expect from Gilliam?"

Reluctantly, Joe returned to face Yellow Serpent. "The Blue Coat leader greets you. Perhaps some day soon he will meet with you. At present he is in council." He fibbed, hoping to smooth things over. It didn't work. The Walla Walla leader saw right through him.

Yellow Serpent spurred his mount so near Joe could see the veins in the angry eyes. He aimed his quirt at Joe's chest. "Your tongue is not straight. The Blue Coat leader is not in council. He thinks Indians are dogs, not worth his while. He will pay for these thoughts. Before the Season of Long Grass he will die. When it happens remember I spoke these words."

Yellow Serpent flourished the quirt. The Indian horsemen wheeled their mounts around and galloped away. Joe watched until they were hidden by a bend in the trail. Yellow Serpent's warning hung in the air like an angry cloud. Chagrined, Joe turned back to camp. Yellow Serpent was right. In Gilliam's eyes Indian people were no better than dogs.

The next morning a sentry galloped into Fort Waters. "War party! The enemy is here!" he shouted, pulling his mount to a skidding stop. Troopers grabbed their rifles and ran to drop behind improvised barricades.

"Hey!" the sentry shouted, "they've stopped. Maybeso, they want to palaver."

"Well, if they're actin' so bloomin' peaceful why doesn't someone go palaver," Adams suggested.

"Good idea," Joe agreed. There was no point in angering any more Indians. He quickly saddled up and rode to the edge of camp. A hundred or more dusky-faced riders sat their horses. The leader held his hand up in the traditional greeting of the plains. The troopers who had accompanied Joe, nervously cocked their rifles.

"Take it easy," Joe cautioned. "These people are friendly." Yet, there was something strange about the horsemen. The leader was unlike the others. He was broad and wore a cap pulled down over his ears. He disengaged himself from the others and rode forward, hunched like he had a pain in his backside. When he came near Joe recognized him -- William "Red" Craig, a mountain man who had taken a Nez Perce wife. He had been a friend of Little Ned. On several occasions Joe had stayed in his Lapwai Valley home. What was he doing with a gang of Indian horsemen?

"Hello, Young Joe," Red greeted. "Nice to see you again. These people are Nez Perce from Wallowa country. They came all this way to pay their respects to Colonel Gilliam. Would you kindly ask if he will receive us."

Perhaps Red Craig's polite manner or respect for the mountain man moved Gilliam into granting the requested audience. After a short wait, the Indian vanguard advanced. Tall in stature and colorfully dressed, they made an impressive entrance. Not to be out done, Gilliam had the American flag run up on a newly erected flag pole. A color guard stood at attention. After the ceremonial smoke, Gilliam asked commissioners Newell and Palmer to address the visitors. Palmer spoke first.

"We greet our Nez Perce friends from beautiful Wallowa. We welcome this opportunity to meet with you. We want you to know why we are here. We come to the plateau to make the laws you have accepted work. We come to bring the mission murderers to justice . . . ."

The presentation was precise and impersonal. The traditional gift giving was omitted. The unspoken message was clear. The Blue Coats meant business. No favoritism or compassion could be expected.

Chief Tuekakas, who Missionary Spalding had given the name Joseph, spoke for his people, the Wallowa band of Nez Perce. "Your words are good and understood. Our people stand for justice. We were the first plateau tribe to accept the white man's laws that say if you kill you hang. We know these words and live by them. We do not want our people to hang by the neck until dead. It is not an honorable way to die.

"Our hearts are saddened by the deaths of the Boston missionaries. We had no part in these killings. The Nez Perce were far away when these things happened. We come to you because the Blue Coats treat us strangely. They act like they do not know us or what we believe. They say they will come into our homes, use our pastures, take our horses. Do you tell them to do these things? Is this the way your justice is done?"

The Nez Perce leader fell silent, waiting patiently for the leader of the Blue Coats to speak. Gilliam uttered a disdainful grunt. The commissioners kept their eyes fixed on the ground. Joe felt ashamed. Like Stickus, Tuekakas had nothing to do with the massacre. Both Indian leaders had accepted the Christian faith, Tuekakas was one of the first Indians on the plateau to be baptized. Both men adhered to the teachings of their new religion far more faithfully than did Gilliam who proclaimed himself a Freewill Baptist minister.

Palmer finally broke the uneasy silence. "We must do whatever it takes to capture these murderers. Innocent people may feel threatened. Some may get hurt. You must let these people do what has to be done. Do not resist the Blue Coats or stand in their way. People with bad hearts hide in your home-land. You must tell these murderous men to give themselves up. If they stay among you we will come after them. Then your people will suffer badly."

Commissioner Palmer sat down. Commissioner Doc Newell stood to speak. Although none were present, Newell's words were directed to the Cayuse.

"When the Cayuse did these terrible killings they forfeited their land and forfeited their possessions. No longer do they have a homeland. Soon they will have no herds. The only thing they will have left is their name, a name that will never be forgotten. They will always be remembered as the 'Bloody Cayuse!'"

A murmur of disbelief swept through the Nez Perce con-tingent. This was unheard of punishment. The laws the white man had forced upon them meted out stiff penalties but nothing like this. The listeners glanced at one another, aghast. Were all tribes to be treated in this manner?

Red Craig, who had married into the Nez Perce tribe, was equally disturbed. He had brought his people to meet Gilliam in the hope of lowering tension on the plateau. Instead, their peaceful intentions were scorned -- actually they received a scolding. It was all Craig could do to keep from lashing out at Gilliam. What was the fool trying to do, gain the enmity of every Indian on the plateau?

Instead, Red Craig calmly got to his feet and held up his hand to speak. He addressed his remarks more to Doc Newell, who at one time had been his trapping partner, than to Colonel Gilliam. "I came with these people because their hearts are good. They have told me they want to smoke the pipe of peace. I think you should. What good does it do to treat these people as en-emies when they want to be friends?

"Your actions have all plateau tribes disturbed. They are afraid to leave their camps. They cannot hunt. They cannot fish. They cannot dig for the kouse root or camas bulb. This is not right. If they do not get food they will starve. The blame will be on this army that is seeking half a dozen criminals. Is this the way we render justice? Should everyone on the plateau suffer because of a handful of wrongdoers?"

Red Craig stopped to glance around the audience. His gaze paused on Colonel Gilliam and the two peace commissioners who sat stone still and silent. Red Craig sadly shook his head and sat down. Talking to these people was like lobbing a rubber ball against a wall. Everything one said bounced away without sinking in.

The council abruptly ended. What was left to say? What could the peaceful Nez Perce delegation do? They had ridden all the way to Waiilatpu to seek justice for their people but no one listened. The Indian council members silently pulled their robes around them, strode out, mounted up and rode away.

Macon Laird, who sat in on the proceedings, shook his head. "That was bloody awful," he said to Joe as they left the council grounds. "I don't understand what Gilliam and the peace commissioners are trying to do. They treat these Indians as if they had no rights at all. Someday you Americans will rue the way you have dealt with these people. After all, they occupied this land long before you arrived."

XXV

*When we see the soldiers moving away and the forts
abandoned, then I will come down and talk.*

Red Cloud, Oglala Sioux

Tuekakas of the Wallowa Nez Perce was not the only Indian leader disturbed by the reception received at the Blue Coat
camp. Stickus, of the upper Umatilla band of Cayuse, returned
from his fruitless meeting with Gilliam bewildered and tormented.
The Blue Coat leader and peace commissioners had treated him
and his party in the same manner they would deal with vermin.
Even the worst of enemies smoked the pipe before making council, but not the leader of the Blue Coats -- it was his way or no
way at all.

Stickus uttered a painful sigh. Peace on the plateau was
as elusive as a Ruffed Grouse, the bird that, to evade pursuers,
buried itself in frigid banks of winter snow. The future looked so
bleak Stickus decided to put more distance between his band of
Cayuse and the Blue Coat forces. This time he led his people
into the hill country. Traveling was torturous. They left the main
trails to force a new path through brush and over rocky ravines.
It was after dark when Stickus finally called a halt.

It was not a suitable place to make camp, but everyone,
including the horses, was ready to drop. Barren of vegetation
and filled with rocky outcroppings, the camp site was bleak and
inhospitable, not a pleasant place for either man or beast. Horses,
already gaunt, nibbled at tufts of dry cheat grass and licked at the
salt corroded ground. These efforts did little to provide suste-
nance or decrease hunger. Humans also suffered. Food was in
short supply. Constant moving had them bone weary. Fear
haunted their every waking hour.

As usual, Michael spread out his blanket away from the
rest. After tending to Magpie, he chewed on a piece of dried

venison and laid down to rest. He thought of Little Fox. Hoping her family would set camp near him again, he watched for the beaver head that Little Fox's father, Beaver Tooth, had painted over the entrance to his tipi lodge. But the nightly coyote chorus lulled him into a doze, then a deep sleep.

Toward morning Michael awakened feeling something terrible was in the offing. He itched all over. His clothes felt uncomfortable, as though he was lying in a bed of nettles. Out of the dawn came ominous rustling sounds, like someone creeping through the grass. Tamsucky!

He sat up straight and reached for his rifle. The rustling stopped but the nettle-like stings did not and his blanket seemed to come alive. He leapt to his feet and pulled it to one side. Out darted a furry object and then another. Michael grunted in disgust. Unable to see in the dark, he had made his bed over the home of a family of ground squirrels. The rodents' fleas were eating him alive.

He shook out the blankets and placed them a good distance away but the stingy itching remained. He took off his shirt and started the fruitless search for fleas. Father Sun rose above the eastern horizon. He stood to say the morning prayer, thanking Father Sun for the new day and went back to his flea hunt until Willakin, the sentry, rode up.

"Stickus holds council. He wishes your presence," Willakin announced.

Long before he arrived at the lodge of Stickus, Michael heard the indignant voices of council members. The angry tone was so unusual Michael picked up his pace. What possibly could be taking place? Standing before the council members was Man of Many Words, the village crier. He was reporting on the abusive words spoken by Doc Newell at the meeting between the Blue Coats and the Nez Perce peace delegation. A Cayuse hunting party had met the returning Nez Perce. The disheartened peace delegation related in detail what had occurred.

The news made taciturn council members livid. When

their peaceful Nez Perce friends were ill-treated by the Blue Coats, what would happen to them -- the Blue Coats' enemy? Arguments sprang up on every side. So vociferous were council members, the normal respect afforded each other was forgotten. The situation they faced was as life-threatening as the measles epidemic that decimated their villages. This time they were in danger of losing their precious herds and homeland.

The only way to deal with these Blue Coats is all out war, the warlike insisted; others suggested they take their herds and families to hideouts deep in the Blue Mountains. A third group wanted to wait before taking action. It was not good to make hasty decisions. "Before we run or fight is it not wise to wait and see what the Blue Coats do?" a gray-headed elder asked.

During the council meeting, Stickus said little, but afterward, in the privacy of his tipi lodge, he was unable to disguise his feelings.

"Bloody Cayuse! So that is what the Blue Coats call us. If we were not peace loving Christian people we would show the Blue Coats how bloody we can get," he stormed.

Kio-noo did not like to see her mate in such anger. "It is not good to say such things. You are a good man. Missionary Whitman was your good friend. You did what you could to save his life. Do not blame yourself that he would not heed your warnings. We must show the Blue Coats we are honorable people by doing honorable things."

Stickus gave Kio-noo a scornful glance. "I tried to tell them. They did not listen." But he knew Kio-noo was right. He could not give up. His people depended on him. Somehow he had to make peace with the Blue Coats.

Late into the night Stickus sat beside the low campfire, searching his mind for ways to keep his people free from the clutches of the Blue Coats. One of Gilliam's demands was the return of the livestock and other items taken from the mission. That was one thing he could manage. He would ask his people to collect these things and hand them over to the Blue Coats.

The following day another council meeting was held. The gathering took place in front of Stickus' lodge. Sitting on mats laid down by the women, the council members formed two circles. Michael sat in the second circle with other youths. After the customary smoke, Stickus spoke.

"The Blue Coats demand everything taken at the mission be returned. I have thought much about this. The people who stole from the mission are frightened. They do not want the Blue Coats to know they did these things. We must help them. We know where many of these stolen things are hidden. Mission sheep and cattle are pastured on the Tucannon. Some horses are at the Red Wolf camp. We will go to these places, get these stolen things. When we have them together we will take them to the Blue Coats. We will show these people who make war on us our hearts are good. Perhaps they will let us return to our homeland on the Umatilla. If not, we then decide what to do -- go to war or find a hideout in the Blue Mountains."

Many elders did not agree. Why should they, the Umatilla Cayuse who had no hand in the mission massacre, go in search of these missionary things? It was ridiculous. Where were these murderers? They were to blame. If they gave themselves up all the troubles would be over. They were the ones who had the Blue Coats so hopping mad. Yet, in the end the council accepted the plan. Few wanted to go to war and many others were too tired of running to make the hard journey into the Blue Mountains. All they wanted was to be allowed to return to their home on the upper Umatilla. It would do no harm to make one more attempt to bring peace to the plateau.

After the meeting broke up Stickus motioned for Michael to remain. "It is important we make a record of these things we give the Blue Coats. You understand the mysteries of talking paper. I want you to make a mark for everything we bring them."

Stickus paused and ran a hand over his face and through his graying hair. "We ask the Blue Coat leader to make his mark on this list. It will show we give these things back. We keep that paper to let people know we are not murderers. We are honest people. We are not 'bloody Cayuse.'"

Michael did not believe returning the stolen possessions would soften Gilliam, and the Blue Coat leader certainly would not put his name to anything that was Cayuse. The Indian fighter was a taker, not a giver. Michael kept the thoughts to himself. He would do as Stickus asked. The task assigned him was easier said than done. Where was he to get paper, pen and ink? Even in the camp of the Blue Coats these things were scarce. The challenge he faced and the itching flea bites nearly drove him crazy.

Michael walked back to his campsite pondering the problem. He hadn't written a word in months. Did he still know how to form letters? Did he still know how to spell? The list had to be done right or Gilliam would laugh in their faces and say they were nothing but ignorant savages.

Michael led Magpie to the nearly dry stream that supplied camp water. On the way he saw the lodge with the beaver head painted over the entrance. He looked for Little Fox but she was not to be seen. Two boys played outside, Little Fox's brothers. What were their names? He tried hard to remember. It didn't matter. He would ask about Little Fox anyway.

Before Michael could open his mouth, the rumble of hooves and a distant cloud of dust sent the campers into a panic. "Blue Coats!" Little Fox's brothers shouted and scampered away to hide. Michael, ignoring his flea bites, jumped on Magpie and galloped toward the approaching sounds of hoofbeats. For a moment it did appear Gilliam's troops were racing pell-mell straight toward the encampment. As the hoofbeats became louder and bobbing heads came nearer it was obvious the animals had no riders. It was a herd of horses, hundreds of horses. The lead drove, with stallions in front, swept across the rocky, rolling plain.

"What fools are driving them?" an outraged voice demanded. Michael was shocked to see Stickus. It was so unlike the usually placid man to raise his voice about anyone or anything, but there was good reason to question these crazy herders.

The lead drove thundered ahead. The space between the village and the lead stallions had dangerously narrowed. The vast herd was obviously running wild. Michael urged Magpie forward, making a beeline for the leading drove. He swung alongside the galloping animals, shouting and waving his arms. The lead stallions only stretched out their necks and ran faster. The herd that followed engulfed Michael and his black and white pony in their midst. At the last moment the stallions veered away from the encampment, slowing down as they approached the hilly ground filled with rocks and brush.

Out of the dust and hail of flying clods emerged three herders looking as wild as the horses they drove. They pulled to a stop and mopped their brows. Stickus walked out to meet them. Michael, who had ridden back, could tell by his quick steps Stickus was furious, and not just because of the near destruction of his camp. When he came near he instantly knew why. The riders were three of the Whitman massacre murderers: Tiloukaikt's two sons who had been given the English names, Edward and Clark, and their friend, Tomahas.

"Ah-ho!" Tomahas exclaimed, catching sight of Michael. The murderer's dark eyes roamed over horse and rider. Goose bumps rose up on Michael's flea-bitten skin. Evil was in this man's blood. He took delight in performing evil deeds.

Stickus strode up. "Why is it you ride in here like crazy people?" he demanded. "Where are you going, and why are you here? The Blue Coats seek you. There is no place here for you to hide."

Tomahas gave Stickus a look of disdain. "If it is peace you want, you won't have it as long as the Waiilatpu band is near. Our people are warriors. We seek battlefield coups."

Michael's muscles grew tense. Stickus should be careful. Tomahas was not one to cross. Once, while Michael tended the mission gristmill, Tomahas refused to wait his turn. In a fit of rage he threw sticks in the gristmill hopper. The resulting clatter brought Marcus Whitman running from the mission house.

The appearance of the missionary had increased Tomahas' rage. He knocked Whitman down and started to pummel him. Even after friendly hands pulled him away, Tomahas acted like a mad man. He cursed the missionary, dancing back and forth, foaming at the mouth like a rabid dog.

"We do not plan to stay. We take our horses to the mountains," Tiloukaikt's son, Edward, who had attended mission school and was more mannerly than his rough companion, Tomahas, attempted to soothe Stickus. "We save them."

"Your father, where is he?" Stickus curtly asked. He distrusted these Waiilatpu people. They had caused all the trouble. It was said Tiloukaikt, the leader, had been the one who started the killing by driving a hand ax in the head of Missionary Whitman.

"He brings another herd. We have plenty-plenty horses," Edward said proudly.

The horsemen wheeled about and galloped away. Stickus glanced at Michael, his face set in a scowl. "There are days when darkness hides the brightness of the sun. Perhaps this is one of those times. We try to make peace and these murderers move in."

Michael did not like the situation at all. These three men were killers, in the same class as Hard Eyes Tamsucky and Joe Lewis. Then there was Tiloukaikt who would certainly follow his two sons. If these six killers joined forces -- the thought sent cold shivers racing up Michael's spine.

All afternoon Michael covertly kept watch on Tiloukaikt's great herd. More herders appeared to round up the scattered horses. They turned the herd to the east where the animals bunched together to graze. Soon pack horses led by women arrived, dragging lodge pole travois on which were piled tipi coverings and packs of belongings.

Tomahas and the Tiloukaikt brothers, who appeared to be in charge, walked around, finally stopping in a flat area and motioning for the women to set up lodges. The triangles of poles for three tipi lodges began to take shape. After coverings were draped over the lodge poles and staked firmly to the ground, the women began to unpack. Out of packs and bundles came robes, food and cooking utensils, everything needed to set up house-keeping.

Stickus, who also watched, made a gesture of helpless-ness. "It is as I feared. They plan to stay a good long while."

Michael remained silent, but knew how Stickus must feel. With the Tiloukaikt brothers and Tomahas camped nearby, any-thing could happen. They endangered the entire camp. Michael led Magpie away. He made camp where he had a view of all three Waiilatpu lodges. That evening he kept vigilant watch, noting who came and went. Toward dusk a figure emerged from the third tipi -- a Tiloukaikt brother. Michael could not tell which one. He wore a white deerskin shirt and leggings. As he ap-proached, the porcupine needle decorations that fringed the gar-ment sent points of light dancing. It was dress only worn for special occasions.

"Where was he going that was so important?" Michael asked himself. From the uncertain way he strolled along it was apparent the Tiloukaikt brother did not know himself. Suddenly, the step of the white clad figure quickened. He made for the tipi with the beaver's head painted over the entrance, Beaver Tooth's lodge.

Michael could not stifle a moan. He took a second look to make certain. Yes, Edward Tiloukaikt stopped at the lodge entrance. He had come courting. Little Fox, the maiden with the impish grin and dancing eyes, was the one he sought!

XXVI

I seek no war with anyone. An old man,
my fighting days are done.

Dull Knife, Cheyenne

Similar to their Nez Perce neighbors, the Cayuse tribe (in the native tongue Cayuse means Superior People) was a unification of bands. A band could be one large village or a cluster of villages in the same general area. The primary social and economic core of a village was the family. As offspring married and formed their own families new villages sprang up. To maintain order councils emerged. The council authority brought the clusters of villages into the composite entity called a band. Bands had the freedom to roam throughout tribal grounds but at the same time kept a home base. During the early missionary years the Cayuse tribe consisted of four such bands.

The middle Umatilla and its tributary, Butter Creek, were the homelands of Young Chief and Five Crows; the upper Umatilla, including the foothills of the Blue Mountains, was where band leader Stickus ruled. The band led by Tiloukaikt lived in the Walla Walla Valley centered at Waiilatpu (Wy-ee'-lat-poo) which in Cayuse means "the place of rye grass." Grasslands along the lower Umatilla was the territory of the legendary and powerful horseman, Buffalo Horn.

Marcus Whitman chose to build his mission at the site of Waiilatpu, "the place of rye grass." Whitman's Nez Perce guide, Tackensuatis, often called Rotten Belly because of an odoriferous unhealed wound he received fighting the Gros Ventre at the Battle of Pierre's Hole, warned the missionary against establishing a mission here or anywhere among the Cayuse. "The Nimapu, (native name for the Nez Perce, meaning Real People) do not have difficulties with the white man as Cayuses do, and you will find it so," Rotten Belly is reported to have said. But Marcus

Whitman had come to minister to the Cayuse and would not be swayed.

Unfortunately, Rotten Belly knew of what he said. From the beginning the Waiilatpu band of Cayuse resented the manner in which the missionaries and their outside friends summarily moved in. The missionary group selected a flat area of fertile land near the Waiilatpu village. Without regard for the needs and custom of the natives, they arrogantly announced through interpreters, here was where they would erect their adobe and wooden buildings that would become the base for spreading the gospels of the white man's god throughout Cayuse country.

Over the years the missionaries were grudgingly accepted, but the fact these white people had thrust themselves into their midst, unwanted and uninvited, was ever present in the minds of Waiilatpu villagers.

On the upper Umatilla, Stickus and his band had not been affected particularly by the presence of the missionaries. Stickus saw them as benefactors. Soon after Marcus Whitman established the mission at Waiilatpu, the Cayuse leader had fallen seriously ill. The ministrations of village medicine men were ineffective so Stickus journeyed to the Waiilatpu mission and placed himself under Medicine Man Whitman's care.

As good Christians, Marcus and Narcissa Whitman took Stickus in and nursed him back to health. Stickus never forgot this. He took up the white man's religion and followed the teachings of the god, Jesus, as nearly as he could. No one on the plateau was more disturbed by the Whitman Mission massacre than the leader of the upper Umatilla band of Cayuse.

Even though he had done his best to save Marcus Whitman from the deadly disaster that was about to befall him and his mission family, Stickus still felt beholden to this good man of God. He had a debt to repay, and he was going to do everything possible to satisfy it, an underlying reason for taking on the task of retrieving the mission's stolen possessions. In addition, he also saw this as a way to force Colonel Cornelius Gilliam to sit down and talk peace with the Cayuse.

At first the searchers who went to collect stolen mission belongings returned empty-handed, but as word got around of the drive's peaceful intent, a variety of mission items emerged. People who possessed the tainted property were happy to get it off their hands. Travois arrived loaded with boxes and barrels of a variety of articles: cooking utensils, bedding, clothing, furniture, tools, even a baby's crib. A scattering of cattle and horses were collected and held in a corral.

A small flock of sheep caused the first major difficulty. They bounced into camp taking everyone by surprise. Bewildered dogs raced out to bark, nipping and snapping at the heels and ears of these strange woolly creatures. Frightened by the ferocity of the attack, the sheep ran helter-skelter among the lodges, bleating and butting, knocking aside anything in the way.

Shelters collapsed. Sleeping robes and clothes became entangled in sharp hooves and were dragged down dusty paths. Pots and food baskets bounced in the air and spilled their contents. A covey of gleeful youngsters ran after the woollies, shouting and throwing rocks. The dogs barked louder. The entire camp turned out to stop the turmoil. Order was finally restored. The youngsters were ordered into the hills. The dogs were tied up. The exhausted sheep followed the bell sheep into a makeshift corral.

Just as calm descended, a batch of pigs came grunting into camp. Their captors, dodging back and forth, were at their wits' ends, attempting to keep them from straying. They tried to herd the squat animals by horse. It didn't work. The porkers went straight for a while, then abruptly turned to dash between the horses' legs. The irate herdsmen dismounted. With locust sticks and sagebrush branches, they goaded the pigs forward. Just as the last pig entered the holding pen a big sow rooted through the pen's flimsy side. She ran grunting among the ramshackle temporary shelters, spreading chaos in her wake.

Soon the entire batch of pigs broke out to run squealing

after the sow.   The dogs had been released just in time to begin another frenzy of barking and nipping.   The pigs were not intimidated.   They rushed the attackers, butting them with their snouts, tossing them into the air.   Howling and barking, the dogs fled, leaving the field to the hogs.

It was meal time.   The pigs were hungry.   They nosed cooking pots over, gobbling down the contents.   They charged into shelters, sniffing and rooting into sparse bags of foodstuffs. Children, who had returned from their banishment in the hills, squealed and shouted.   The pig drovers, angry and weary, began to beat on the animals with any weapon at hand.   Those who could find them, armed themselves with war clubs.   Stickus, who foresaw impending disaster, ran through camp shouting.

"Stop!   Stop!   These creatures called pigs are different from horses and cattle.   They dig in the dirt like badgers.   They need a special corral."

Women and children were instructed to pound a circle of closely spaced stakes into the ground.   After much running around and waving of arms, two men got a rope around the sow's leg and pulled her, snorting and squealing into the pen.   Soon the other pigs followed.

Each arrival of stolen goods brought Michael out to count and record the numbers.   In place of ink he used a pot of chokeberry root dye borrowed from Kio-noo.   It was purplish-brown in color but made reasonably good marks.   His writing instrument was the end of a bulrush stalk.   Laboriously, he printed the inventory on a scroll of whitened buckskin.   When the last entry was made, Michael presented the list to Stickus.   Although the Cayuse leader could not read, he critically examined the list.

"It is good," he grunted thoughtfully.   "Blue Coat Chief Gilliam will be much surprised.   He make his mark here."   Stickus put a finger on the bottom of the scroll.

"We show Blue Coats we are not ignorant savages.   We go to school.   We learn white man's language and ways.   Why do they not learn ours?   Is it because our homes are not made of sticks and stones? Is it because we are do not plow and plant but are happy to take what Mother Earth gives us as it is?"

On another piece of whitened buckskin Stickus had Michael write a message to Gilliam telling of the spoils his band had collected. "Tell Blue Coat leader on third sunrise we bring many stolen things to Touchet Crossing," Stickus instructed. When the message was completed to his satisfaction, Stickus sent Willakin galloping away to deliver it to the Blue Coat camp.

Over the next few days everything collected was taken to Touchet Crossing. Michael was amazed at Stickus' firm belief Gilliam would appear. Michael attempted to explain Gilliam's irascible nature. He would no more respond to a message from the hated Cayuse than he would fly.

To Michael's astonishment on the third day Gilliam and a detachment of volunteers rode up to stop on the far river bank. Waving a white flag, Stickus and Willakin forded the shallow stream. Gilliam's orderly, Jasson, heavily armed, met them at the edge of the water. Stickus held out the inventory list. In sign language he explained what it was and what it said. Neither Jasson nor Gilliam understood.

"Jennings, front and center," Gilliam ordered. "What's this man up to? He sends a message he holds many items stolen from the mission. Now he comes and presents this rag of buckskin. You speak the language. Ask him what the devil is going on."

Joe gave Stickus a friendly nod. He glanced around for Michael. He was not in sight. "Colonel Gilliam greets you and asks what you desire?"

Stickus returned Boston Joe's nod with a curt nod of his own. He still did not know what to make of this young man. He must have a powerful medicine of some kind. He should have been shot as a deserter, yet the Blue Coat chief kept him by his side. Stickus put away thoughts of Boston Joe and explained the need for Colonel Gilliam to make his mark on the buckskin.

"Stickus greets the Blue Coat leader and wishes him long

life," Joe interpreted. "He wants the Blue Coat chief to sign for the things he brings."

Gilliam stared across the open space. "Who the hell does this man think he is, Napoleon Bonaparte? Like all the others, he and his people are little better than common savages. Put my signature on a piece of buckskin? I should say not. What does he think this is, a peace treaty pact? This meeting is for the purpose of returning stolen mission property, not writing up a Cayuse Bill of Rights."

Stickus did not understand but knew the Blue Coat leader was angry. The opportunity to prove his people were honorable was slipping away. He raised his hand and spoke again.

"Stickus says you may leave your command to someone else. If he has no record the next Blue Coat chief may not believe he returned these things."

Gilliam uttered an obscenity. "Where did he get the idea I'm leaving? I have half a notion to take him prisoner and give him the bull whip. Maybe then he'll turn over the murderers he's hiding."

Joe shifted uneasily in the saddle. The warning Yellow Serpent uttered crossed his mind. Did Stickus also believe Gilliam would soon die? He had anticipated Marcus Whitman's death. Did he know of a conspiracy to murder Gilliam? The thought sent a chill running up Joe's spine.

"It won't do any harm to sign a receipt for the goods," Joe said hurriedly. He wanted to bring the meeting to an end. He did not like the setting or the proceedings. Not all of Stickus' people were peace loving. The place had the smell of ambush. Beyond the fringe of hills warriors could be waiting. Gilliam's men already were outnumbered.

"I don't know why a written record is needed," Gilliam protested. "Hardly one of them can read or write."

"Not many," Joe agreed. "It won't hurt to look at what they have written."

"All right! All right! Give me the list."

Gilliam unrolled the whitened buckskin scroll. "Would you look at that! Whoever made this has artistic talent."

"Michael Two Feathers probably did it," Joe said.

"You mean that renegade deserter? Is he present? Before I sign I want to see the man who wrote this."

Michael, half hidden by a patch of brush, watched from the far bank. When Stickus signaled, he forded the river and rode up on Magpie. He avoided looking at Joe. When Gilliam was in this kind of mood no one could predict how he would react. He saluted the colonel.

"Michael Two Feathers at your service," he said in perfect English. "Do you find fault with the inventory?"

"Hmm! Respectful cuss, aren't you?" Gilliam growled, his neck beginning to bulge and take on the all too familiar reddish glow. "Well, don't think I'm taken in. You're the young whippersnapper who brought the message a thousand warriors waited up river to wipe out my troops. Well, your little ruse did not work. I should have had you shot as a traitor because that is exactly what you are. Shame on you. You turn your mission school education against those who gave it to you. I'll sign your bloody inventory but mind you, the next time our paths cross it will be for the last time."

"Yes, sir," Michael said. Surprisingly, from somewhere, Jasson produced a quill and ink. After Gilliam signed the scroll he handed it to Jasson. With a scornful smirk, Jasson handed it on to Michael. Michael saluted the colonel and reined Magpie away. Out of the corner of his eye he glanced at Joe. Joe shook his head in disbelief. His young brother entered the lion's den and walked away unscathed.

The Cayuse band rode from Touchet Crossing in a pleasant mood. The expression on the face of Stickus was one of content. He had returned the stolen property with dignity. His people could hold up their heads. They had proved to the Blue Coats the Umatilla Cayuse were trying to do right. They were not bloody killers. They were honorable people.

The feeling of a job well done was contagious. The men joked and laughed. They were happy to be free of the pigs and sheep. It delighted them to see these short legged creatures give the Blue Coats trouble, too. At first the pigs refused to cross the river. Blue Coat horsemen were forced to rope them and pull the stubborn beasts through the water. When released, the pigs charged through the Blue Coat ranks like demons were on their tails. Riders chased after them hollering, "Sooee! Sooee! Pig-pig-pig -- sooee!"

The pig call delighted the Cayuse youth. For miles they rode along shouting, "Sooee! Pig-pig-pig -- sooee!"

When the column neared the hill country camp, Stickus held up his hand. The horsemen stopped. To the south and east of the rocky ridge of hills where Stickus' band was camped hundreds of horses milled about. Thousands of hooves churned a cloud of dust that spiraled up like prairie fire smoke.

"Tiloukaikt's main herd!" The words passed from one horseman to the next. Mutters of anger rippled through the column of riders.

"Let us have patience," Stickus cautioned. "Tiloukaikt's sons say they will move on to the mountains. Perhaps tomorrow they will be gone."

Stickus and his men continued forward. The camp, nestled in the hills, came into sight. New tipi lodges had been erected. Several horses waited beside them. Men mounted the horses and rode toward the column. Tiloukaikt's two sons and Tomahas led the way. The other two men looked familiar. They turned to face the sun. Michael sucked in his breath.

"Oh, no!" he muttered. Tamsucky! Joe Lewis! These two murderers and deadly enemies had returned. For certain they would seek revenge.

DEATH ON THE UMATILLA

XXVII

The shrill war whoop was changed to the melancholy death
song . . .while a number of their lifeless brothers who
lay on the field, heard not their mournful elegy.

Captain Maxon describing last hours of the Battle of Touchet Crossing as reported

in OREGON SPECTATOR, 1848

Stickus and his horsemen were not the only ones startled by Tiloukaikt's great herd and the presence of Tamuscky and Joe Lewis. A Hudson's Bay man on the way from Fort Colville to Fort Walla Walla, attracted by the great pyramid of dust, was astonished to see the immense number of horses spread across the rocky, rolling plain, by far the largest collection of equine he ever had seen. He took out a spyglass and scanned the vast herd.

"Jeez!" he muttered to himself. "Every Indian nag in the Northwest must be here." He turned the spyglass on the horsemen. He recognized Stickus. The Cayuse on the upper Umatilla never had this number of horses. Then, afraid he would be discovered, he tethered his mount out of sight in a draw and crawled up to the high ground to scrutinize more closely the gathering of horses and Indians. He had helped rescue survivors of the Whitman Mission massacre. The gruesome tales they told were imprinted on his mind. This gathering looked suspiciously like people on the run. If they were the criminals he wanted to know.

"Oh-oh," he said to himself as the scene came into focus. "I'm right." Many of the horses were from the herds of the Waiilatpu band of Cayuse, and most of them Tiloukaikt's animals. This was not their destination. The pasture was not good. They were off to the Blue Mountains. Yep, Tiloukaikt's two sons were present. By jove -- so were Tomahas, Tamsucky and Joe Lewis! Old man Tiloukaikt also probably was around. Keerist! Six murderers in one spot. If Gilliam's army was alerted he could bag the whole kit and caboodle in one fell swoop.

Hezekiah Brown was the man's name. He knew the importance of what he had seen. Hurriedly he mounted and urged his horse into a gallop for Fort Walla Walla. He reported the discovery to Factor McBean, who immediately sent a rider to the volunteers' camp at Fort Waters. Gilliam had retired for the night. Major Lee took the report. Reluctant to awaken Gilliam, he waited until morning to relay the news. Gilliam received the delayed report with the temper of a disturbed wasp.

"I told you and I told you those Bloody Cayuse are no good," Gilliam ranted to anyone within earshot, his red neck nearly bursting his tight-fitting collar. "There they were acting so pious, peaceful and innocent. All the time they were hiding the murderers -- si-six of them," he spluttered.

"Sure, they returned stolen mission property but it was a ruse. I keep thinking of that smooth talking half-breed, Two Feathers. Damn him! I'll bet it was his idea. Roust the men out. Get them ready to march. Before sundown I want those murderers, Stickus and that damned Two Feathers, bound for the hangman. We'll execute them right here on the mission grounds where the bloody cutthroats carried out their evil deeds."

Gilliam's orders did not set well with the volunteers. The men were exhausted from dealing with the unruly pigs and sheep. Since the legislature saw the campaign as a short police action, many only had signed up for three months. Already their enlistments had run out. Everyone in camp was owed back pay. Spring was just around the corner. The farm folk were anxious to return home and start plowing and planting. Others were downright disgusted and homesick.

"Blast it all! I'm too long in the tooth to run back and forth like a scalded cat," Adams complained. "I signed up to go solderin', not playin' nursemaid to pigs and sheep. What's ol' Gilliam after now, tryin' for a flock of chickens? Wants to ketch them whilst still on the roost, is that it? Damn me! Why cain't he run a proper war."

"Quit growling, old timer," Jasson scolded. The hairy

knob in his pelican neck did its usual dance, the two long hairs springing out of it fluttering like signal flags. "This time the boss means business. All the murderers are together in the camp of Stickus. The colonel's goin' to round them up once and for all. Think of it! We can go home. You'll be able to plow your fields and spend as much time as you want with your old woman and kids."

As soon as the troops were fed, allocated ammunition and mounted, Gilliam led them out of camp. The reported location of the Indian camp was hazy but Gilliam insisted it had to be north across the Tucannon River, most likely at the confluence with the Snake.

Near midday the volunteers came to a bluff. At the base lay an Indian village. Gilliam called a halt. For a moment he studied the encampment. No one sounded an alarm; no sentries stood guard. Kids played along the stream bank. A few horses in a makeshift corral lazily switched flies. The usual camp dogs did not come out to bark.

Joe, who rode in front with the scouts, gave the village a quick inspection. This was not a Cayuse camp. "Palouse," he said, breathing a sigh of relief. "These people are peaceful."

Gilliam put a spyglass to his eye. "Don't be so sure. We took them by surprise. They look like folks on the run to me."

"A temporary camp," Joe explained. "Probably a band here for a bit of fishing. After winter months that they call 'The Cold Time,' these people store their winter mat lodges and drift from place to place. Sometimes they travel as far as Blackfeet territory east of the Rockies. They like to hunt buffalo with the Nez Perce."

For a moment officers and scouts surveyed the terrain. Along the edge of the river were large freshly dug holes. Joe identified them as storage places for surplus fish. Above the river lay fish nets, spears and dipping seines.

"I don't give a hoot what label you give these people. They're still redskins," Gilliam finally declared. "It's our business to sort them out. Let's get cracking."

The officers gave the command to move forward. Insolently, Gilliam led the troops into the Indian camp. He pulled up and demanded to see the chief. When the Palouse leader appeared Gilliam called on Joe to interpret.

"Tell this man we know six or more men involved in the Whitman Mission massacre are in this camp. Don't take any 'we are innocent' guff. Tell him we want the murderers turned over nice and peaceful like. If he does we'll leave and do his people no harm. If he doesn't . . . ." The threat was left hanging in mid-sentence.

After passing on the gist of Gilliam's message, Joe translated the reply. "The chief knows nothing of murderers or the business at Whitman's mission. He says they are peaceful people. They camped here to fish and hunt."

"Humph!" Gilliam grunted in disgust. "These bloody plateau Indians are all alike. Not a one of them had anything to do with the massacre. Well, I'm not buying it. You tell him he speaks with a forked tongue. If he knows what's good for him he'll turn over these killers or tell us where they're hiding out. There'll be no peace in these parts until we have them in hand."

Joe again spoke to the Palouse leader. In the background a group of young men stared boldly at the troopers and fingered their weapons. A chill raced up Joe's spine. These young bucks were anxious to count coups. The slightest misstep could set them off like a pack of hungry wolves. Why did Gilliam place his men in these stupid predicaments? The old Palouse leader drew his blanket around his shoulders and repeated they had nothing to do with murderers. They were peaceful people. They did not want trouble with the Blue Coats.

"Balderdash!" Gilliam exclaimed when Joe translated. "I don't believe a word the old man says." He abruptly reined his horse farther into the Palouse camp. "We're not leaving until we take a look around."

Joe could feel the hair on the back of his neck bristle.

The Palouse people were highly independent. An unwelcome intrusion was an affront. Besides, Gilliam's force was outnumbered. If they wished, the youthful warriors could cut them down to the last man.

At the edge of the Indian camp Gilliam came to a pasture where a sizable herd of horses grazed. He pointed to the animals with his riding crop. "Round them up," he ordered. "If these redskins won't cooperate we'll give them a damned good reason to do so."

Joe's heart sank. No tribe on the plateau took more pride in their horses or guarded them with more diligence than the Palouse. Before the day was out they would be after their herd with a vengeance.

Joe was right. Hardly did the volunteers drive the Palouse herd beyond the first ridge when a party of hooting warriors descended on the column. The attackers discharged their guns and disappeared into the hills. Just as the troopers breathed sighs of relief, the attackers were back again. This time they rode nearer. Rifle fire was accompanied by showers of arrows.

"I'm hit!" a volunteer rifleman cried out and fell from his horse.

Throughout the day the harassment continued. That evening Gilliam called a halt in a meadow filled with clumps of willows. All day it had rained. Every twig and branch was soaked. The exhausted, miserable, shivering soldiers who attempted to take shelter under the willows wished they had remained in open country. The wintering, leafless trees not only allowed the rain to pelt the troopers but also funneled water down the branches and trunks and onto their heads. They were unable to light fires. One trooper did and paid for it. A Palouse marksman put a bullet through his hand.

The attackers circled the meadow. The slightest movement brought dozens of arrows and a hail of bullets. Hunkered behind a tree trunk, Joe tested the Palouse shooting skills by exposing his hat, thrusting it out from behind a tree trunk on the muzzle of his long barreled rifle. A bullet made the hat jump. The man behind him uttered a painful yell.

"Dammit, Jennings, quit playin' around. Yuh're drawin' fire," Adams complained.

When they weren't shooting, the Indian warriors shouted taunts and uttered bloodcurdling war cries. "What are they saying?" Macon Laird asked Joe during a moment of quiet.

"They call us cowards. We have dogs for mothers and skunks for fathers. We come into their peaceful camp and steal their horses. We are not warriors but blue jays who talk nonsense and eat offal. Tomorrow they will lay us out. Bugs and ants will feed on our insides. Crows and buzzards will pick out our eyes. They say other nice things, but that's an example."

"What extraordinary imaginations. Cannot say I blame them for giving us a roasting. Gilliam jolly well bought a peck of trouble. The way things are going I am thinking we will be lucky to get back to Fort Waters."

"Yeah!" Joe agreed. "The situation is worse than most of these people realize. The Palouse are first class warriors. They'll stay on top of us until they get tired and then will be back for more. Many blunders like this and we'll have a real war on our hands. All the tribes on the plateau will band together. If that happens Colonel Gilliam will wish he was back in Florida fighting the Seminoles."

By morning Gilliam admitted his mistake. He ordered the livestock the troops had taken to be released. He expected the attackers to take the animals and leave. Instead, they redoubled their attacks. From time to time Palouse warriors veered so near troopers could see the whites of their eyes. One volunteer after another was hit. Miraculously, none was killed.

The attackers did not go unscathed. Amidst war cries came the mournful chant of death. At Touchet Crossing the Palouse assaults became more intense. Realizing the Blue Coats were about to escape, the warriors rode wildly into their midst, firing point blank. Gilliam ordered the volunteers to dismount and take cover. For more than an hour the men groveled in the sand unable to move. Macon Laird's hat sailed away, an arrow pinning it to a bush. "I say, old boy, this is a bit dicey," the Britisher dryly observed. "It appears we are up against a pretty sticky wicket."

"It's pure hell, yuh mean," Adams said. His yellow beard had turned a muddy brown. "Believe me, this's me last battle. If I get out of this alive I'm leavin' fer good. Ol' Gilliam can carry on this silly war by hisself."

Either too weary to continue or out of ammunition, the attackers withdrew. "Now's our chance, men," Gilliam shouted. "Make haste. Get across the river while you can."

Even without the enemy shooting into their midst, the crossing was not easy. The recent rain had swollen the river. At the water's edge the horses pawed and snorted. When riders forced their mounts into the stream, the current snatched them up. Eyes wide with terror, downstream the animals were swept, finally able to struggle ashore on the far bank. Getting the wounded across was especially difficult. Horses carried two riders, one rider holding a wounded comrade in the saddle.

"Help! Throw a rope!" the shrieking cry rang out. Joe turned in time to see a horse carrying double stumble and fall back into a foamy whirlpool. Two troopers flailed away trying to keep their heads above water. Macon wheeled his big bay around. He reached for the wounded man, pulling him up by the shirt collar. The other man was thrown a line, but too late. Uttering a desperate cry, he sank out of sight, disappearing in a swirl of foam.

On the far side of the river over a ridge a band of warriors came howling. They galloped pell-mell into the water and released a barrage of arrows. An arrowhead pierced Macon Laird's big bay's wind pipe. The horse struggled up the near river bank. Desperately heaving for breath, the big animal dropped to its knees. Macon thrust the wounded man onto another rider and turned to save his precious bay. The wounded animal attempted to rise but couldn't. The bay fell back to lay gasping like a grounded fish.

"Come on," Joe urged. The Palouse were forming to make another attack. He pulled the grieving Englishman away. He shot the dying horse and boosted Macon up on his own mount.

"My saddle! My bridle!" Macon cried.

"Leave them. Let some Palouse warrior enjoy the spoils."

When the last man was across, Gilliam rode up to the river's edge and shook his fist at the enemy who continued to shoot and shout taunts. "You've won this day, but I'll be back," Gilliam yelled. "Next time I'll not pussyfoot around. We'll shoot you down and burn your village. "I'll teach you a lesson you'll not forget or my name is not Cornelius Gilliam."

"If he's countin' on me ta hep teach 'em, he kin fergit it," a shivering youth muttered. "My enlistment is up. I've had a belly full of Injun fightin'. It's time fer plowin' an' plantin'."

The youth was not the only trooper sick of the war. Within a few days more volunteer enlistments ended. Rather than stay on, they made ready to return to their Willamette Valley homes. Tom McKay, disgusted with the manner Gilliam mismanaged the campaign, said his French Canadians also would leave.

The reduced ranks and shortage of supplies forced Gilliam to cancel another foray into Indian country. Instead, he announced he would return to the valley to garner supplies and recruits. Upon his return he would go after the redskins tooth and nail.

XXVIII

If your mothers were here in this country . . . suckled you and
while you were suckling some person came and took your
mother and left you alone . . . how would you feel then?

Stickus, Cayuse

In the hill country camp Stickus was even more upset by the turn of events than Colonel Cornelius Gilliam. After returning from the meeting at Touchet Crossing he closeted himself in his lodge. He hated to venture outside. The sight of Tiloukaikt's herd and the presence of the murderers' lodges turned his blood cold. His people looked at him with reproach. They were sick of living in constant fear. They wanted to return to the familiar home grounds on the Umatilla. They were worried about their herds. The pasture had been eaten bare. Water was scarce and their food baskets and pouches were scraped clean.

Stickus poked at the fire. Returning the stolen mission property had accomplished nothing. Now that the murderers were in camp the feeling of having done the honorable thing had vanished. The Blue Coat chief was right. His people harbored the killers of the missionaries, but what could he do about it? Everyone was afraid. When he talked of taking the murderers or driving them away, no one supported him. They were as afraid of these evil men as they were of the Blue Coats -- more so because the killers were only a few lodges away.

"We cannot touch them," Beaver Tooth had said. "It will make big trouble, cause bitter feeling. It is best to wait. Soon Tiloukaikt and his people will go away by themselves."

He shouldn't have listened to Beaver Tooth. He had friends in the Tiloukaikt camp. It was said Edward Tiloukaikt desired Beaver Tooth's daughter for a mate. Poor maiden. Didn't Beaver Tooth know Edward was one of the murderers, a man hunted by the Blue Coats? But of course Beaver Tooth knew. He was a greedy person. He wanted a share of Tiloukaikt's herd. Even as a boy, Beaver Tooth's greatest desire was to possess more horses than anyone in the village.

"Why do you sit here like an old woman?" Startled, Stickus looked up to see Kio-noo standing over him. What had come over her? He was so astonished by his mate's outburst his jaw sagged and his mouth flew open.

"You act like a sick dog," Kio-noo continued her harangue. "Get up and do something. The campsite is not good. People want to leave. They wait for you to take them where water and grass is good."

So this is what things have come to, Stickus thought, women speaking to their men like man had no brains. This was intolerable. He jumped to his feet and raised his hand, but habit was stronger than his anger. He refused to fight with his mate. He went outside and glanced around the pitiful camp. He was suddenly ashamed. Kio-noo was right. The presence of the murderers had turned his blood to water. Until he started acting like the leader of the band, Kio-noo had every right to treat him like a child. Yes, he had to lead his people out of trouble and do it now.

Stickus went to the lodge of White Crow, the elder who looked after the spiritual needs of the band. "We must leave this place and its dangers behind," Stickus informed him.

"My brother your words are spoken well," White Crow said. "What about them?" White Crow pointed his lips toward the Tiloukaikt lodges. "Wherever we go they will follow."

Stickus nodded grimly. "Your words are wise. Let us hold council. We will speak about this in my lodge."

That evening the elders and responsible young men of the upper Umatilla band gathered in the lodge of Stickus. When everyone was seated Stickus took his pipe from its pouch hanging from the center lodge pole. He solemnly filled the bowl with a special mixture of sweet grass and tobacco. He lit the pipe and took two puffs. He handed it to the elder on his left. When the last man had had his turn, Stickus carefully knocked the ashes from the bowl and placed them on a flat rock near the fire. He replaced the pipe in its special bag. The brief ceremony was a tradition handed down from one generation to the next. It was the prelude to discussions on serious matters such as the one they now faced.

"It is necessary we leave the hill country," Stickus began. "This is not a healthy or happy camp, but we cannot wander off like a hungry grouse pecking around hoping a grain of food will turn up. We must make this move wisely. Our people are weary of traveling here to there. Why should we worry about the Blue Coats? We have done nothing wrong. I say we should return to our homeland on the Umatilla."

There was a murmur of surprise. White Crow gave Stickus a sharp glance. "The Blue Coats stand in our path."

"They will not if we do what they wish," Stickus replied. "The Blue Coats seek the six murderers who live in our midst. The Blue Coats say they will leave when they have these people in their hands. We will give them these people, take them to the fort at Waiilatpu. This will please the Blue Coats. They will leave. We can return to the Umatilla and live in peace."

Michael, who sat with young men in the second circle, could read the council members' minds. They knew the peril their people faced. They also knew it was serious business to attack their own kind. They were also afraid to seize an important tribesman like Tiloukaikt. Tiloukaikt was a powerful and wealthy man. He was also ruthless and had surrounded himself with cold-blooded killers. Tamsucky, Joe Lewis, Tomahas and the Tiloukaikt sons had killed once and would not hesitate to kill again.

The silence in the lodge grew unbearable. Michael could hear the next youth's breathing. Outside a dog barked; a child cried. In the distance came the lonely notes of the nightly coyote chorus. Finally, White Crow, his craggy face creased with concern, spoke.

"Our brother speaks wisely. We must do what is right. Let us take our weapons and rid our camp of these people who give trouble. We are great in number, they are few. I say we move in the hours before first light."

"It is not our job to capture these people," a round-faced man named Short Nose argued. "It is wrong to turn our own over to the enemy. If the Blue Coats wish to take these men prisoner, let them come and do it themselves."

"That is just what we do not want," Stickus retorted. "The Cayuse people have brought this down on our heads. It is the Cayuse people who should bring these troubles to an end. If we allow Blue Coats to search and find these murders in our midst we will have earned the name they give us -- 'Bloody Cayuse.'"

"Pouf!" Short Nose's companion scoffed. "We should do as the Palouse. When the Blue Coats come, we chase them back to their Waiilatpu fort. They are like toothless dogs, all bark and no bite."

One man after another voiced his objections and departed. Only seven remained: White Crow, Willakin, the brothers Cut Lip and Fish Hawk, an elder named Black Horse, Michael and Stickus.

Stickus glanced around the circle of men who remained and shook his head. "Our numbers are small. These are bad people we face. Are we strong enough to seize these evil men and take them to Waiilatpu?"

Willakin raised a hand to speak. "While they sleep we pounce upon them like a night owl on a mouse. Tie them, stake them like one does in breaking a wild horse. When the sun rises we put them on pack mares and ride to Waiilatpu. Finished." He brushed his hand as though cleaning off dirt. The brothers, Cut Lip and Fish Hawk, gesticulated their approval. "Willakin's words are good. We take their weapons, pull their fangs like we would poisonous snakes," Cut Lip said.

"Oh-ha!" Fish Hawk agreed.

The seven men looked at each other, their eyes in solemn

agreement. It was done -- no more talk needed. White Crow, Black Horse, the brothers and Willakin left to snatch a couple of hours sleep and prepare their weapons. Stickus did not move from his place beside the fire. "I send these men into great danger," he said. "Blood may flow. Death may come. Is it right to risk these people's lives?"

"Is it better to let the murderers stay and have the Blue Coats find them in our midst?" Michael asked.

Stickus glanced skyward. "Let us rest. Father Sun will soon rise."

In the quiet, dark hour before dawn, the men threaded their way to the far side of the camp. Except for a few inquisitive dogs that came to sniff, their passage went unnoticed. On the slope above the Tiloukaikt lodges Stickus held up his hand to stop. The tipi lodges loomed large against the horizon. A cool breeze blew in from the north. Dressed only in hunting shirt and leggings, Michael shivered. The idea that seemed so good in the warmth of Stickus' lodge suddenly appeared foolhardy. Any moment he expected the murderers to come raging out of their tipi lodges and cut them down. Instead, a voice called from the darkness.

"You come too late. The people you seek no longer are here." The blanketed figures of Short Nose and his companion came forward. "We warned them to leave. They have gone. The women and herders will follow with their lodges and horses. Our troubles are finished."

"Our troubles are not finished," Stickus angrily replied. "The Blue Coats will still come. They will tear our village apart searching for them. When they do not find them . . . ."

"You do not see things clearly," Short Nose interrupted. "We will send a message to the Blue Coats. We will tell them the mission troublemakers are gone. The Blue Coats will leave us alone. They will search for them elsewhere."

"Hah!" Stickus retorted. "Send the Blue Coats a message! They will say it is a trick. There is no Cayuse alive they will believe."

"Send the mission boy." Short Nose motioned to Michael. "He has marched with the Blue Coats. They will believe him."

"No! The Blue Coat chief will never believe me," Michael protested. "He believes me a traitor."

"That is true," Stickus said thoughtfully. "They will not listen to the mission boy yet they do listen to the Boston brother. The Blue Coat chief keeps him at his side."

Michael started to object. He hadn't thought about Joe. It might work. Gilliam depended on Joe, called on him whenever a situation dealing with Indians occurred. If somehow he could get a message to Joe he might make Gilliam accept the truth. It was worth a try.

"All right. Exactly where have these murderers gone?" he asked Short Nose. "That is the first thing the Blue Coat leader will want to know."

XXIX

*If the few left are not reinforced . . . they will be in danger
of being cut off and the Indians will be down upon
the settlements.*

H. H. Spalding, letter to parents of Narcissa Whitman, 1848

Gilliam's plan to return to the Willamette Valley set into motion a hum of excited activity among the volunteers. The air itself expressed a future of promise. The Season of First Blossoms was at hand. Leaves and buds emerged. Formations of geese and other migrating birds skimmed overhead. Flocks of them glided down to feed in the old mission grain fields.

The men who had served out their enlistments were especially pleased. They were going home. Hurriedly, they made ready to leave, patching and polishing boots and equipment. They packed meager belongings and told innumerable tales of what they would do when they arrived in the Willamette Valley.

Amidst the flurry of preparations for departure, a messenger rode into camp with saddlebags loaded with mail, the first to arrive since Gilliam's army left The Dalles. Among the letters were several for Sandy Sanders and one for Joe Jennings.

Macon Laird was in camp to receive them. He glanced at the handwriting. His heart gave a painful lurch. Sandy Sanders had been dead a month and still Tildy had not been told. Macon placed the letters for the dead man to one side. It was cruel to continue keeping Tildy ignorant of her husband's death. It was not really his business, but he couldn't stand by and do nothing. He found Joe in the pasture working with battle wounded horses.

Joe glanced at the handwriting. "Of course you know who it's from." Macon's tense expression confirmed it. Grief over the death of his big bay had cracked the British reserve. Macon had become almost human. It was obvious he was anxious to hear what Tildy had written. Was she all right? Was

Baby John, the child Macon sired, healthy and well? These would
be questions uppermost in the Britisher's mind. Joe glanced at
Macon, who, in an attempt to conceal his emotions, had turned
to study the distant haze covered hills.

Perversely, Joe watched his companion suffer. He de-
served it. What right did he have, taking advantage of an innocent girl who never before had encountered a suave man of the
world? And poor innocent, unsuspecting Sandy, had doted on
Baby John, glorying in him, planning his future.

"Aah!" Joe inwardly groaned. Perhaps Sandy's death was
a blessing in disguise. If he ever had learned the truth about his
precious son's origins it would have broken his heart.

"Aren't you going to read your letter?" Macon finally
asked.

"Ah! Yes. How thoughtless of me." Joe still took his
time. He dabbed liniment on an inflamed arrow wound, soothed
the horse with a few pats and turned it loose. He sat on a fallen
fence rail and slit the envelope open with his pocket knife. A
flimsy piece of paper fell out. Macon scooped it up and handed
it to Joe. Deliberately, Joe unfolded the paper and begin to read.

"Dear Joe,
I hope this finds you and Sandy well.
We miss you both very much. Take care of
Sandy, for me will you, Joe? He is so innocent
in the ways of the frontier. He knows nothing
of making war. We can't wait for your return.
I saw Bithiah the other day. She . . ."

Joe read the remainder of the letter to himself. It was too
personal to share with anyone else. He quickly folded the paper
and thrust it into a pocket. He wished he never had received it.
Every word pierced his heart. He had not watched over Sandy,
now he was dead. He had not spoken for Bithiah's hand, now
she was someone else's wife. He had not introduced Michael to
the family as he should have, now he was a member of the upper
Umatilla band of Cayuse. He had made a mess of everything he

touched.

　　That night, by firelight, Joe began a letter to Tildy. Jasson was leaving with the volunteers the next morning. He had promised to take the letter and deliver it. Macon fretfully smoked his pipe and watched Joe agonize with the words. He had the greatest urge to take the pen from Joe and write Tildy himself. No, that would not do. Having the tragic news come from him would be cruel.

　　Macon got up and walked away. Why had Joe refused to read the entire letter to him? Did Tildy mention Baby John? Did she mention him? Of course not. She could not. She did not know her husband was dead. He strode back to the campfire and stood over Joe.

　　"Old man, you are a miserable coward," Macon blurted. "A true-blue brother would deliver the news of Sandy's death in person and damned soon. Why do you treat your sister this way? It is rotten, you know."

　　Joe flushed. An angry retort was on the tip of his tongue. How dare this Britisher call him a coward? He slowly and carefully counted to ten. He had no intention of making a bad situation worse by fighting with Macon Laird. "You're quite right; I'm a coward. I'm what you call a cad."

　　"So sorry, old chap. I am out of sorts. But you have to quit blaming yourself for Sandy's death. So he took a bullet meant for you. In battle that happens all the time. The best way to clear your conscience is to go to Tildy and explain the way it happened. You will feel better and so will she. It is best you pack up and leave in the morning with the departing volunteers."

　　"It isn't just Tildy. There's someone else I can't face. There's a girl in the valley I love and hate at the same time. If I see her I fear I might do something stupid, like kill her husband. Every night I lie awake wishing it had been him who got shot instead of Sandy. Now maybe you can understand why I can't go. It has nothing to do with Tildy."

　　"It is this Bithiah person, is it not?"

"Who told you that?"

"You may not realize it, but you have a habit of talking in your sleep."

Joe grimaced. What other secrets had he revealed? He started to ask, instead, remained silent. He really did not want to know.

Macon shook his head. "So sorry old boy. Why have you kept this awkward affair secret?"

"I can't stand to think about it, let alone talk about it. Makes me look like a complete ass."

"My dear fellow, you cannot let this ruin your life. Think of the people you are hurting. Granddad Jennings may not have much time left. You will never forgive yourself if he leaves this world before you see him again."

Joe didn't answer. He went back to the torturous task of writing. Macon knocked out his pipe and put it away. "Quite so! Quite so! I bloody well forgot myself. I have no business giving advice. Mention in your letter you have asked me to deliver it. It will make me feel more comfortable when I hand it to Tildy."

##

Captain McKay and his French Canadians were the first to leave. Before dawn they marched away. They were tired of living cheek to jowl with the Willamette Valley volunteers. They distrusted and disliked Gilliam. His erratic leadership kept them constantly on edge. His attitude toward people with Indian blood made them furious. At the rate Colonel Cornelius Gilliam created enemies the entire Northwest would soon be embroiled in war.

Gilliam's decision to erect a fort also irked them. They refused to lend a hand. Why should they help Americans rule this land which, for decades, had been the province of Hudson's Bay? The campaign was supposed to be a police action, to arrest the Whitman Mission murderers and take them in for trial. They saw no reason to establish permanent fortifications like some occupying power.

Joe watched the French Canadians leave with a feeling of shame. Gilliam had not treated them fairly. As far as he knew, Gilliam hadn't even thanked them for their efforts. To make matters worse, the colonel didn't have the decency to get up and see them off.

When the end of the departing column disappeared from view, Joe turned back to camp. Macon Laird was trying to get a bridle on the pale-faced mustang, that had replaced his bay killed at Touchet Crossing. Every time Macon approached with the bridle the mustang reared and jerked away.

"Here! Let me give you a hand," Joe said. He seized the mustang by the nostrils and squeezed them shut. For a moment the horse opened its mouth to catch its breath. Macon slipped the bit into the open mouth and the bridle strap over the ears.

Getting the saddle on proved more difficult. The wild horse circled around and around avoiding the saddle blanket. Joe seized the horse's head and clamped down on an ear with his teeth. For a moment the horse stood paralyzed. Macon quickly threw the saddle on and cinched it tight.

Joe shook his head. "This critter'll kill you before you get to the valley. I'd better tag along and lend a hand, at least until you get to The Dalles."

"Jolly good! That is the spirit. Perhaps by then I can talk you into going all the way."

Colonel Cornelius Gilliam did not look forward to leaving with the same eagerness as his men. He was bone weary. He had spent most of the previous night writing standing orders. During his absence he feared chaos would rein. Waters and his fellow officers had the judgment of pea brains. They couldn't even site a latrine. The one Waters had ordered dug at Waiilatpu was downwind from the mess quarters. Sometimes at meal time the odor was so strong the men accused the cook of urinating in the soup. Then there was that damned Lee. All he thought about was spit and polish inspections. He even had the men braiding horses' tails and burnishing their hooves.

Gilliam wagged his head in disgust. When he got to the valley he had half a notion to resign. No one appreciated his work. The last meeting with the officers was a disaster. He could see the smug looks, mocking smiles . . . . It was too shameful to think about. Major Lee was the worst.

"Isn't the casualty list high for the results realized?" he asked of the Palouse fracas, his voice smooth as silk. Dammed snot-nosed know-it-all. Someone should take his pants down and give him a swat with a belt.

Then there was that old maid, Palmer. Sanctimonious prig, worried that the Palouse would join the enemy. Then the Umatilla and Walla Walla would ally themselves with the Cayuse. "Like a row of dominoes one tribe after another will fall in with the hostiles," Palmer had predicted.

The ignoramus Doc Newell had put in his two cents worth. The Nez Perce were good friends with the Palouse. They were certain to become involved. When that happened there would be an Indian uprising that would be impossible to control.

Tom McKay, that damned Catholic half-breed. He didn't like the way the entire campaign had been conducted. He said little, but his manner spoke for him. Gilliam was glad McKay and the French Canadians had marched ahead. He never wanted to see them again.

The colonel swore out loud. When he returned he would run the campaign exactly the way he wanted. Anyone who attempted to interfere would get the back of his hand. He would wipe every blistering redskin in the Northwest off the map. He put away his portfolio, handed the standing orders to Lieutenant Colonel Waters and mounted the bridled and saddled horse that Pelican Neck had readied for him at the front of the headquarters tent. He led the valley bound troop away toward Fort Walla Walla, his thoughts as grim as the expression on his face.

The reception at Fort Walla Walla did not improve Gilliam's frame of mind. Head factor McBean facetiously asked about the Palouse encounter.

"It's none of your business," Gilliam huffily replied. "It's over and done with. The Palouse got a proper bloody nose."

"That's not the way I heard it. Perhaps your officers dressed up the report. Maybeso, they were afraid to give you the facts."

"I know what I'm talking about. I commanded the troops myself. I didn't lose a single man," Gilliam retorted. "You've lived in this country long enough to know you can't believe a word Indians say. In my book redskins are the greatest liars in the world."

"Hmm!" McBean grunted. "I see. I see. However my source was not Indian. He had no reason to lie."

"This is mon-monstrous," Gilliam stammered. "Produce your informant. I will challenge him."

"Here he is. Hezekiah Brown, fresh from Fort Colville." He turned to a huge man wearing weathered buckskins. He gave the broad back a slap. "Hezekiah! Meet Colonel Cornelius Gilliam, commander of the American army post at Waiilatpu."

The huge body swung around. A thick matted beard hung down to his chest. "Howdy, pardner!" The voice boomed from a thrust-out belly. Hezekiah offered a hand covered with hair as dark and almost as thick as his beard.

"Glad to meet any fightin' man, even though he's been through the hopper like a cob of corn. From what I hear tell those Palouses had yuh pinned down like a cow caught in a bog. Still, yuh're lucky as sin. Yuh tackled old Badger Claw in his lair an' got away. Not many kin say thet."

"The Palouse aren't so tough," Gilliam said indignantly. "We marched into their village and took a herd of horses right from under their noses."

"Yeah, but they took the horses right back an' a leetle more. Here, looksee. Yuh seen this before?" Hezekiah pointed to a tooled leather saddle and silver decorated bridle. "That's part of the spoils. One of yer men left it at Touchet Crossin'.

Mighty careless, 'less the Palouse was too hot ta handle."

Glumly Gilliam looked down at Macon Laird's saddle and bridle. He always knew that damned Britisher would cause trouble. Before he could think of a suitable reply, Macon Laird and Joe Jennings walked in.

"I say, my saddle! My bridle!" Macon exclaimed. "How marvelous. I never thought to see them again. Did you bring them in?" he asked the big Hudson's Bay man.

"Yep! Traded fer 'em on the Tucannon. Feller I got 'em from said the saddle was too weighty fer Palouse mustangs. I wouldn't take the saddle without the bridle, so he let 'em both go fer 'nother two dollar. If'n yuh want 'em back I'll give 'em to yuh fer what I paid."

Colonel Cornelius Gilliam spun on his heel and walked out. He silently cursed the decision to stop at Fort Walla Walla. Loudmouthed McBean and that bearded buffoon, Hezekiah, would soon make certain the disastrous fiasco with the Palouse was common gossip. When he returned with reinforcements he had half a mind to occupy the fort and send McBean and his hangers-on packing.

The more Gilliam thought about McBean's snide remarks, the more indignant he became. He had been right all the time. Hudson's Bay and their Catholic friends were in cahoots. Already they had managed to close the Protestant missions at Lapwai and Waiilatpu. Next, they and their Indian friends would make a drive to rid the territory above the Columbia of all Americans.

By God! He would show them. They might make fun of him now, but just wait . . . . All the way back to the bivouac area Gilliam thought of ways to square accounts with Hudson's Bay and their damned Catholic allies. Little did he know his plans would never be carried out. In less than twenty-four hours he would be dead.

DEATH ON THE UMATILLA

XXX

I am the master of my fate:
I am the captain of my soul.
William E. Henley

"Little Fox rode away in the night," Straight Arrow bragged to Michael. "She has a mate, the son of Tiloukaikt. We now have many horses. Make us rich like Buffalo Horn."

Michael stared at the boy in disbelief. Just yesterday he saw Little Fox. She smiled. She joked. Her voice was as cheery as the song of Meadowlark. The bright eyes had the twinkle of a chipmunk. Now she was gone, given by her father to that murderer, Edward Tiloukaikt. How could Beaver Tooth do this to his precious daughter?

The loathsome, insensitive act made Michael sick at heart. He swung up on Magpie and roughly wheeled his four-footed friend about. Everyone had been afraid of the killers and let them do as they wanted. He had acted as badly as the others. He hadn't wanted to tackle them either. Now, it was different. They had Little Fox in their midst.

Michael urged Magpie away, only to pass near Stickus. The Cayuse leader stood in front of his lodge. He had just finished his prayer to Father Sun, grateful for this new day, hopeful for the good it would bring. Michael's rage turned to shame. He had neglected the morning prayer. He pulled Magpie to a stop, slid down to face Father Sun. "When you forget the gods, you have forgotten why you have been given the privilege of living on Mother Earth," Grandfather Lone Wolf had scolded when as a child Michael had awakened and raced away to play before saying his morning prayer.

Reciting the prayer gave Michael time to reflect. Riding after the murderers by himself was certain to end in failure. The plan Stickus and the elders had settled on was the action to take, and it had to be quickly done. He mounted Magpie, bode farewell to Stickus and turned on the trail toward Waiilatpu.

Michael forced himself to think of the task ahead. The key was finding Joe. And when he did find him, would Joe be able to report the murderers' whereabouts to Gilliam? If he did make the report there was no assurance Gilliam would believe him. The colonel was certain to ask how he received this important information. Honest Joe would tell him the truth. It came from Two Feathers. That alone would make Gilliam swear the information was not true. It was another Two Feathers' trick to lead them on a wild goose chase.

Michael dismissed the pessimistic thoughts. Don't trouble trouble until trouble troubles you, was a quotation he remembered from school. Right now he had to concentrate on finding Joe. That alone was like searching for a kernel of corn in a harvested field without disturbing a flock of feeding crows.

It was near midday when Michael rode up to overlook the ruined mission grounds. For a moment he studied the fortification that had been constructed from the old Whitman Mission buildings. How strange it was to see it loom above the grounds where the peaceful Whitman home and outbuildings had stood. The fields where had he so often toiled were laid waste. Scattered debris lay everywhere: broken wagons; pieces of oxen yokes and harnesses; burnt timbers; odd pieces of rusting iron; and scraps of paper fluttered all over the formerly spick-and-span compound. The wind sent a paper sailing up the slope to wrap around a bush. Michael picked it up. It was a page torn from a mission school book. The weather faded print was barely legible. It was a nursery rhyme.

> *"Cock a doodle do!*
> *My dame has lost a shoe,*
> *My master lost his fiddle stick,*
> *And knows not what to do."*

Michael turned the page over. On the other side was another rhyme.

"Oh where, oh where has my little
dog gone?
Oh where, oh where can he be?
With his ears cut short and
his tail cut long,
Oh where, oh where is he?"

A lump rose in Michael's throat. It was a rhyme little Helen Mar and David Malin chanted as they skipped along ringing a bell to scare birds away from the garden rows. Now Helen Mar was dead and little David Malin had been adopted by the British man, Macon Laird.

Michael mounted up and started away when a harsh command shattered the silence. Halt!" Michael winced. What he feared had happened. For a split second he debated whether to make a run for it. He knew the voice. It was that of Pimple Face, the troublemaker who hated him. The odious volunteer had taken an arrow in the buttock while on patrol out of Fort Lee. His wound, although not severe, left him with a limp. His hatred for Indians equaled that of Colonel Gilliam.

"Two Feathers! What traitorous skullduggery're yuh up ta taday?" The pimply-faced sentry stepped out from behind a cluster of trees. Menacingly, he waved the barrel of his rifle, a satisfied smirk on his face.

Michael inwardly groaned. He had to outwit the man or his mission was certain to fail. "I came to see Colonel Gilliam," he said. "I have a message to be delivered only to him."

Pimple Face was not at all in a good frame of mind. He had had his heart set on leaving with Gilliam and the troopers who left Waiilatpu for the Willamette Valley, but at the last minute Lieutenant Colonel Waters had insisted he stay. His enlistment time would not end for another two weeks, he was told.

"Besides," Waters added. "We need experienced hands to garrison the fort while Colonel Gilliam is away. When he returns with reinforcements, that's when you will be free to leave."

Stunned by the turn of events, Pimple Face had uttered

an obscenity at which Colonel Waters had taken offence. "Just
for that you're on guard duty for the remainder of your enlistment." Now to see his old nemesis, Two Feathers, come sneaking over the ridge was the last straw.

"Listen, yuh blasted redskin, I ain't takin no guff. Thet
no-good brother of yers tried thet same message trick. It didn't
work fer him an' it ain't goin' ta work fer yuh neither. Yuh'll see
who an' what I tell yuh ta see, an' thet's the inside of the fort
stockade. Now get off thet horse nice an' easy like. Don't try
an' pull any tricks. I'd jest love ta put a bullet in yer bird brain."

Michael tied the reins together to stall for time. The last
thing he wanted was to leave Magpie in the clutches of Pimple
Face. "I wish you'd call out Joe Jennings. If I can't deliver the
message maybe you'll let him."

"Joe Jennings! He ain't here, neither is yer British friend
nor all yer French Canadian blood brothers. They went skitterin'
away yestiday. Probably nigh onta the Umatilla by now. Maybeso
farther, Colonel Cornelius Gilliam's leadin' 'em. He'll be hurrin'
'em along as fast as he kin. Quit yer lollygaggin' an' git off thet
speckled turkey egg of a nag. There's no place fer a horse in the
stockade." Pimple Face cocked the rifle.

Michael kicked Magpie in the ribs. The startled horse
lunged ahead, straight at Pimple Face. The soldier yelled and
went down, firing the rifle as he fell. The bullet whistled harmlessly into the air. Before Pimple Face could recover and reload,
Michael and Magpie were out of range.

Soon after leaving Fort Walla Walla Gilliam led his troops
across the Walla Walla River. The column wended its way through
the rocky gap that channeled the Columbia River west, almost
directly toward the Pacific Ocean. The volunteers passed the
twin columns where Cayuse legend claimed cunning Coyote had
turned two fisherwomen sisters into stone. Except for a fringe of
trees at the river's edge, the terrain was bleak and uninviting.
Large blackened rocks lay strewn about as though vomited from

some subterranean pit of fire. The river bank sloped up to end at
an escarpment. A coyote, outlined on the horizon, looked down
on the troop and yapped a mournful cry. In the sky high-flying
birds circled over the river, then over the cliffs and back again.

"If Michael was here he would see the lone coyote and
the circling birds as signs of a kill," Joe observed.

"Perhaps there will be. Those damned Cayuses could be
waitin' in ambush," Adams said.

"I shouldn't think so," Joe replied. "The Cayuse who
occupied this land are gone. Those who aren't on the banks of
the Touchet and Tucannon rivers have probably taken refuge in
the Blue Mountains." Joe said with assurance, but at the same
time he, too, had an ominous feeling of trouble ahead. Was it
because he dreaded meeting up with Bithiah and her husband?
For certain, he would travel no farther than The Dalles. Irritated
with himself, he kicked his mount into a trot and rode to the head
of the column. Gilliam greeted him with a curt nod.

"I see your British friend has his saddle back. I suppose
you had a good gabfest with the rascals at Fort Walla Walla,"
Gilliam growled.

"Yep. It was good to see old McBean again."

"Talked about the Palouse business, I suppose?"

"I believe it was mentioned."

"You know damned well it was. There's one thing I don't
understand about you, Jennings. You're an American but you
hobnob with Indians, Englishmen, Canucks and breeds like they
were kin. Where does your loyalty lie? That's what I would like
to know."

"I don't mean to interrupt, colonel, but isn't that someone ahead, perhaps one of McKay's men with a message?"

Gilliam held up his hand to signal halt. A rider on a horse
lathered with foam loped up the trail. "Hold up!" Gilliam commanded when the rider came abreast. "Where are you going and
what's your mission?"

"I have a dispatch for Colonel Cornelius Gilliam. "My

orders are to deliver it to him personally."

"I'm Colonel Cornelius Gilliam."

The rider hesitated.

"Come on! Hand it over," Gilliam ordered.

Gilliam ripped the seal open. He stared at the paper so long Joe wondered if Gilliam's eyes bothered him. He finally thrust the paper in a pocket and gave the messenger a curt nod. "Message received. Fall in and join the column."

For the remainder of the day the troop marched in silence. Everyone wondered what Gilliam's message contained. From the way Gilliam acted something portentous was in the wind.

The volunteers came to Buffalo Horn's pasture lands on the lower Umatilla, peacefully passed through them and forded the river. A short distance from the Umatilla, at a picturesque spot with a view of Horse Heaven Hills, Gilliam held up a hand, calling a halt. He didn't want to catch up with McKay and be forced to camp with his troop of half bloods.

The men fell out and began to make camp. It was still light. Several took their rifles and went to hunt, hoping to bag meat for the pot. Hardly did they leave when rifle shots rang out and then a shout. "There's a damned Injun!" a hunter shouted. "He's forded the river an' makin' signs he wants ta powwow."

Gilliam, who leaned against the tailgate of the wagon re-reading the message brought by the lone horseman, angrily glanced up. "It's looks like that renegade's black and white pony. What the devil does he want?"

"I'd better go see," Joe said, also recognizing Michael's Magpie.

"No!" Gilliam said sharply. "Let the traitorous half-breed ride in by himself. I'll bet he doesn't have the guts."

Michael hesitated. He could see Joe, but why did he not come out? Gilliam was holding him back. Unmindful of the many hostile eyes fixed on him, Michael resolutely urged Magpie forward. He had been sent to deliver a crucial message -- nothing was going to stop him from carrying out his orders.

XXXI

It is not right to exult over slain men.
Homer, ODYSSEY

The camp on the lower Umatilla was so tense with suspense, the air, itself, seemed to stand still. A single word, a false move, a sharp intake of breath -- almost anything could cause the nerves of this apprehensive, frustrated, defeated band of volunteers to snap. The animal instinct to lash out, to give vent to their discontent, easily could be unleashed on this renegade half-breed who entered their camp as guilelessly as if enjoying a leisurely ride along the riverside.

Joe grimly watched his Nez Perce brother's approach. He knew Gilliam hated him, in fact had sworn to kill him the next time they met. Yet, Joe couldn't help but feel a surge of pride. This was the way of the true Indian warrior. No one could doubt Michael Two Feathers' courage. In the eyes of fellow tribesmen, every step into the enemy camp earned the youth battlefield coups.

The troopers cocked their rifles, the muzzles tracking the horseman with trigger fingers tensed. The ominous clicks as hammers were pulled back sent a chill up Joe's spine. It would be just like one of these idiots to shoot.

Major Lee also sensed the danger. He licked his dry lips. "Easy men. He comes peacefully. Let's hear what he has to say."

Michael rode through the gauntlet of volunteers, his eyes fixed on Gilliam who continued to stand at the back end of the supply wagon. He dismounted and led Magpie until he was within a dozen feet of the colonel. He stopped and tossed the Blue Coat commander a salute.

Michael's calm, determined soldier-like demeanor, infuriated Gilliam. This damned half-breed had been a thorn in his side the whole campaign. Where was that infernal rifle? He reached inside the wagon, his hand falling on the loaded gun. He wouldn't shoot the rascal down in cold blood, but he'd sure scare the bejesus out of him. He gripped the rifle, pulling it forward.

Everything happened so fast Michael could not recall afterward exactly what had occurred. There was an explosion. The rifle, with its muzzle smoking, fell to the ground in front of Gilliam. For a startling moment Gilliam's gaze met his. A complete look of disbelief shone in the colonel's eyes. Slowly his body crumpled, falling into a heap.

Stunned, Michael stepped toward the fallen man. He was crouching over the body when Jasson rushed up. The skinny trooper's eyes bulged. He stared at Michael and then at the smoking gun, his behaired Adam's apple jumping up and down. "Keerist!" he shrieked. "You killed the colonel."

Macon Laird and Joe Jennings, who had witnessed the incident, could not believe what they had seen. Quickly, Macon dropped to his knees to check the colonel's pulse. Major Lee and more volunteers crowded near. "He's dead," Macon announced, "an unfortunate accident. When the colonel pulled the rifle from the wagon the trigger must have caught on something, accidentally discharging the gun."

"Accident! Hell! I saw it all. That damned half-breed murdered him," Jasson screeched, although everyone had seen that Michael Two Feathers came unarmed.

"All right! Disband. There'll be an inquiry," Major Lee ordered. "No, not you two," he motioned to Joe and Macon Laird to stay. "Go on there's nothing you can do here," Lee continued to shoo the muttering riflemen away. Michael stood transfixed.

"This is a bad situation," Lee said to Joe and Macon when they were alone. "I don't know if I can control these men or not. If they have a mind to lynch the Indian lad . . . well . . . ." He glanced apprehensively at the cluster of agitated troopers.

Michael pulled Magpie near. He understood Major Lee's predicament. If the major didn't take action the men surely would. They had spent months in the field and had nothing to show for their efforts. Killing the man who they thought murdered their commander would ease their frustrations. He glanced around. He was on the edge of camp. The volunteers' horses were either hobbled or tethered. If he could get beyond the first ridge . . . .

Michael leaped on Magpie, reined him around, and was off at a dead gallop. Furious shouts and scattered shots followed, but in the gray dusk the troopers' aim was bad. The dodging target was soon lost in the thick sagebrush.

Jasson was furious. "Dammit, we can't let that murderin' Injun git away." He ran for his horse.

Adams spit in disgust. "Go get him, brave one. I hope yuh find yer way back to camp."

Major Lee was now the ranking officer. Most of the men waited for his orders. "Go back to your campsites. It was a terrible accident," Major Lee informed them. There was no doubt in his mind but that Gilliam accidentally had shot himself. He noticed the communique the messenger had delivered. He slid the paper from under Gilliam's lifeless hand. He read the message and shook his head. Wordlessly, he handed it to Macon.

"You are hereby directed to hand over command of the Oregon Militia to Major H. A. G. Lee and return forthwith to Oregon City . . . ." Macon read aloud. "Hmm, relieved of his command was he? No officer likes to receive orders like that. Do you suppose it drove him to commit suicide?"

"No!" Major Lee said emphatically. "It was an accident. This campaign has been disastrous enough without even suggesting such a thing. There's no need to reveal the contents of this message. I'm the ranking officer. It is only natural that I should take over. We shall proceed on to the valley as planned, taking the body of Colonel Gilliam with us."

The death of their commander left the volunteers in a state of shock. They hadn't particularly liked the man, but the sudden and strange way he died unnerved them. Silently they dispersed, stoked up the campfires and began to prepare the evening meal.

Jasson, who had been Colonel Gilliam's orderly since the

volunteer army first had been formed, was the exception. He took the death of Gilliam personally. He did not for a minute believe Gilliam accidentally killed himself. He was murdered. Two Feathers had not only killed Gilliam but also destroyed his importance as Gilliam's orderly. Jasson could not rest until he extracted vengeance. In a fury, he saddled and bridled his horse. He galloped over the ridge, but soon the dark expanse of rocks and sagebrush defeated him. Slowly he retraced his steps.

"Poor Pelican Neck," Adams commiserated. "He's lost his place in the sun. As Gilliam's right hand man, he was a some-body. Now he's gotta come down outta the clouds an' be a no-body like the rest of us."

Joe, who had sensed disaster when Michael first appeared, scolded himself. He should have prevented this. If only he had gone and escorted Michael in it would not have happened -- or was it meant to happen? He remembered Yellow Serpent's pre-diction. "Before the Season of Long Grass the Blue Coat leader will die," he had said. How could the Walla Walla leader have known? Then there was Stickus insisting that when Gilliam was gone he had to have something to show the Blue Coat chief who was to follow. Joe shook his head. These Indians with the power to see into the future were a mystery he would never understand.

Back at the campsite where Macon and he had intended to spend the night, Joe methodically collected his gear. He led his mount up and cinched the roll on the saddle. Macon Laird silently watched. "You are going after Michael?" he finally asked.

"Yes. He believes he is accused of killing Colonel Gilliam. He has enough on his shoulders without having to bear that bur-den, too. You'll have to go on to the valley without me. You'll deliver the letter and make excuses, won't you?"

"I promise to do the best I can. Should you start now? It's nearly dark. Michael's probably half way to the Tucannon."

"No, he'll be waiting over the next hill. He knows I'll follow." Joe shook hands, mounted up and rode away, ignoring Jasson's disapproving glare.

After a short ride Joe heard the shrill bark of a coyote. He gave an answering bark. Out of the darkness floated a ghostly phantom. "Hello, brother," Joe greeted. For a long while they rode silently, unmindful of where they were going.

##

Colonel Cornelius Gilliam's death came at a time of year when, under normal conditions, the future on the plateau held the most promise. The Season of Long Grass was beginning to show. Already Mother Earth had painted brooding Horse Heaven Hills an eye-soothing green. Wild flowers burst forth in a rainbow of colors. Along the borders of Butter Creek and the Umatilla River, white-petaled flowers dangled from locust tree branches like clusters of grapes, their perfume so heady it turned the air sweet as honey.

This wondrous change in scenery did little to uplift the spirits of the region's citizenry in spring, 1848. The Whitman Mission killers were still at large. In the rocky, rolling hills of the out-country, Stickus, who wanted peace so badly, impatiently paced back and forth in front of his makeshift lodge, awaiting word that would allow his people to return to their homeland on the upper Umatilla. The thought that he never would lead his band back to their home grounds, nearly drove him mad.

##

Camped deep in the Blue Mountains, the daughter of Beaver Tooth, Little Fox, cried herself to sleep. "Oh! Two Feathers," she wept. "I am locked in the lodge of Edward Tiloukaikt; will I ever be free to see you again?" Little did she know her predicament would take an incongruous turn. Down the trail devious, murderous, covetous, Joe Lewis would slit the throats of his three Cayuse companions, including Edward Tiloukaikt, and steal everything they possessed.

In a sparse camp on the Butter Creek pasture lands of Five Crows, Joe Jennings and his Nez Perce half brother sat up half the night. Where were they to go? What were they to do? There was certain to be another attempt to capture the Whitman

Mission murderers. Should they try to get involved? Joe glanced at his brother's dark profile. Would he be allowed to march in the ranks of the Blue Coats again, or would he even want to? His heart went out to his brother. The life of a half-blood, torn between two worlds, was grim indeed.

##

In the camp of the volunteers Macon Laird sat by a campfire, smoking. He slid a blue envelope from a pocket and sighed. He had promised Joe he would deliver the letter to Tildy. How was he going to do it -- boldly knock on her door? How would she receive him? Would she hold Sandy Sanders' death against him? How would she feel about him taking Sandy's place? And most worrisome of all, would she accept David Malin, the half-blood boy who had survived the Whitman Mission massacre and whom he had adopted and now awaited him in Fort Vancouver?

Macon puffed on his pipe and stared into the night. What would it be like living in a homesteader's cabin -- one built by a man you had betrayed? He knocked out his pipe and put it away. That was something he dare not think about.

In the same camp Major H. A. G. Lee sat with pen in hand and journal on his knees. He thoughtfully scratched his chin with the pen quill and stared into the flickering fire. What could he say that would explain the shocking events of the day?

He wrote down the date, March 28, 1848. He paused again to scratch his chin, then hurriedly wrote: "Death on the Umatilla - Colonel Cornelius Gilliam. Major Henry A. G. Lee takes command." He stared at the blank space left on the page and grimaced. What else was there to say? The Gilliam conducted campaign had been a disaster. The volunteer army was no nearer to capturing the Whitman Mission murderers than the day they set out from The Dalles.

Major Lee closed the journal and grimaced. Soon another campaign in search of the killers would begin. For certain he would be involved. If he suffered as many ups and downs as he had in the first campaign, it might well drive him over the hill.

DEATH ON THE UMATILLA

AUTHORS' NOTE

Colonel Cornelius Gilliam was real. His character was much as portrayed. Lieutenant Colonel Waters and Major Lee were officers in his command. Gray Eagle, Yellow Serpent (Peopeo-mox-mox), Five Crows and Stickus were Indian leaders of note. The raid at The Dalles and the Battle of Sand Hollows took place as did the fruitless running fight with the Palouse.

According to official records, Colonel Cornelius Gilliam met his death much as described, accidentally shooting himself while withdrawing a rifle from a wagon. Upon the colonel's death Major Henry A. G. Lee took command of the volunteers, and along with Captain Tom McKay and his French Canadians, accompanied Gilliam's body to the Willamette Valley.

Whitman's Mission at Waiilatpu, WA is now a National Historic Site beautifully maintained by the National Park Service. Visitors stroll the old compound grounds and past the Great Grave that holds the remains of massacre victims in silence and with a feeling of reverence. Little wonder, the spirits of those who gave their lives here seem to rise up and walk with them.

Old Fort Walla Walla, the Hudson's Bay trading post (pictured on front cover) that played such an important role in the events of the time, has disappeared under the waters backed up by McNary Dam on the Columbia River. McNary Dam is located not far from the mouth of the Umatilla River where Colonel Gilliam was killed.

Umatilla Crossing, where the Cayuse escaped after the Battle of Sand Hollows, is now pleasant, locust tree shaded Fort Henrietta Park and picnic area at Echo, OR. (Fort Henrietta was a military stockade established by Oregon volunteers and destroyed in 1855). Not far from the old stockade emigrant wagon wheel tracks are still visible in Mother Earth.

ABOUT THE AUTHORS

Bonnie Jo Hunt (*Wicahpi Win* - Star Woman) is Lakota (Standing Rock Sioux) and the great great granddaughter of both Chief Francis Mad Bear, prominent Teton Lakota leader, and Major James McLaughlin, Indian agent and Chief Inspector for the Bureau of Indian Affairs. Early in life Bonnie Jo set her heart on helping others. In 1980 she founded Artists of Indian America, Inc. (AIA), a nonprofit organization established to stimulate cultural and social improvement among American Indian youth. To record and preserve her native heritage, in 1997 Bonnie Jo launched Mad Bear Press which publishes American history dealing with life on the western frontier. These publications include the Lone Wolf Clan series: The Lone Wolf Clan, Raven Wing, The Last Rendezvous, Cayuse Country, Land Without a Country, Death on the Umatilla and the forthcoming The Mounted Riflemen.

# #

Dr. Lawrence J. Hunt, a former university professor, works actively with Artists of Indian America, Inc. In addition to coauthoring the Lone Wolf Clan series, he has coauthored an international textbook (Harrap: London) and authored four mystery novels (Funk and Wagnalls), one of which, Secret of the Haunted Crags, received the Edgar Allan Poe Award from Mystery Writers of America.

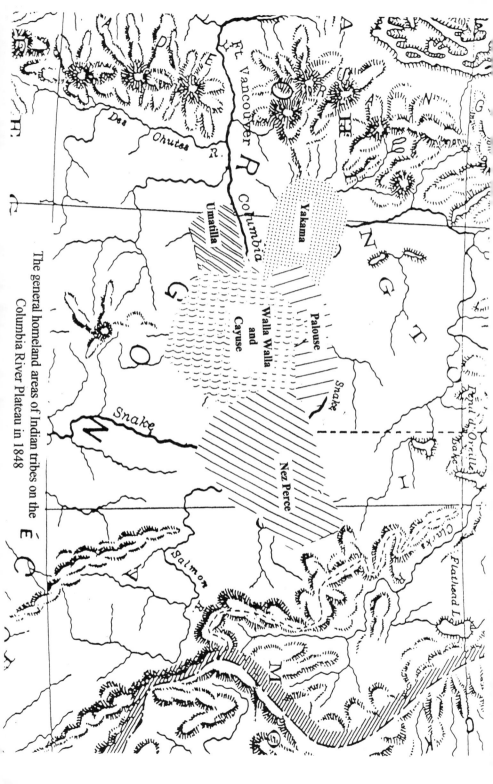

The general homeland areas of Indian tribes on the Columbia River Plateau in 1848

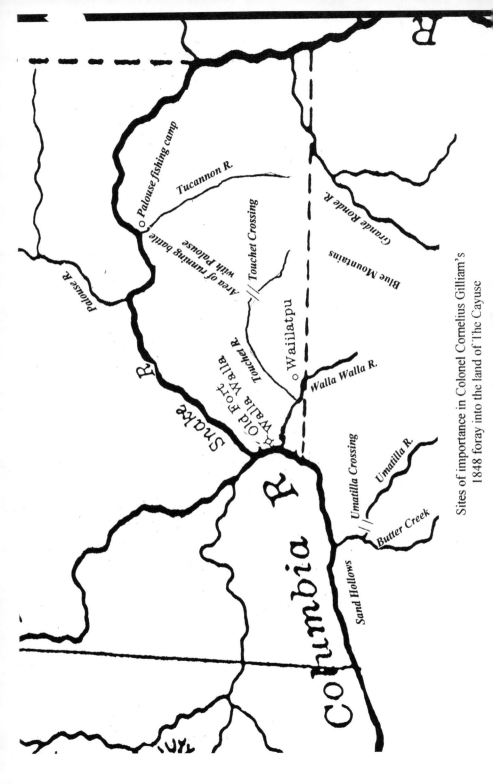

Sites of importance in Colonel Cornelius Gilliam's 1848 foray into the land of The Cayuse